Viking W

**Book 6 in th
Dragon Heart Series
By
Griff Hosker**

Published by Sword Books Ltd 2015
Copyright © Griff Hosker Second Edition
The author has asserted their moral right under the Copyright, Designs and Patents Act, 1988, to be identified as the author of this work.
All Rights reserved. No part of this publication may be reproduced, copied, stored in a retrieval system, or transmitted, in any form or by any means, without the prior written consent of the copyright holder, nor be otherwise circulated in any form of binding or cover other than that in which it is published and without a similar condition being imposed on the subsequent purchaser.
A CIP catalogue record for this title is available from the British Library.
Cover by Design for Writers

Dedication

Thanks to all the Time Team programmes! You keep me straight on most things. And thanks to my readers who also make sure that I am as accurate as possible. Thanks to the British Museum for the excellent exhibition of 2014.

Prologue

I am Jarl Dragon Heart of Cyninges-tūn. I was born to a Saxon father who enslaved my mother, the daughter of one of the last Warlords of Rheged. I had never had an easy life. After being taken as a slave from a river in Northumbria I had become a warrior. I had become one of the Norsemen feared in Britannia and called a Viking. I had raided and I had fought both Saxons and Hibernians. I had sailed to the farthest isles and I had also visited Constantinopolis. There the Norns, the weird sisters who weave our destinies, set me and, my son Arturus, in place to save the life of the Emperor Nikephoros. *Wyrd*. It had not only saved his life it had made my fortune. I wondered what the Weird sisters had planned for me now!

Chapter 1

The first seven days after leaving Constantinopolis saw a rapid improvement in my health. The wound I had suffered defending the Emperor completely healed. We were anxious to get back to our home having trade well in the richest city in the world. We had gold, we had weapons and we had spices. Our hold was full. Below the deck of the long ship our shipwright had constructed a large space where we could hide a healthy cargo. When we reached the land of the Franks we would trade for those things we could not make ourselves.

Josephus had been a slave we had rescued. Although we had returned him to his home in Constantinopolis he had chosen to journey with us to our home. He was a fine captain and I felt it was *wyrd* that he had so chosen to be one of us. He had kept us safe on more than one occasion for he had knowledge of the seas, the currents and, most importantly, the pirates who preyed on lone ships. Of course our ship was not a tasty morsel to be easily digested. We were a drekar, a long ship and we had the finest warriors on board. However, we were well laden and I knew that we had to keep our wits about us if we were to survive the long journey home.

When we made it through the Pillars of Hercules and left the balmy blue waters of the inner sea and were entering the grey stormy seas of the west, I felt a huge sense of relief. These colder waters were what we knew. There had been the danger of Barbary pirates and Moors when we had sailed the blue waters of the Inner Sea. As our ship moved with the motion of the larger waves I knew we were on the way home. The Allfather was smiling on us for the seas were gentle and the waves did not threaten to engulf us. The winds were favourable and the men did not need to row. I was at the steer board with Josephus, Aiden, Arturus, my son, and Haaken. Josephus was watching young Erik Short Toe as he steered. The young sailor was becoming quite a skilled navigator. Josephus and I intended him to become captain of *'Heart of the Dragon'* when Josephus left the sea.

Haaken idly rubbed the socket of his empty eye. He did it when thinking. "I am not sure that we should return to Frisia. Rorik will not forgive us for the destruction of his boats."

"I know but I do not fear him!" Rorik was a Norse like us but there the similarities ended. He was without honour and had tried to capture us in his port. He then pursued us as we left to make the journey east. He was desperate to defeat us. The Allfather would not let such a man defeat us.

Haaken laughed, "No one would dare to say that Jarl Dragon Heart but it may be prudent to avoid returning there. Rorik rules and at the very least we would be cheated."

"Why go there anyway?"

We all looked at Aiden. The young Hibernian was something of a galdramenn. When he spoke he was worth listening to. He read well and had spent every spare moment when were in Constantinopolis examining objects and books in the many libraries there. My warriors had spent their time drinking and wenching!

"Carry on with your thoughts, Aiden. They are normally worth listening to."

"We know that we do not have good trades there. They rob us and we only went there for convenience. They are pirates and they only act as middlemen for others. We need to ask ourselves what is it that we need."

"Weapons?"

Aiden shook his head, "No, Haaken One Eye, for Bjorn Bagsecgson makes weapons which are now as good, if not better than the Frankish ones we used to buy. We can supply our own iron ore from the lands of the Saxons. We need not weapons."

He was right. "We need pots for cooking. We know that they make good ones in the land of the Franks and the Al-Andalus."

Aiden nodded and looked at Josephus. "Then do we know of a port close by where we could trade gold for them?"

"Aye Olissipo is a fair port and they trade with the people of Britannia. It is a few days up the coast."

Aiden seemed pleased. "And what else do we need?" He smiled, "Not want, but need,"

The question perplexed me for I needed nothing. I had my weapons and my armour. We had plenty of gold. That seemed to me to be enough. Haaken, too, looked lost for words. Aiden, however, had the answer. "We can grow rye and oats in the land to the north and south of Windar's Mere. That is not enough for our farmers for most of our land is not suitable for crops. It needs animals. I come from Hibernia and there we prize cattle. Why do we not get a good bull and a cow? We could use the low land for those." He grinned at Haaken, "I know that Haaken One Eye enjoys his meat."

"That is true but we have more land which is higher up and only suits sheep."

Aiden shrugged, "Then trade for better quality sheep with finer wool."

This all made sense. "You have spoken wisely, Aiden. Where would we trade for those?"

"Gwened, it is the land of those who fled Britannia when the Romans left."

I was suddenly interested. "Did they not return to Rome?"

Josephus shook his head. "No they live still with the same language as the Welsh and the Cornish and they have a small part of the land of the Franks which Charlemagne cannot get his hands on."

This was getting better and better for Charlemagne had closed his ports to the Dane and the Norse. It was *wyrd*. "And what would we trade with them? Gold?"

"No, Jarl, the spices. They are more valuable than gold to those who have not the access to Charlemagne and his trade."

I looked at Aiden, "Well galdramenn, is there anything else?"

He smiled, "No, Jarl Dragon Heart. For myself the gold and silver we have been given by the Emperor is more than enough."

When we reached Olissipo it looked like an African port. There were many dhows amongst the larger traders. We were the only long ship and we attracted much attention when we entered the harbour. The men had taken their shields from the side to show that we came in peace and no one made any threatening moves towards us. Had we seen this city first it would have seemed exotic but we had visited the most exotic city on earth and it just seemed interesting.

Although Aiden and I had some Greek we took Josephus with us. He had been a sea captain for many years and could speak many languages. Haaken and Snorri came as guards for we took both gold and silver with us. We were of some interest to the locals. The Angles and the Norse did not often venture this far south and we looked unusual. I had learned that a smile made us a little less intimidating. I wondered about shaving off my beard for Aiden seemed to look much like the locals did. I had oiled it and trimmed it when in Constantinopolis but my men looked like hairy bears.

As with Frisia and Constantinopolis, there was a market area where you could buy whatever you wished. There we were welcomed, especially when we started spending our gold. Although we were looking for fine pots we were on the lookout for anything we could not make ourselves. Aiden found some fine needles which were expensive but could be used for his and Kara's healing as well as sewing. Josephus recommended we buy some of the orange fruit which was in abundance as well as the lemons. "They keep men healthy on a long voyage and they remain fresh for some time."

They cost us copper only. When we did find the pots, I let Aiden haggle. He was very good at it. I would have given in much earlier than he did but he negotiated not only a good price but delivery to the ship. He gave one small gold piece only and the rest would be paid upon delivery. The fine clothes we had bought in Constantinopolis meant that we had little else to buy, although I did buy some lace for Kara. Her mother had always had an eye for such things and I suspected that my daughter would like it too. Our last visit was to the wine merchant. They did not make good beer here but the wines were acceptable and we bought several amphorae of them. The containers themselves would be useful when the wine was gone.

By late afternoon we were done and we made our way back to the ship. Snorri had sharp eyes. "We are being followed, Jarl Dragon Heart."

I was not surprised; we were strangers and we had shown that we had money. My men's hands were full but I did not think they would try anything in a public street. There were guards on the street corners; each of them was armed with a wicked looking sword.

However I was relieved when we saw the drekar. My men were stretching their legs on the jetty. Although they were not wearing armour I knew that their size would intimidate those who were following us. I wanted to see who they were. We lowered the amphorae and fruit to the jetty. Josephus knew how to store it so that we were well balanced; he and Erik would see to the loading. The goods we had brought from Byzantium were neither heavy nor bulky and we had plenty of room in the hold. My ship builder had done a good job with the last ship he had ever built. His spirit was in the hull even now.

I stretched and turned so that I could see the men Snorri had spotted. They were not Arabs. They had the olive complexion of someone who lived in the Inner Sea. There were four of them and they were sailors. I knew then that it was not only our cargo they coveted, it was '**Heart of the Dragon**' herself.

The pots arrived just before sunset. Aiden checked every item before handing over the gold. The merchants left happy and Aiden was also pleased with himself. My men were disappointed when we did not have the night in port. They knew better than to argue and we planned to sail just before darkness fell.

Haaken and Cnut stood by me at the rail as Josephus and Erik Short Toe prepared the ship for sea.

Cnut pointed to two small ships across the harbour. They both had a lateen sail and a second, smaller one. "I think the men who followed you are on those ships."

"Aye, they look like greyhounds, do they not?"

Arturus had been listening. "Then why do not we not leave quickly and sail north as fast as we can?"

"If we do that, my son, then they will know that we suspect them. This way we will leave and sail slowly north. They may become overconfident thinking that we are unaware of their intentions."

Haaken mused, "What I cannot understand is why they would risk taking on a dragon ship. Are they mad?"

"It may well be that they do not recognise us for what we are. Perhaps they think they are tougher than barbarians like us."

"All set, Jarl Dragon Heart. We are ready to put to sea now."

"Then set sail." I waved and smiled at the men who were hanging around the harbour. We looked like satisfied merchants who were heading north having had a successful trade. We were the only ship leaving harbour. However, I knew that the ships with the men we had seen would follow us out. They were set on piracy. They would learn to their cost that you do not hunt the wolf unless you are a cunning hunter.

We progressed with just the sail and I let my men rest. I had a feeling that we would be fighting before too long. I had seen no need for armour but we all donned our leather byrnies and wore our cloaks. The Ulfheonar fought better in the wolf skin! We had all eaten well and we lounged on the deck as we headed into the sunset. Our two pursuers would wait until dark to leave and approach us from the darkening shore.

I strapped on Ragnar's Spirit. For the first time since the fight in the palace it felt comfortable and my wound was itchy enough to tell me that it was healing well. I slipped a dagger inside my boot and checked that I had another in the sheath on my shield. I suspected that we would be outnumbered when the would-be robbers arrived.

The wind came from the land and was pleasantly warm. It also sped us on our way north. Josephus was an experienced captain but he would not wish to risk the rocks on this coast. Erik was seated on the top of the mast and looking astern and not ahead. He had sharp eyes and he would spot the two ships first.

"I will be glad to be home, Dragon Heart."

"Did you not enjoy the east, Haaken?"

"I did but I miss my wife. She should have given birth by now and I may have a son to greet me."

I felt guilty. I had lost my wife and baby on my last trip away. I forgot that my men had their women to return home to. "We can stay at home until the winter is finished. I see no reason to go raiding."

"We have done well, Jarl Dragon Heart. If the Allfather wills it then we will have a good harvest of grain and we can hunt."

"Unless, Cnut, we have another wolf winter."

He shuddered despite the warm breeze. "I have never been as cold as that winter, Jarl. I think that the gods were punishing men."

"Punishing for what?" Aiden was ever the thinker.

"As a punishment for those people who follow the White Christ."

I laughed, "I do not think the gods would punish all for such an act. Besides he punished us and we did nothing wrong."

"All I am saying is that the winter was the worst I had ever known. The ones in Norway were not as bad."

"We survived and we are stronger. The ones we lost are still there." Kara was not meant to have children but she had become a volva. She spoke with the dead. When we had returned from our last voyage we had found a mystic on the islands off Cornwall and I had learned much about myself. I was happy that the gods and the spirits still spoke with me.

"I see them, Jarl."

"Where away, Eric?"

"One is inshore and the other is to the west. They mean to attack on both sides at once."

"You have done well; now come down." As he slithered down the stays I said, "To arms, we will have company soon."

We did not have a full crew. We had been on a voyage to trade and not to war but, even so, I had enough warriors on board to defend both sides if attacked. What I would do would be to make the odds come in our favour. "Josephus, I want some sea room. When the inshore ship comes close then make it look as though we are going to head in shore too. As soon as he begins to turn put the steer board hard over and we will go across the bows of the other one."

"That is risky, Jarl Dragon Heart. I would not wish to take out the hull on the rocks."

"Do not worry we watched this ship being built. She has a lower draught than you think." He nodded and spoke with Erik. "Archers to the side of the ship. We will cross the bows of the boat to the west. Take out the warriors gathered in the bows."

The archers moved to the left side of the ship. Arturus asked, "What will the other ship do?"

"Why she will try to attack our stern. That is where we shall be. Josephus, on my command head north again."

"Aye, Jarl Dragon Heart."

Erik said, loud enough for me to hear, "The inshore ship is closing."

"Ready Jarl Dragon Heart!"

"Archers prepare."

I knew that this would all take place really quickly. Even though I was expecting it, the turn to steer board was so severe that I thought I might lose my footing. I kept my eye on the inshore ship. He did not wish to ram us and so he began to lower his lateen as he turned to steer board too. A moment later and Josephus put the steer board hard over the other way. I saw that the other ship had turned in to shore, too, to match our move. There was confusion as we suddenly appeared across his bows and the captain of that ship took in some sail. No-one was paying us any attention as the archers released their arrows and flight after flight sailed towards the ship which was less than fifty paces from our stern. The deadly missiles fell on to men who were not wearing armour. The pirate ship almost lost way as the sailors who were hauling on ropes fell to our arrows.

"Now, Josephus!"

We turned north and caught the wind again. We leapt like a spurred horse. The second pirate had put on more sail and was now less than forty paces from our stern. His companion had almost stopped and would take some time to catch us. "Archers, rain death upon them. The rest of you come to the stern and protect the crew with our shields."

The second ship closed to almost touching distance. I picked up a javelin and hurled it at the large warrior who was whirling a hook attached to a piece of rope. They hoped to grapple us. The javelin threw him back into the others. The arrows began to pick off the pirates in the boat. They had all gathered close to the prow and there must have been almost thirty men there with more behind. At that range, and with my superb archers aiming at the bows, it was almost too easy. Two hooks did catch the stern rail and we slowed slightly. Had the other ship been closer then we might have been in trouble. As it was the four men who tried to climb along the ropes fell to their deaths when Haaken and Cnut severed them. As soon as we were released we began to move away from the pirate. More pirates fell to the arrows and I saw the captain realise the futility of pursuit. He put his tiller over and headed south to his consort. They were defeated.

Chapter 2

We lowered the sail when the coast of this new land hove into view. Josephus had never visited here before and none of us knew what sort of welcome we would get. The people here were isolated. As we had neared the coast I was amazed at how similar it was to the coast of Cymru.

Cnut was sceptical about the potential success of the venture. "It seems a risk to me, Dragon Heart. We know not if they have such beasts as we need and, even, if they will wish to trade them. Would it not be better if we just stole them from our neighbours?"

"We both know that bulls and rams are prized and kept safer than gold. Any we stole would not make our animals stronger and that is what we need; strength. We have riches Cnut, let us use them. Would you rather we squander them on warrior bands to adorn the arms of our warriors?"

He became self conscious and laughed. He had many warrior bands, "No, Jarl Dragon Heart, as usual you are right. Besides it is easier to take warrior bands from the warriors I kill than to steal cattle and drag them unwillingly home."

It was a narrow harbour and would be hard to leave in a hurry should we need to. They had used two natural spits of land and, by depositing more rocks there, made a narrow entrance. I had to admire their engineering; it would also make sure that there was a good current to sweep away silt. I wondered, as we entered, if Cnut was not correct. Was this well done? I saw a few ships in the harbour. There were constructed and rigged like the Saxon ships; they were broader in the beam and shorter than our drekar. They were not fighting ships, they were traders and that gave me hope that perhaps we could trade with these strangers.

"Aiden, you are more likely to speak their language. Haaken come with me and we will try to speak with someone in authority." I remembered Frisia. "Josephus, try to find a berth where we can leave easily and we can protect our vessel from surprise attack."

"Aye Jarl Dragon Heart."

We tied up at the end of a jetty. We had some way to walk to the buildings but that suited me for we would be better able to examine the place. We did not go dressed for war. We had just our swords strapped to our waists but we wore the fine clothes we had bought in Constantinopolis.

"Cnut, take charge and remember the last port we entered. Just try to be pleasant."

He shrugged, "As I will not understand a single word they say and they will not offend me, that should be easy."

We walked down the wooden walkway to the gates of the town. We smiled at the other sailors and merchants we saw but they scowled back at us. Our hair and our beards might be slightly less unruly but we were Norse and, as such, dangerous. We were renowned throughout the western seas as pirates.

Word of our arrival must have spread for some armed warriors were waiting at the gate. Aiden spoke. We had rehearsed what we would say. I picked out a few of the words the mailed warrior spoke and I gathered that we were not welcome. I was about to tell Aiden that we would return to our ship and try another port when Aiden smiled and said, "Jarl Dragon Heart, we are to be taken to their leader." I nodded, feeling relieved until Aiden added. "They want our swords. We are to be treated like prisoners until they have questioned us."

Haaken's hand went to his blade. "No Haaken. Let us see what the weird sisters have planned for us." I took out my sword and said, "Aiden tell him that this is a special sword. I will be angry if anything happens to a blade touched by the gods."

Aiden explained. He said something and then pointed to the heavens. I saw the guards' eyes widen. He nodded and took the blade and scabbard carefully. We were marched between the two lines of warriors up the steep path which lead to a stone citadel. It looked to be Roman in origin. The stonework and the design were similar to many we had seen at home. I could see the looks we were receiving; it was as though we were some sort of monsters which had been captured. It was always the same.

The guard who had brought our weapons placed them on the table in the hall which I could see had been a Roman Praetorium at some time in its long ago past. A few moments later a man a little older than me came into the room. He spoke with Aiden.

"This is Judicael and he is the headman of this town. He is the lord." I bowed my head slightly. "He wants to know what we are doing here."

"You have told him?"

"Aye, my lord, but he is suspicious."

It was too warm for my cloak and I never think well when I am hot. I took off my cloak. I did not expect Judicael's reaction. His eyes stared at my neck. He turned and said something to the warrior who had brought us from the jetty. He said something to Aiden.

Aiden spoke and then said to me, "I have told him your name. He seems interested in you now and yet he was not before."

I could see no reason for the interest. I was dressed as the other two were and I had only taken off my cloak. I did not feel threatened at all by the attention but I was curious. Was this the Norns again? Judicael appeared curious more than anything. A much older man came in. He looked to be even more ancient that Ragnar had been. He looked at me and then came to touch the wolf pendant hanging from my neck. It had been made by Aiden and copied from one we had found in the tomb at Wyddfa.

He spoke to me and Aiden answered him. "He asked where you got this from and I told him."

The old man sat down and appeared to be treated deferentially by the others. He and Aiden spoke for quite a while. Occasionally Aiden said something and the old man would look at me and then back at Aiden.

"What is going on Jarl?"

"I know not, Haaken, but the old man appears interested in the wolf."

They stopped speaking and turned to us. I saw that Aiden was smiling. The old man reached under his tunic and took out an identical wolf pendant to mine. My mouth must have dropped open in amazement for the old man laughed.

Aiden spoke. "This is Caradog son of Llenlleog. Judicael is his son. It seems that Caradog's father served with your ancestor, the Wolf Warrior. He was given this for his service. It appears we are welcome guests now." He added quietly, "They are a suspicious people." Almost immediately our swords were carefully returned to us. Wine and cider were brought in as well as some bread and cheese. We ate and I was questioned. In truth Aiden answered most of the questions for he knew all that there was to know about the caves, the body and the sword that we had found. The Norns had been spinning well for had we landed anywhere else we would have had no welcome. The people here were the only ones who had any connection with the wolf pendant I wore. It was *wyrd*. Once again my long dead ancestor appeared and seemed to have a hand in my future.

When Aiden mentioned the cave and the witch then Caradog showed the same degree of shock as I had. It turned out his father had been in the cave and visited the witch. I was about to say that it could not be the same woman when I realized that I knew too little about that world. I was a warrior. I was not someone who was comfortable in the spirit world. My mother and her tales of her father and grandfather suddenly made far more sense to me. I realised how little I really knew and, not for the first time, I regretted not speaking more with her when she had been alive. Her stories of her family had seemed interesting only because of the combat. I saw now there was more to it.

It was dark when we finally left. We had not had time to discuss the animals we wished to buy but that did not matter for we had done the important part. We had opened the way for talks and we were safe. It had turned out to be a good day.

Once back on *'Heart of the Dragon'* we told our friends all that had happened. Even Cnut appeared to be affected. "I am sorry that I doubted you, Jarl Dragon Heart. We were meant to come here. It is *wyrd*." He touched his wolf amulet to protect himself from the wrath of the Norns; just in case he had offended them.

Haaken was almost beside himself with joy. "I shall have more tales to tell! When I am no longer a warrior because I am as fat as Einar Belly Shaker, I shall live well and people will pay me to tell them the tales of Jarl Dragon Heart and the magic the Norns wove around his life."

The trading the next day went well. It seems they wanted spices more than gold for Charlemagne and his stranglehold meant they were too expensive to buy. However, we could not buy a proven bull. They were valuable and their owners regarded them jealously as prizes and symbols of power. Caradog, however, owned his own herd and he had a young bull, less than two years old. He told Aiden that the bull was meant to be traded to us for it had fought off an attack by a wolf pack. He had heard the stories from Aiden about my name of the Viking Wolf. He also traded us four heifers. The ram and the sheep were easier to obtain for they had those in abundance and we had a fine ram and ten ewes to take home. We handed over a mixture of pepper, cumin and the yellow spice which made all food so colourful as well as some of our gold and silver. We were not cheated and we still had more spices to trade if we needed them.

We stayed for four days and Caradog would have had us stay longer. There was kinship between us. We were from different stock but we were both islands fighting the rest of the world. We fought Saxons and other Norse. They fought Charlemagne and the Franks.

It transpired that our presence proved to be an even more propitious event. They had traded with Cornwall for years but Rorik and his pirates had made that harder. Many of their ships had been attacked and their crews slaughtered. Trade had dropped off as a result. In return for some of the drinks they made they asked us to escort one of their vessels to Cornwall. Aiden proved a master negotiator. His time in Constantinopolis had been well spent. We agreed to escort the ship if they carried our animals in their capacious ship and Aiden promised that they would be escorted back to their home port. It was an agreement which suited everyone. After we had returned home then the knarrs of Trygg and Siggi could return to trade some of our weapons for more animals and "**Dragon Heart**" could escort them. We now had a new trading partner. Escorting the slow moving cargo ship would mean a slower journey back but, as Cnut pointed out, we would not have the smell of the animals to contend with.

Haaken had laughed, "No Cnut, you are right. It is just your belching and farting which will keep us awake!" The Ulfheonar laughed.

The harbour entrance seemed wider going out than when we had entered. We needed no oars for our ship was much faster just under sail. We kept inshore of the cargo ship; especially when we passed the rocky islands to the north of Gwened.

As we neared the stretch of water close to Frisia we kept a good watch and it was rewarded when Erik saw sails. Two small threttanessa appeared on the horizon. My men went to the oars and we rowed to position ourselves between the cargo ship and the drekar. We were bigger but I had no doubt that they had larger crews. I knew without even closing with them that they were Rorik's ships. Although we had sunk two of his ships on our way south he had others and he was both ruthless and powerful.

"Keep your weapons handy."

"Do you think he will seek revenge, Dragon Heart?"

"Probably but he will need more than two threttanessa to achieve it. He will attack us only if he thinks he can win. We will have to make him believe we have a bigger crew than we do."

I let the cargo ship have more sea room. It headed towards the north west and I kept Josephus heading our ship north. My men had had much rest and we could row for a long time. Cnut kept a steady and even pace as we watched the drekar approach. When their sails were lowered a little I knew it would not come to blows. He wanted to talk.

"Take in the oars but watch for tricks. Have arrows ready if he tries anything."

I saw Rorik as he stood at the dragon prow of his drekar. "You survived then, Dragon Heart."

He had not known where we were going and I assumed that he was fishing for answers. I kept him guessing. "So it would seem and you have another drekar now."

"You still owe me two ships. I will take that waddling duck who is your consort in payment."

"I think not, Rorik. Let us just say that my belly is now full and I have no need to destroy any more of your ships but a word of warning. If you approach this wolf too closely, it bites!"

I could see that I had angered him. He drew his sword and pointed it at me. "This is not finished yet, Jarl Dragon Heart. I will have weregeld for the men and ships I lost."

I laughed and the sound carried to his crew. "Then teach your men how to swim!" I turned to Josephus. "Let us head home, your former master appears unhappy."

"He was ever so and I am glad that he has been punished for he was cruel." We soon caught the knarr and we headed to Cornwall so that our new friends could trade for the Cornish tin they needed.

As we left Cornwall for our home Aiden told me of the conversations he had had with Caradog. "It seems, Jarl Dragon Heart that our arrival was foretold. Caradog's father, Llenlleog, when he returned to the land of the Bro Waroc'h, said that a wizard had told him that a descendant of the one who wielded the sword would come one day. They had almost given up waiting. It was the wolf pendant which told them that we had finally arrived."

"*Wyrd* and we knew nothing. I wonder how many other events are waiting for us."

"I know not Jarl but it seems we are all marked in one manner or another. The caves, the wolves, the islands they are all strands in the webs the Weird Sisters have woven."

I was overjoyed to see Úlfarrston. Pasgen was the headman of the port which was closest to our land and they were our allies and friends. Descended from the old Britons of Rheged they guarded the southern entrance to our lands and protected our ships. I saw the knarrs of Trygg and Siggi bobbing in the estuary. I felt relieved. The captains and their families had been driven from their homeland and taken refuge with us. They were now part of our family.

"Cnut, take the Ulfheonar back to Cyninges-tūn. I need a crew to escort our friends and the two knarr back to our new allies."

"Aye Warlord." He turned to the warriors. "Let us get this drekar unloaded. We will not leave this for the jarl to carry."

"Josephus can you manage another voyage for me?" He nodded, "It will be the last before winter."

"Of course, Jarl Dragon Heart but I am happy to sail over the winter too."

I shook my head. "You will be more valuable to me making maps for young Erik here to use when he becomes captain!"

While they saw to the ship I went ashore to the settlement with Aiden and Arturus. I had seen little of my son on the journey back for he had been closeted with Aiden. Aiden was teaching him to read and to speak other languages. Arturus was ambitious and I knew he wished to rule the people after me. He would be better prepared than I had been.

"Aiden, you will need to return with Josephus to Gwened for you have the words."

"Of course."

"Jarl, may I accompany him?"

"You can and I am happy, Arturus, but why?"

"My education is lacking. I am a fair warrior but I need to exercise my mind. We have learned much on this voyage and I believe I can learn even more."

"Do not forget you are a warrior first. Our people need our protection."

He smiled, "I can do both; I can think and fight."

I saw Aiden roll his eyes but I admired the confidence of my son. I had not had as much confidence when I was the same age. "Then go with Aiden and think how to get the animals safely from the ship!"

Trygg and Siggi were waiting for me with Pasgen. A horn of beer awaited me. I found myself looking forward to it. I had not had a decent horn since I had left on my long voyage. They allowed me to drink before they began to question me. It took three horns for me to tell them all.

"You wish us to return with **'Heart of the Dragon'**?"

"Aye Siggi, have we much to trade?"

"There are some farm implements and weapons as well as combs and some tunics made by the women. They have been spinning under the direction of Kara."

"How is my daughter?"

All three laughed, "We are just thankful she is not a warrior for she rules in your stead with a hand of iron."

"And you, Pasgen; is there anything for you to trade?"

"Aye my lord. Not much but enough to make us some profit."

"I am sending my son and Aiden. If you trust their judgement then they will handle the trades for you."

"I do not think it matters what we trade just so that we can find new markets. We have prospered since you have been away."

As I took a swallow of my fourth horn I laughed, "Perhaps I should stay away more often then Pasgen."

"Oh no, Jarl, I meant no offence."

"And I took none. It is the ale. I have been drinking wine since I left here." I tapped his arm with my hand to show that I was not upset. "I am pleased and with the new bull and ram we should have better animals. What we need is a supply of salt. There are salt flats to the south of the land of the Bro Waroc'h."

Pasgen shook his head, "A waste of a ship. The bay to the south, where we get our shellfish, already provides some salt. It would not take much effort to produce more."

"Excellent, then we can salt our spare meat. I would not have another Wolf Winter where the people starve."

The crew of my ship came in with the two suits of armour given to myself and Arturus. I had almost forgotten them but they took the breath away of my three companions. "This is the armour of a king!"

"No, Trygg, an Emperor; for it was an Emperor who gave it to me." I was not certain when I would wear it for I was used to my blackened wolf armour. This was not made of mail but square pieces of overlapping metal. The lower part was still mail but the lamellar armour extended down the arms. It was lighter than mail and yet it covered more. There was also something the Greeks had called greaves, which protected my lower legs.

The three of them examined the armour. Siggi nodded, appreciatively. "You should have it blackened like your mail armour, Jarl. It is lighter and you would be an even greater warrior wearing this."

I wondered if he was right. Certainly it would be much easier to repair. I would have Bjorn Bagsecgson examine it. If we could make armour like this it would make us even stronger.

"Pasgen, I would have you make the crew of this ship welcome tonight. Throw them a feast; I will pay for it. We need to make the links which bind our peoples like links of iron. I will leave my son and Aiden here to translate. I know that you will watch over them."

"Aye Jarl Dragon Heart."

"And I will leave the animals here tonight so that they can recover some of their strength for the journey tomorrow. They will need penning."

"We will do that for you. Will you not stay with us?"

I shook my head, "I am anxious to see my home and my daughter."

"I understand." A look of sadness passed over Pasgen's face for he remembered when I had come home to a house of the dead and discovered most of my family dead in my hall.

I took one of the ponies we kept at the port and, wrapping my wolf cloak about me I set off to make the journey home.

Chapter 3

Although night was falling we had made the track to Cyninges-tūn both wide and easy to follow. It meandered between the oaks and the beeches. The pony trotted along happily. Even when night fell he seemed quite happy to head through the tall trees and, once I reached the water my land opened up. The moon had risen. The old man that was Olaf looked down and I saw his reflection gleaming across the shining water of Cyninges-tūn. I felt at peace. I knew from my daughter, Kara, that the spirit of my dead wife, Erika, lived between the mountains. I felt her presence whenever I returned home from a voyage. I heard a voice telling me to stop. I reined in the pony, which seemed surprised and I dismounted. I put the reins under a large rock. I was totally alone. I could see the lights from the two villages many miles ahead; they were glowing like tiny candles in the dark. I walked to the water and took off my boots, my sword and my clothes. I just walked into the water.

The pony happily nibbled the grass at the side of the water and I walked slowly into the Water of Cyninges-tūn. I felt the icy cold creep up on me until I was chest high. I lay on my back and allowed the water to wash over me. Putting my arms and legs out I floated. With my eyes closed I felt as though I was cocooned somewhere safe and as the sounds of the night disappeared, I went deep within myself into a dark black hole which suddenly filled with light as I heard Erika's voice.

'You have come back to me, my warrior. You have done well. Ragnar and your mother are both pleased with you. You made the right decisions even when others doubted you. You are fulfilling your destiny. You are the Wolf Warrior reborn.'

I tried to speak in my head but nothing came. It was as though I had been struck dumb. There were so many questions I wanted to ask and I could not.

'I am always close to you, my love, but I can enter your head when you are in water or in the cave of the dreamers; the place of the dead. Kara can ask the questions which fill your heart. Now you

must go. You have much to do. Danger comes to this land and it comes unseen. Trust your heart and not your eyes. We have only one friend now and the enemies of our people are gathering to take what we have built.'

And then the sounds of the water returned. The gentle neighing of the pony reminded me of where I was. I stood and walked from the water. The air felt warmer, somehow. I rubbed myself dry with my tunic and then dressed. The pony seemed eager to get home and we make quick time.

The gates were closed and I stood patiently waiting for the sentry to see me. It was Magnus Tostigson and he was embarrassed that he had not seen me quicker. That was not because I was jarl but because had I been an enemy then all would have been in danger.

"I am sorry jarl. I was…"

I shook my head as I walked through the gate. "Do not make something up. Be more vigilant in the future. Just because the Ulfheonar are back does not mean that there is no danger." The words of Erika rang in my ears. "There is danger all around."

Kara and her healers had their own hall but she must have known I was coming for she almost ghosted next to me as I walked towards the fire in my home. "I am glad that you are safe." She put her arm through mine and, for a moment, she was the tiny girl clinging on to her father returning from the wars. She leaned up and kissed my cheek. "You smell different. Is this perfume?"

"In the east they oil beards and put sweet smelling herbs in the waters in which they bathe."

She laughed and it sounded good. "I like it. Do not apologise. The men here all smell like goats. You must keep it up." As we entered the hall she said, "Mother has spoken with you."

At one time I would have been surprised, but no longer. "Aye, I went into the water and she came to me."

"I have seen the danger too. It comes from all around us. The north, south, east and west."

"Not just Northumbria and Eanred then?"

"No, although that snake is not yet scotched. Our land is attractive and we have made it so. Others covet what we have." She sat me down on my chair and poured me some beer. "I have had the men improving the defences here but I fear that Windar's Mere and

Ulla's Water will require more work for they lie to the east and enemies would strike them first."

"You have done well my daughter. We have brought many riches back for you. Aiden bought not only spices but herbs and potions from the eastern doctors."

"He and Arturus are still at Úlfarrston?"

I nodded. "They have another short voyage to make. It will be a month or more that they will be away."

"Then rest and I will go and have a word with Magnus Tostigson. He was not paying enough attention to his duties."

I shook my head. She knew things which others would not even notice. "No Kara, he knows his mistake. He will not make a second."

Laughing she left saying, "You are far too soft for a fierce warrior whom Saxon mothers use to terrify their children."

I was relieved when the animals came. With winter approaching I did not wish to risk the animals and we built some pens on the fell side close to the water. I had my men construct some byres for them. We would cosset these fine animals for they would ensure our survival. In the spring they would begin to give us the new herds and flocks. I would work out, with Aiden and Scanlan, the best place for them. The bull and the ram, however, would live within my walls; they were like gold and they would be protected as fiercely.

Over the next few days Kara tried to get me to rest after the gruelling voyage and the battles which had given me new scars but I shook my head. "I am more aware now, than ever, that I was brought here for a purpose. I will stop when I go to the Otherworld. Do not fret over me, daughter. I am happy in my work."

I left my new armour with Bjorn and took the Ulfheonar north to visit with Thorkell the Tall at the outpost to the north of our land. He was the guardian of the northern passes. Raiders could still come from the coast but the greatest danger came from the Picts and the men of Dál Riata to the north. As I led my Ulfheonar north I told Haaken and Cnut of my wife's words and my daughter's warnings.

"Then why are we going north? We should do as Kara suggested and build up Windar's Stead!"

Haaken laughed at his friend, "They are hidden. Did you not hear the jarl? We know not when they will come or who they are. They could come from any direction. They might even come from the north."

"And securing our northern borders will allow us to look to the east. Hopefully we will find a world at peace and a Thorkell who is bored."

Even though we were in our land I had Snorri and Beorn Three Fingers scouting ahead. It did not do to be surprised. We had appeared unseen in Saxon lands before now. We would be vigilant.

I was surprised when we reached the hill fort. Thorkell had had his men and slaves working to improve it. I saw his ship, *'Great Serpent'*, in the river beyond. It was reassuring. We paused on the slope which overlooked the fort to examine the new defences. He had added another ditch and I could see a channel leading from the river. Cnut nodded his approval. "He has made a dam so that he can flood his ditch. That is clever, Jarl."

"Aye, Cnut. I think our old comrade will not be caught by surprise as he was by Wyddfa." As we made our way down I saw that he had towers too and we had been seen from their tops. Our wolf cloaks told them who we were but I was pleased when more warriors joined the six sentries on the walls.

We had to twist and turn to cross Thorkell's ditches. It was ingenious. Any attacker would be subject to arrows and stones whilst he was approaching the gates and walls. Thorkell strode towards us to greet us. "Jarl, it is good to see you. Where is Arturus Wolf Killer?"

"He and Aiden are on a trading mission. He is growing. He is now a warrior and a man."

He led me into his fort. "Aye he is and I now have a baby son. Soon I will train him as you trained Arturus."

"Good." I spread my arm around his defences. Inside the fort looked to be as well managed as the outside. "I see you have made the fort stronger. That is good."

His face darkened. "We need to. Come to my hall and I will tell all."

Thorkell had been Ulfheonar and was a blood brother of my men. We all sat and enjoyed his ale. After we had thanked him for his hospitality he told us of their trials and tribulations. "The drekar stops the Hibernians from coming too close to our river and our land. We keep a crew aboard and it patrols our shores. Not long after you left they sent a couple of ships to raid for slaves. We hurt them badly and they have not returned but we have found that the men of Dál Riata cross the river upstream and raid the farms there. They have taken many slaves. We cannot reach them quickly enough to deter them. The land to the south is safe for the high passes protect too but the east is where we now have few people. They have moved closer to the fort."

"Your numbers have not increased then?"

"No, Jarl."

I had come at an opportune moment. "They have taken people and animals?"

"Aye. The land to the east is not suitable for grain. We have our grain farms to the south and the west. They occupy the little land before the mountains rise." He looked at me curiously, "You have some plans in mind?"

"Aye, it was something Cnut said when we were trading for a bull and a ram. He wondered why we did not steal from our neighbours. It seems the men of Dál Riata were listening to him and they are stealing from us. We will go north of the river and teach them a lesson."

"You will bring your army north?"

I shook my head. "I have one boat crew at sea with my son and Aiden and the other protects our valley. My daughter has seen war in the future and danger from the east." He frowned. "It is not here yet but you and your men will have to guard this frontier alone. We will try to make it secure for you now."

"But you only have the Ulfheonar!"

Haaken shook his head indignantly, "Have you forgotten so soon what we can do? Fear not Thorkell, if the jarl can save the Emperor of Byzantium with just his son and a slave to help him then he can deal with cattle thieves."

Thorkell laughed, "You are right to chastise me, old friend. There may be just thirty of you but I would not be the men north of the river. Do you need any of my men as guides?"

"No, Thorkell but we will need some of your boys to wait for us when we return with the cattle and the slaves we will free." He nodded. "Now tell me where they will be."

We had created our own maps and Thorkell took one out. "They have a hill fort here." He pointed to a place north of the estuary.

"But the land twixt the rivers and the hill fort are where they farm. They do not have forts. They rely on ditches and the fact that we do not cross north to fight them as their protection."

"Then they will learn how the Norse makes war. Keep your ship in the river. It can keep watch for them. We will leave in the morning."

Late summer was the time of the rains and the land north of the fort was wetter than it would normally have been. It would make the enemy more complacent. We crossed the river further upstream using a raft bridge we quickly constructed. We left Thorkell's boys there with orders to keep the raft on the southern side of the river. Snorri and Beorn Three Fingers loped off towards the north west. We had no supplies and only had our bows as extra baggage. We would live off the land. My men were ready for this. They had had little opportunity to use their skills for some time. They wanted honour, treasure and, most importantly, to fight.

"We want animals on this raid."

"No slaves then?"

"No slaves. They will slow us down and provide a distraction. I want the land between the fort and here as empty of people as the land to the east of Thorkell."

"The men do not like to kill women nor children."

"I know Haaken. We may not need to. If we take their animals then they will flee to their neighbours."

We found the first farm on the first evening soon after the moon had risen. Snorri returned, "Beorn watches the farm. They have cattle, pigs and sheep. There is a wooden enclosure. It is to keep out the wolves and not men."

"Good. Lead on."

We ran through the night not making a sound. Animals and birds knew that we were there but the humans on whom we preyed had no idea. We arrived in the depths of the night when all would be soundly asleep; hopefully any sentries they might employ would be easily dealt with.

We found Beorn who spoke quietly, "They have a young warrior on guard in the pens. They have a hall and I think there is a hut with slaves within but I am not certain."

"Cnut, take half of the men and go around the far side of the ditch. You will take the hall and we will capture the animals. When they are secure we will join you."

Cnut and his half moved silently like shadows.

Snorri was an expert with a knife and he slithered along the ground towards the unsuspected warrior. I think that the warrior was actually asleep, leaning against the tree and seated on the wall, for Snorri reached him and slit his throat without even the slightest of movements. I signalled for Stig Sweet Tooth to watch the animals while we slipped over the low stone wall towards the hall. I say hall but it was more of a large roundhouse. That meant only one entrance. There were three other smaller huts and then the one I took to be the slave hut for it had a bar on the outside. I waved for Tostig Stigson to watch the hut. Cnut and the others appeared. I left them to the hall. Waving Sigtrygg Thrandson and four warriors to one of the other huts and Haaken and three to the second, I took my remaining three warriors to the last hut.

I had not reached it when there was a shout from the large round house and Cnut and his men began their work. The door of the hut closest to me burst open and a warrior rushed out with a spear. He took Ulf Green Eye by surprise and the spear head scored his mail as he was knocked to the floor. I sliced Ragnar's Spirit horizontally; it bit into his arm and then into the side of his naked chest. He was a tough warrior and he reached out to grab me with his left hand. I plunged my blade deep into his chest and gave him a warrior's death. I peered into the hut which was lit with a glowing fire. There was a woman and three children cowering at the back of the hut. I pointed to the north and shouted, "Go!" it was not their language but they understood. The woman grabbed a handful of belongings and fled with the children. I had no doubt that, once we left, she would return and collect everything of value.

I wasted no more time on the hut for I could examine that at my leisure. I led my men to the large round hut. As we ran I heard the screams and cries of the women and the children as they fled to the north. It was the one direction without my warriors. I knew that they would spread stories about our numbers which would be exaggerated. They would speak of a horde of Vikings rather than the handful we were. That could only help.

When the farmstead was secure we went to the slave hut and I nodded. The bar was lifted and the door opened.

"It is Jarl Dragon Heart of Cyninges-tūn, you can come out." A dozen slaves, the adults all yoked came fearfully out. The children clutched at their mothers. I took off my helmet to make me less fearsome. Since my beard and moustache had been trimmed in Constantinopolis and my hair tamed, I looked less like a wild troll. I had decided to keep my slightly more human look. Kara's words had convinced me that it was acceptable. I smiled.

One of the women dropped to her knee and took my hand. She kissed it. "We knew that you would come for us, jarl."

I recognised her. "You are the wife of Arne No Thumb."

She nodded. "He was killed when they took us."

I looked at his three young boys. "Will you go back to your farmstead?"

She shook her head and I could see her fighting back the tears, "They took our animals and burnt our home. With winter coming we would die."

"Then return with me to Cyninges-tūn. My daughter can find work for willing hands and when the boys are grown we will build you a new home."

The eldest said, "I would be an Ulfheonar, Jarl Dragon Heart."

"And you will be. What is your name and how many summers have you seen?"

"I am Haaken Arneson and I have seen seven summers."

"Then in five summers you can begin your training." The boy and his mother nodded gratefully.

"Cnut, find four men to escort the animals and our people back to the river. The boys of Thorkell the Tall can take them to Thorkell's Stead."

"Aye Jarl Dragon Heart."

When the animals and the people had gone it was much quieter. I had not expected much opposition. That would come when they knew that we were in their lands. "Sigtrygg, set sentries. We will rest here for a few hours and then seek the next farmstead."

It was at times like this I missed Aiden. Often he would help me to plan our next moves. I had to do it alone. There were just eight slaves we had freed and the same number of animals. There had to be far more in this land. I had hoped to achieve more in my first raid. I prayed that we would become lucky the next day.

We could all survive on but a few hours of sleep. When I awoke Snorri and Beorn were preparing breakfast. They had killed the fowl that we had not been able to send back to Thorkell and the smell of their cooking flesh put an edge on my appetite.

"When you have finished eating find us a bigger settlement. I want to make a bigger impact."

Haaken stretched and said, "Why?"

"I want the army of whoever controls this part of the land to come looking for us. We need to give him a bloody nose. That way he will seek easier targets: the Saxons perhaps."

"His army may be too big."

"It matters not how big it is. When I was in Constantinopolis I discovered then that the size of an army does not matter; it is the quality of the army which is most important. Bardanes Tourkos infiltrated a huge army of killers into the palace but we defeated them."

He laughed, "You nearly died and you had to flee to the Ulfheonar to finish them off."

I smiled and took the leg which Snorri proffered. "And we can do so again."

Cnut, who had been listening, looked confused. "We have no Ulfheonar to run to. We are all here."

"We have Thorkell, his ship and the land to help us. I want the leader of the Dál Riata to pursue us intent upon our destruction. We will flee and draw him into a trap. That is why I asked for the ship to stay on the river and for the boys to watch for us. They can bring Thorkell and '**Great Serpent**'. We will destroy them."

"You are confident, Jarl."

"Aye Sigtrygg for I know the mettle of the men I command. When I fought the rebels and assassins of Bardanes Tourkos I saw men who were paid well but fought badly. You are hardly paid and yet you fight like none I have ever seen. That is why I am confident."

The four men sent to escort the animals returned at dusk as did Snorri. "Jarl Dragon Heart I have found a collection of farms. It is along the coast close to a stream which leads to the sea. There is no wall around it but they have a ditch and they have many cattle that are penned."

"Are there warriors?"

"They carry swords and there are twenty or thirty men who live there. It looks like a prosperous place. We saw thralls." He paused. "I saw Tostig Olegson. He has lost his hand."

These were our people. I had fought alongside Tostig when he was still a warrior and before he had chosen to be a farmer. It was also a target which might attract the attention of whoever ruled in these parts. "How far away is it?"

"Fifteen miles. We can run there in four hours."

I laughed, "You might be able to do so, Snorri but we will take an hour or so longer than that. We will wait for Beorn to report until we set out. You have done well. Get what rest you can."

Beorn arrived soon after sunset. "I have found a farmstead. It is up the valley to the north and they have many sheep there."

"How many warriors?"

"I saw none."

"And how far away is it?"

"Perhaps four or five hours of running."

That decided me. "We will strike at Snorri's village and then we mark our way up the valley to Beorn's farmstead. I think they will follow us. The survivors from this farmstead should have reached other villages by now and they will investigate. They will follow us west to the village but we will have gone by the time they reach us. We will send the animals back from the farmstead of Beorn."

It seemed simple as I said it but I did not know what the weird sisters had planned for us. As usual they interfered with my idea and strategy. Perhaps I had not learned enough in Constantinopolis.

We set off after dark. I went at the rear for I wished to see my men in the night. They were almost invisible. The black armour and the wolf cloak hid us from view. If the full moon came out and illuminated the land we would be seen. If not then we would be hidden. We would not be merely wolf warriors we would be ghost warriors.

Snorri halted us a mile or so from the village. We could smell the smoke and the animals. As we waited and adjusted armour and shields we heard the faint noise of conversations within the village. It must have been close the time when they all went to their sleeping rooms. We heard the people of Dál Riata as they said, '*Good night*' to each other.

The herd was in a pen to the north and Erik Dog Bite and Tostig Wolf Hand took Bjorn Carved Teeth, one of the newer Ulfheonar, to secure the valuable animals. The rest of us spread out in a half circle with me in the middle. We crept through the night; our weapons drawn and our shields ready. The fire in the centre of the village was already dying and they had one sole sentry in the middle. Snorri's arrow plunged into his back but he shouted a dying warning to the others. It made little difference. We were in the village in an instant. As warriors emerged, weapons in hand, from the huts we attacked them. As with the other settlement we let the women and children flee. Although there were more men this time I suspected that these had been drinking for they fell easily to our blades. When they had all been despatched and any treasure recovered, I ordered the village to be burned. The dry roofs soon caught fire and night became day with the fierce flames.

"They will see this from many miles away. They may even see it from their hill fort."

"I hope they do, Cnut, for they will hurry here and we will be gone. Let us go north and take the animals with us."

"They will make a noise and alert the next village."

"And the villagers will flee and the word will spread that the Vikings are raiding. What will they do then?"

"They will try to catch us."

"Precisely."

We gathered the handful of slaves. Tostig Olegson was so grateful I thought he would weep. He had all of his own family alive but his brother and nephew had both died. "Give me a sword, Jarl Dragon Heart. I only have one hand now but I can use it. I will not be taken so easily a second time!" We gave all the men weapons. The women and the children were given the task of leading the animals.

In the end the animals remained remarkably silent as we headed to the lonely farmstead. It was the dogs which woke the inhabitants. There was a shepherd boy with the sheep and when the dog warned him of our presence then he shouted the alarm. The farmer and his people fled. This time there were no slaves but the flock was a large one.

It was coming on to dawn and my men were tired but I had another task for them. "Erik Wolf Bite, I want you to lead the animals and our people to safety. We will stay here and slow down the men of Dál Riata. Keep going until you reach the river and then ask Thorkell to bring his men to the river for we will be bringing them the ones who destroyed his farms."

"Aye Jarl Dragon Heart."

They moved swiftly out. I knew they would not keep the pace up all the way to the river but they did not have far to go. It was less than twenty miles to the safety of the bridge. They had freedom to spur them on. I had been a slave and knew that freedom was a better master than slavery.

My men looked all in. "We can rest but first I want to prepare this place to receive visitors. Snorri and Beorn go down the trail and lay traps. The rest of you deepen the ditch and plant stakes. Cover them with the bramble bushes."

I joined my men and we worked hard to create defences which they would not be expecting. They too would be tired but the difference was that we were expecting them. They thought that we were fleeing and they were just following us. They would not expect us to fight them. I made them all rest after two hours of hard work. Snorri slept down the trail in the branches of a tree. He was a light sleeper and he would warn us of the arrival of our pursuers. We had all eaten the food the farmer had had prepared for his family and all of us fell asleep as soon as our heads hit the ground.

They reached us just before dawn but we had had some rest. Snorri woke us when he heard their approach. We all hid behind the wall. Four of my men had bows and they would begin the attack. The men of Dál Riata fought as the Hibernians did. They used a wild attack and prized individual combat. My men also liked that but they could be disciplined and today they would be as disciplined as the bodyguard of Emperor Nikephoros himself.

The men of Dál Riata tried to come silently up the trail. Perhaps they hoped that we had rested and they would catch us asleep. They were, however, unable to do so silently. We heard them. Readied, behind the small fence to keep in the animals, we waited with swords ready to wreak death upon the men of the Dál Riata.

They were far too noisy and we were ready. As soon as they hit the ditch they screamed their pain and my archers let loose at targets no more than ten paces away. They screamed as the barbed arrows ripped into naked flesh. We remained silent. We knew the benefits of silence. It created uncertainty and fear. Warriors who are not Ulfheonar do not like stepping into the unknown. The men of Dál Riata knew nothing of what they faced. As soon as the first warrior who survived the traps climbed over the fence I sliced horizontally with Ragnar's Spirit. He went to the Otherworld in an instant. As soon as they realised that we were waiting I heard a voice shouting orders. I knew not exactly what they said but I guessed that they warned them that we had not fled and we were standing to fight.

The second warrior who launched himself at me over the dying body of the man before him thought that he had me as he sailed through the air with sword raised. I held my shield for protection but Ragnar's Spirit sliced through his poorly made sword and it split in two. As he landed behind me I brought the sword down to dissect his head which did not have the protection of a helmet. The sounds of battle were mixed with the cries of the men of Dál Riata. It was a brief combat. My archers were still picking their targets and men were dying before they could fall into the deadly ditch. I saw that there was no-one before me. All that I could hear was the sound of the wounded and the dying.

"Light torches! Let us see what is here!"

It was a horrific sight which greeted us. Our superior weapons, tactics and armour had ensured complete victory. No one had escaped either a wound or death.

"I need a prisoner who can walk and another who is going to die. The rest can go to the Otherworld."

I heard the sighs as men were killed. Torches were lit and I went to Haaken and Snorri who had two prisoners. One had a bad cut to his leg whilst the other had been gutted and would not last an hour.

I went to the dying warrior. "I can put a sword in your hand and send you to the Otherworld if you answer me but one question."

His hands were trying to hold in the guts which were desperate to spill out. He nodded.

"Give him a sword." Cnut put a short sword in his hand and he smiled.

"A name! Who is your leader?"

"Fiachnae mac Neill," he winced, "and he will eat your heart!"

I nodded and Sigtrygg slit his throat. I turned to the other one. "We will bind your leg and send you back to your Warlord."

"He is our king!"

"Whoever he is tell him this. If he ventures south of the river again he will feel the wrath of Jarl Dragon Heart and the wolves will feed on his flesh!"

He looked at me in surprise. "That is all? I can go?"

"You can go!"

His leg bandaged he hobbled off as fast as he could go; grateful, no doubt that he had survived an encounter with the Ulfheonar.

When he had gone I said, "And now we sleep."

Cnut shook his head, "We should run as fast as we can."

"Why?"

"This Fiachnae mac Neill will know that we are here and he will seek us out! He will bring his whole army!"

Haaken laughed so hard that tears poured down his cheeks, "Cnut, my friend, we are sending a man with a wounded leg to run twenty miles to report to his king! Can he fly? Is he Myrddyn the wizard? The jarl is right. We have two days before this Warlord reaches us."

"Exactly. We rest and then head towards the river, slowly. We tease them; we tempt them and we draw them on and when we are ready then we slaughter them and show them how the Norse makes war!"

My men suddenly shouted and cheered; we had won and we had won easily. How the Norns must have laughed.

Chapter 4

We all had a good day and a night's sleep and then we headed east before dawn had broken. Beorn and Snorri left to keep watch on our enemies. We knew that as soon as they heard what had happened to their warband they would rush after us. They would not stop until they reached and then they would be so full of anger that that they would throw themselves upon us to wreak their vengeance on these barbarians who had dared to invade their land. We would be fresh. We left a clear trail and went slowly. Twenty miles in one day was not difficult and we camped five miles from the river. Stig Sweet Tooth met us and told us that all was in place. Thorkell had both his ship and his men ready to support us. All that we lacked was the numbers Fiachnae would bring.

We found a good defensive site some three miles from the river. Sigtrygg Thrandson discovered it; he had a good eye for such things. It was almost made for us. *Wyrd*. There were trees behind us and a stream which meandered to join the two rivers. It was autumn and the rains had made the ground to our left swampy. My men cut branches from the woods and planted them to our right. When the Dál Riata came they would come for me. My wolf shield would draw them on. When we had sent the messenger back we had left it in plain sight. I was the one, in the black armour and the mail mask who had spoken to him. They would know who the leader was and they would seek me out. We would fight in a wedge and they would die. At least that was the plan. When we looked north we saw some of the standing stones placed there by giants. They dotted our land and they were a good omen for us. It meant that the old ones and the old ways ruled in the land in which we fought. The giants and the gods were on our side.

We ate the last of the fowl we had killed and we waited. I needed a bath. I needed a shave and my hair combing. Constantinopolis had changed me. I was not the same warrior who had defeated Rorik and fled south. I was now used to a little more civilisation than before. I was becoming the warrior painted on the wall of the tomb. *Wyrd*!

They reached us late in the morning. Beorn reported their numbers. There were over a hundred of them. Had we been anyone other than Ulfheonar we might have been worried for they outnumbered us by three to one. My four archers had ten arrows left to each of them. I turned to them, "I want every arrow to strike home; a death or a wound for all forty arrows. Do that and I know that we shall win!"

"We will not let you down."

"The rest of you must be patient. They will climb this hill and be eager to die. Send them to the Otherworld."

I knew that Ragnar's Spirit needed sharpening. I checked that I had my two daggers and seax close to hand. If I had to I could fight as well with those weapons. I regretted not wearing my new armour. It would have been much lighter. I was just happy that Haaken had persuaded me to wear the mask of mail. It made me look even more terrifying.

We stood in a shield wall with the men angled back from me. Snorri raced up the bank. "They are half a mile behind. There are four mailed warriors and the rest are the hairy arsed barbarians we might have expected!"

I laughed for Snorri had grown from the young ship's boy into an Ulfheonar without peer. I banged my shield with my sword and roared, "I am Jarl Dragon Heart! Flee while you can for if you come here then you will meet death!"

Their leader, whom I took to be the warrior in the mail with the two handed sword shouted something back and they raced up the hill. The archers' arrows flung back those at the front. My archers knew what to do. They avoided hitting those with armour; they were harder to kill. They aimed at the rest who were half naked and the ones they hit died. The warband was thinned, almost decimated, as it came towards us. We waited patiently. They had seen our numbers and thought that they could beat us but they reached us with a third less men than they started.

The ones to our right struck the hedges. They became stuck in the branches and brambles; my archers used the last of their arrows to slaughter them. The ones to our fore fell as we scythed them down with our superior swords and spears. I heard their leader shout something and men ran to our left. There they became stuck in the sticky swamp. This was the moment for me to unleash the beast that was the Ulfheonar. "Ragnar's Spirit!"

We hurtled down the hill. They could not believe that they were being attacked. They outnumbered us still! A warrior ran at me and held his sword up to stab me. I smashed down with Ragnar's Spirit. The blade of my foe folded and buckled and my sword continued down to rip into his unprotected shoulder. I stepped over his body and looked for another enemy. I went for Fiachnae mac Neill; he had a chieftain's torc about his neck. I held my shield before me. He swung his sword wildly over his head. I ducked beneath it and punched with my shield so that he fell backwards and then plunged my sword into his throat. I began banging my shield. The fighting stopped as the remainder of Fiachnae mac Neill's stared at us. The men of Dál Riata saw their dead leader and the other mailed warriors lying slaughtered on the ground. They had had enough. They fled and took back tales of the monster that was Jarl Dragon Heart. The threat to the north was gone, for a while, at least.

I took the torc from the dead leader's neck. It was made of gold. It would be used to make wolf pendants for my new warriors. We would take the weapons and the helmets but they were of poor quality. These men were brave for they fought with inferior equipment and training. It was no wonder that we always won. We put the bodies in the farmstead and fired it. Their spirits would go to the Otherworld where they would talk of the disaster which had struck them. We headed back to the river leaving a pall of smoke behind us.

Thorkell and his men were waiting anxiously at the river. He looked behind me after we had crossed. "Where are the men of Dál Riata?"

"They fell or they fled. Their chief is dead. I daresay they will appoint another but I am also sure that they will find much easier targets in the future. I do not think they will bother you for some time." I looked at the land around me. "This would make a good farm. We will leave you some of the animals. Why not have a tower built here." I pointed to the Roman wall in the distance. "Use some of that stone to make a good base and deepen the ditch. If you did that you would have cattle that would produce both milk and meat in great quantities. The tower would give you warning of an attack and provide a refuge from danger." I turned Thorkell so that he could see his own fort in the distance. "If you built another tower on your citadel then they would be able to signal back and forth."

He nodded. "You are ever the thinker, Jarl Dragon Heart and you make me feel foolish for not having thought of that."

"Let us say I have been doing this for a long time and Prince Butar was a good teacher. Some of your people wish to come south to Cyninges-tūn."

He nodded. He was a wise and thoughtful jarl. "I understand. Ulla the wife of Arne No Thumb has spoken to me. He was a fine warrior and his sons will be too."

I nodded, and we headed back to Thorkell's Stead. "We have a new bull and a ram. Tell your farmers that when their animals come into season they can bring them to Cyninges-tūn. I would that we could create better, hardier animals. That way we increase our wealth and the prosperity of our people."

We knew that we could not hurry south as quickly as we had come north. We had some families who wished to live either at Windar's Mere or Cyninges-tūn. More importantly we had many animals to move. It would not do to risk such valuable beasts. It happened that we reached the col which lead to the Grassy Mere and the Rye Dale in the late afternoon. We headed for the Mere and the stead of Harald Skullsplitter. He had been a mighty warrior but when he had married, his wife, who was as small as he was huge had persuaded him to take up a stead on the Grassy Mere. It was, as we discovered, one of the most beautiful spots in the whole land. As we watched the sun go down we saw the high mountains reflected in the red water. I thought that Cyninges-tūn was the idyllic home but this one was almost as good.

"Well Jarl Dragon Heart, I see that you have had a successful raid."

"Aye Harald and I hope that the Dál Riata stay north of the river." As I drank the well brewed ale I looked at the cluster of huts and halls which ringed Harald's stead. "How many warriors can you muster if we need an army?"

He gave me a sharp look. He understood war for he had fought with Prince Butar and stood with me in a shield wall. "War is coming?" I told him of the prophesies and Kara's words. "We have twenty men here." He smiled, "My two sons take after their father but they have no mail yet. Then we have four other warriors who are, like me, old."

I patted him on his enormous shoulder, "Let us say veterans and warriors with experience."

He nodded, "It sounds better but it does not mean that we could fight all day as we once did; then there are four others who can use a sword. As for the rest," he shrugged, "they can use bows and slings well."

"Good. Keep them well trained. I will try to get you some mail for your warriors. At the very least all shall have a helmet." When our new animals have bred we shall have a source of leather which will make fine armour."

"We are at your command, my jarl." He spread his hand around. "When I lived in Norway I dreamed of a place like this but I called it Valhalla. Now we have found a Valhalla here on earth. We would not live in paradise but for you and Prince Butar."

"And he watches us even now Harald. He would be pleased that we had achieved all that we have."

I sent the animals and families to Cyninges-tūn with the Ulfheonar and I went with Haaken to visit Windar. He and Ulf, in the next valley, were vital to my plans and they needed to know what was in my mind.

Windar was no warrior; he had fought alongside me but he made a much better leader of men in peace than a warlord. Consequently he looked more like Einar Belly Shaker or Gram the Fat. He greeted me warmly. As we went into his hall by the Mere he said, "Is this a new fashion, Jarl; the trimmed beard and hair? I almost did not recognise you. And Haaken too."

"We stayed in the east and there the people dress differently. We just adopted the style."

"It must take a lot of care."

"It does but we are warriors and we have the time." I had to smile at Haaken who appeared to have taken some offence at Windar's words.

"Come Jarl, I have some fine ale for you to taste."

Haaken sniped, "I can see that you have partaken of more than your fair share."

If Haaken thought he had offended our host he was wrong. Windar laughed and said, "It would be churlish of me to give poor ale to a guest and I have to try it all."

Haaken finally smiled. Haaken was a difficult man to dislike.

"Windar, war is coming."

"The Northumbrians?"

"I think not but in truth I do not know. We have received word from the spirit world and it warned of an enemy from the east. I know that you thrive here on farming and fishing but I want you to increase your vigilance over the winter. I hope this will not be a wolf winter but whatever the Allfather sends our way I want to know of any movements on our borders. " I pointed to the two rivers which ran into the mere. "Use the two rivers as defensive ditches. Keep them clear and deepen them. If you have small portable bridges you and your people can come and go but you will deter an enemy. Make sure your defences do not fall into disrepair and train your warriors."

"I am afraid that many now use their axes to fell trees and not men but I will begin to have the men trained. We will keep you informed by boy riders."

"If it is another wolf winter then we know that will keep enemies from our doors but if it is mild… How many men are there here and at Ulla's Water?"

"Men? There are at least ninety. Men who can fight? That would be less than fifty. Warriors? Perhaps thirty."

The paucity of the numbers made my heart sink. "That is not good enough. I want all ninety training to be able to fight and defend this land. They need not be able to fight in a shield wall but I want all ninety armed and trained." He nodded. "If war comes from the east, Windar, then you will be the first to know." I paused. "And your people will be the first to die!"

"Do not worry Jarl Dragon Heart, we will not let you down. But tonight, you will stay here as my guests and I will try to get Haaken the Stick to be at least half my size!"

As we headed over the ridge to our valley I thought on the words of both Harald and Windar. They had said *'let me down'*. I was not the reason why they fought. They fought for our people and our land. I realised that the legend of Dragon Heart and Ragnar's Spirit had masked our true motives. I would need to do something about that. I was not the important one. The people were.

When we reached our home I saw an immediate difference. Kara had worked as quickly as her mother in days past. The new families had been housed and she had the Ulfheonar building new halls for them. I could see that we would have to spend some time extending our walls or we would become too crowded. There was room at the western end of the Water but that had a tendency to flood. Our eastern hall was built on higher, rocky land and was drier.

I went to my hall and removed my armour. My daughter joined me. "It was well done father. The families you brought have suffered much and they need time to recover." She smiled, "And here we have many warriors looking for wives. I think that the widows will soon have a warrior to watch over each of them."

"Good. And the animals?"

"We had a large enclosure built on the other side of the Water. The grass is good and both the cattle and the sheep will benefit. The pigs I kept here. One of the sows was about to give birth."

My daughter had all the domestic arrangements in hand. After she had taken me on a tour of the new buildings and I had greeted all the newcomers I left her. I needed to find out about weapons. "I will go to see Bjorn. I am keen to know about the new armour."

Bjorn had begun with one small workshop making and repairing armour. Such was his skill that he now had four such workshops by the Water. One of the smiths specialised in jewellery but the rest made armour, helmets and swords. When we needed tools for farming we made them but such was Bjorn's skill that we were able to trade his weapons. We just made sure that we did not trade them to our enemies. Our new trading partners, the Bro Waroc'h in Gwened, would trade us both animals and pots.

The smiths both stopped working when I entered Bjorn's smithy. He scowled at them. "The Jarl does not want to speak with you sweaty lumps! Carry on working." He winked at me. I knew that the two smiths who had stopped working were his sons.

I clasped his arm, "Good to see you again, old friend. Did you have a chance to look at the new suit of armour I sent to you?"

"Aye, Jarl. At first I thought it was flimsy and not as good as our mail." He shook his head. "I could not be more wrong."

"How so?"

He took my old armour which had been sent there for repairs after our skirmish with the Dál Riata. "This is the best armour I ever made." He held up the shoulder. "Do you see how each clump of mail is held together with an individual rivet? This took many hours of work for many smiths. I oversaw them all. It is good mail but it takes many, many days to create."

He then took another suit of mail. "Now this is one you captured last year from the Saxons. I have yet to use it. Notice how the mail is just linked with other rings. It is lighter but, as you well know, one blow can slice through the links and render it useless. That can happen to the armour I made but it is less likely. Now let us examine this armour you brought."

"They call it lamellar armour."

He nodded and I saw him store the word. "It is so light that I thought that it would be useless but it is cleverly made. Each metal plate moves with the body and is secured by a piece of metal wire. The same kind we use in the mail and we manufacture. Each plate overlaps so that the most vulnerable part is the neck. There the plates should be exposed and could suffer damage. But see here, how they have fitted a metal plate across each of the shoulders and the plates which protect them. It cannot be cut by a sword, unlike the mail, even my mail. It can be bent but the armour will remain whole." He stepped back to admire it. "And the best part is we can make it in two days if we have the metal plates ready to hand. Why even women could put it together." He hurriedly added, "Not that we would risk the wrath of Thor by doing so." He touched his Hammer of Thor amulet to protect himself from ill luck.

"I knew it was good. The guards of the Emperor wear it. I did not know how good it actually was."

He pointed to the shoulders. "You will need to have more padding around the neck to avoid chafing."

I nodded, "I remember now that the guards had a kind of scarf wrapped around their necks."

He smiled. "You did not wear it did you, Jarl Dragon Heart? I think that you did not even examine it all in full."

I shook my head, "No, how did you know?"

"Let me show you." I was just wearing a tunic. He took a padded one from the chest in which we had brought the armour home. "Put this on first." The padded tunic was much lighter than my leather one and allowed me to move easier. Bjorn smiled at my surprised looks. Now put on this." He handed me what looked like another tunic made of cloth save that the bottom half was well made mail.

"This protects my legs and yet it is light."

"Now this." He wrapped a silk scarf around my neck. I could barely feel it.

"This will not stop a blow."

"It does not need to. Lift your arms and I will put on the, what did you call it? Lamellar armour." He slipped it over my arms and fastened it tightly at the side. He then began to fit the shoulder guards and the arm protectors. "This is the difficult part. You cannot do this alone. You need another to help you." He dropped to his knees and fitted the greaves. "Now walk around and lift your arms."

"It feels as though I am not wearing armour."

"I know. I tried it on first." He saw my smile and shrugged, "How else will I be able to make them for your warriors?" I laughed and he then said, "Turn around." He placed the metal hood made of mail over my head. At first, I could not see but then the eye holes fell into place and I could see easily. "Either your helmet or the one they gave you fits on the top. Yours will give even more protection but I fear you would be hot. Come to the water and see your reflection."

I went outside and saw, in the bright autumn sun, a warrior who was totally armoured from head to foot. You could not even recognise that it was me. I took off the mail hood. "This is excellent. And you say that you can make them?"

He smiled and led me inside. Like Aiden when he is demonstrating new skill he took a cloak from his bench and there was one set of armour already made. "There. It took just two days. I will have the boys making the plates and we should be able to get it down to one day to put it together. I did not bother with the skirt of mail for I thought the body and arm protection was more important. And the mail mask has not been made yet."

"And you are right about the bodies and the arms. What about the iron that you need?"

"The metal from the captured byrnies is good enough. It does not matter if it bends so long as it is not cut. We have enough metal for twenty sets of this armour."

"Good, then make it and we will pay for them in gold. They will be worth it." I was about to leave when I had a thought. "Would it be possible to make the plates in black and, perhaps copper?"

"Aye, but why?"

"We could have a wolf on each front if we used the different colours. When Aiden returns I will ask him to design one."

Bjorn liked it and he grinned. "Of course. I should have thought of that." He rubbed his hands together. "Right boys; we have some armour to make."

I also spent whole days with Rolf and with Scanlan. Scanlan had been a slave we had freed but now he ran the farms and saw to the day to day organisation of my stead. He lived in the western settlement and was the unofficial headman. Rolf had been my oathsworn until he was seriously wounded and now he commanded the defences of Cyninges-tūn. I felt secure with him watching over my people. He lived in the eastern halls. I had two reliable deputies when I was away.

"We need a larger enclosure for the new settlers, Rolf. We should take down the old one and make a new one a hundred paces further out."

Rolf shook his head, "With respect, Jarl Dragon Heart ,that is not necessary. We just make another enclosure further out. The people will be just as secure but we will have two gates through which an enemy must come. If we take up the old walls and rebuild them it is a waste of time. Let us start with new wood and a new ditch. The old ditch can be used for drainage."

He was right, of course. He lived in the settlement more than I did and he understood its needs. "Good idea. I want the protection in place before veturnætur. There is something symbolic about the onset of winter. I would not wish a Wolf Winter on my people again." I turned to Scanlan. "When Aiden returns I will put him in charge of the breeding of the new animals but you are to see to their distribution. The animals are for the people. Make sure that the most deserving are given the first offspring. We need to work out rates for the services of our bull and our ram. That will be your task. Have Maewe organise the women to produce woollen garments for us to trade. It will bring in much gold."

They both went away happily and I felt content for I was in command again. My people were all working together and I hoped that Nature would be in balance once more.

Chapter 5

Aiden and Arturus returned four weeks after veturnætur. I had missed both of them. They brought with them more heifers and another ram. This one was smaller but I was assured by Aiden that the wool it produced would be even finer. Josephus came with them. I determined to make his life as pleasant as possible. I had promised him a life away from the sea and in comfort. I saw, in him, parts of both Ragnar and Olaf the Toothless. Both men had looked after me and I would pay them back.

Kara divined my thoughts for she fussed over the old man like a mother hen. She chastised Aiden and Arturus for making him walk from Úlfarrston. It was funny to see the huge warrior Arturus was becoming recoiling before his sister's scolding tongue.

They were both pleased to come with me to the Water where they could tell me all that had transpired during their voyage. Kara made sure that Josephus was warm, fed and had a chair by the fire. We left him dozing comfortably.

"The men of Gwened are keen to get hold of more of our weapons. They offered to trade us horses for they have good horses there."

I shook my head. "It would be an unnecessary expense. The ponies we capture in the hills are more than adequate for our needs. And what of Rorik? Did you see him?"

"Not a sign, although Caradog did say that the northern coasts of their land had been raided by men dressed much like us."

That I did not like. I did not want us to get associated with the likes of Rorik. "We need a standard so that people know who we are."

"I think, father, that people know exactly who we are."

"They know our armour and they know our shields but only when the Ulfheonar are there. We will have banners made for all our leaders. Mine will be the black wolf." I took them to the workshops and showed them the new armour. All three of us had seen it before but until Bjorn had examined it we had not looked at it closely. Arturus was as excited as I was when all the parts were inspected.

"Aiden, I took some gold from the men of Dál Riata. I would have golden wolves made for my Ulfheonar. Our meeting with Caradog has shown me the value of such things. And you must oversee the breeding of our new animals. I have asked Scanlan to manage the distribution of them."

"Aye Jarl."

"And what of me, father. Do I have no role to play?"

He surprised me. My young son had grown into a man and he was challenging me. "You have many skills and attributes, my son. I would have you train the young warriors."

"The Ulfheonar?"

"No, for that is a skill that only a few, like you, can achieve. A war is coming and we know not whom we will fight but we will need many warriors. The Ulfheonar are small in number and they can win the battle. If we do not have enough warriors in the field then we will lose the battle. Train all the young warriors so that when we go to war every warrior is better than those that we face; then we shall win."

I said the words and I meant the words but I did not know if I had convinced him. He smiled, "I will do as you wish, Jarl Dragon Heart and we shall win."

Rolf had finished the work on the new wall. I could see that he had put much thought into it. The shape of the land meant that the new halls and huts were lower than the old walls. That in turn meant that the new walls were lower too. When he took me around the ramparts of the old walls he said, "See, Jarl Dragon Heart, if we are assailed then archers and slingers here can support those on the lower walls. If they fall then an attacker would be attacked by missiles all the way here."

"You have done well old friend. I think the new settlers will be safe there."

The villagers who lived within my walls were not the farmers of my land. The farmers lived well beyond my wall. Inside we had the cheese and butter makers. We had the ale wives; their husbands had fallen in battle and they lived together to brew the ale for the two villages. There were the women who worked under Kara and the two Saxons who had been nuns of the White Christ; they produced potions and healed the sick. There were the men who lived in the huts by the lower Water and fished for the food we ate all year. There were the smiths by the upper Water and finally there were the women who worked with Seara to spin the wool which they wove into garments. It was a strange mix of women who had lost husbands and the men who worked as smiths.

Whilst the rest of the land huddled indoors during winter my village was a hive of activity. The days were shorter but the workers could toil within their walls after dark. For Bjorn and his smiths the cold was welcomed for it made their forges a more tolerable place to work.

For the Ulfheonar it was a time to making warrior bands and new weapons. It was a time to train and it was a time to hunt. Each day might be short but they ranged far and wide hunting for food and being vigilant for enemies. At night they would tell their tales and sing their sagas of our battles and our lives. This winter had many new tales. The new warriors who had recently joined my ranks sat in awe as Haaken, Aiden and Sigtrygg told of Byzantium and Frisia; of pirates and sea chases; of treasure and glorious deaths.

And when I retired to my empty hall, for Arturus had now joined those single men who stayed still in the warrior hall, I tried to speak with my wife, my mother, Butar and Ragnar, but they did not speak with me. Kara divined that this troubled me and she came one evening as I sat by my fire with my horn of ale in my hand. "Father, I know what troubles you." I looked up, not in surprise for I knew that she was a volva, but in anticipation. Kara did talk with the spirits and she would give me the answers I sought. "The spirits do not speak with you for there is nothing to tell. The wolves will not come this year. The land will not die." She shrugged, "The Norns may yet interfere but if they do then that is *wyrd*. You need to heal yourself from within. No one else can do that for you. The land is at peace but you are not for you still struggle to come to terms with my mother's death. You berate yourself for not being here for her. These dark nights are for you to make your spirit whole once again for your people will need that spirit and that strength."

She stayed a while longer and we spoke of more inconsequential matters. After she had gone I knew that she was right. I had always been alone. When I had first collected the fish on the Dunum I had been shunned by the other children. My mother had slaved for the

Saxon she called husband and I had grown up inside my own head. When I had lived with Ragnar it had been a lonely existence with a man who slept more than he spoke. When I grew I became the warrior and the leader. That was my lot in life and Kara was right. My life changed on that longest night of the year for I looked into the fire, drank my ale and thought of my life leading up to this point. When I awoke I felt better.

Kara's predictions came true. The winter was mild. We had a smattering of snow and the Water remained ice free. The animals on the lower fells did not die and the sheep were all ready to lamb earlier than normal. Bjorn finished all of the armour. It meant my Ulfheonar would be the best protected of men. Their old mail was given to the new warriors who would now be a formidable force too. Arturus had done a fine job of training, during the short winter days, the young warriors. He had identified their skills and we now had warriors, archers and slingers. I was pleased that they all looked up to my son. I had another leader for my men. He was especially proud of the twenty or so warriors. He had taken great delight in showing them how to wield a sword, spear and defend with a shield.

The first flowers which rose from the ground told us that it was time to see to our ships and for Aiden and Scanlan to look to the new animals. I looked at my new armour. I would not need it yet but soon I would put it on and send fear into the hearts of our enemies.

'*Heart of the Dragon*' was a new ship and her timbers were sound. It did not take us long to make her seaworthy again. Erik Short Toe had spent the winter with Pasgen so that he could watch his pride and joy. He could not wait to get to sea again.

Josephus, too, had enjoyed being fussed by Kara and the women over the winter but the sea was in his blood and when we told him we were ready to sail again he looked suddenly younger. He begged to be allowed to go to sea again. The winter had been good and he was well rested. He needed to feel the wind in his face and the sea in his nostrils.

The goods we had gathered and produced during the winter were sent to the ships. The two knarrs would carry them and we would be their escort. We needed more iron now for Bjorn had used it all. That would be our priority. As the ships were being loaded I asked Aiden where we would find iron.

"We know there is some along the Dunum."

"That is a long way to sail and the Northumbrians are our enemies."

"There is much in Mercia and the land of Gwynedd."

"Good then we can try there."

Josephus said, "Jarl Dragon Heart there is another trading centre where you might find iron as well as other useful goods. I have spent the winter with your people and I know what they need."

"Where is this place?"

"Lundenwic, where the Tamese meets the Fleot."

"It is Saxon is it not?"

Josephus nodded, "It is a disputed port. The Mercians and the men of Wessex both claim it. The men of Essex were not strong enough to hang on to it but the people who live there carry on with their trade. They welcome all; even the likes of Rorik. He used it for he could get higher prices for the spices he stole."

Aiden pulled one of the old maps and writings we had found in the Roman fort. "Look, Jarl, here. There are iron workings just south of it. It is likely that we will be able to find some there. And it will save us having to cross to Frankia and Frisia. Rorik may have more ships by now."

"I will do as you both suggest. We will visit King Selfyn when we have tried this Lundenwic. We will take a full crew though. If we are to sail into a disputed port I would not suffer at the hands of a warlord."

Trygg and Siggi, the captains of the two knarrs had both heard of the port. "Josephus is right. It is a good port but I am glad that you take your warriors for there are many cut throats down there."

"You have sailed up the river?"

"No, Jarl but we have spoken with other captains who have."

"Load your ships and we will sail tomorrow."

Rolf had journeyed with us. "Take charge of the settlement Rolf."

He laughed, "I will watch over it, Jarl but your daughter makes all the decisions these days."

"Does that offend you, old friend?"

"No Jarl. She does not interfere with the defences and it is poor Scanlan who has to suffer the sharp edge of her tongue."

"Make sure that Thorkell and Windar know that we will be away. They will need to keep a close watch on our borders." I regretted not being able to take '***Great Serpent***' too but Thorkell would need that drekar to guard our northern frontier. The shipwright, Bolli would be building me a new one while we were away. Two drekar would make us too large a morsel for pirates such as Rorik.

Every bench was filled as we left Úlfarrston. Pasgen had sent his two ships with us to trade too. I knew that it would be slow; the four knarr were not the fastest of ships. We had enough warriors to put six on each of the ships as well as four boys. The sixteen boys had all been trained by Arturus and were fine archers.

Erik had grown over the winter. He had spent many hours going over the whole of the ship and he knew it as well as his own hand. Josephus was able to doze his way south with just a few questions from Erik. Erik had two assistants: Kurt and Karl. Both were agile and lacked the frame to be warriors. Like Erik they longed for a life at sea. They could become captains, eventually, like Erik Short Toe. I had plans to increase our trade and that meant more ships.

We were always wary when we sailed close to the island of Mann. Our former friends now shunned us and we had been attacked before now. My wife's brother, Erik was jarl there but he was no longer my friend. We passed that and Cymru safely. When we sailed through the islands at the end of the world I could not help looking for the cave of the witch. No smoke came from the island and I wondered if she lived still. Perhaps she had been a spirit sent from the Otherworld.

After many days at sea we began to edge around the headland which would take us into the land controlled by the kings of Wessex. We had heard that they still had a king of Sussex but we were now passing through a land of dispute and war. We wore mail and hung our shields from our ship. We were prepared for trade but we were ready for war.

The river appeared as wide as the Rinaz. That suited us for we had room to move if danger threatened. We sailed at the rear of our small fleet as the oars could take us quickly towards any danger. We saw many ships. Most were like our knarr and were small. We saw one Saxon warship but it only sported ten oars on each side. It sailed away when we entered the main channel. There were many settlements along the side of the river and all looked to have protection in the form of wooden walls.

Josephus took the steering board for he knew these waters better than any. His rheumy eyes looked a little sharper these days. He was back in his element. "Erik, there is a Roman Fort called Lundenburh and beyond it is the port. Have Karl and Kurt keep a sharp look out."

"Aye, master."

The river narrowed somewhat and began to twist and turn with large loops. There were settlements at each loop. I had never seen so many villages and small towns before. It was no wonder there was a dispute going on here. This was land worth fighting over. We would need to be wary for we had already fought for King Selfyn against Coenwulf of Mercia. He would remember me.

"Captain! I see the fort and the anchorage!"

"Cnut, take up the stroke we will be the first to land in case there is trouble."

My rowers powered through the water and soon overtook the four tubby knarrs. I saw men fleeing from the jetty as we approached and the ramparts of the Roman fort filled with armed Saxons. I saw people crowding to get in through the gate. They knew little of our ways. Had we come to raid we would have come before dawn and silently. The first they would have known would have been when we appeared with bloodied weapons in our hands.

There was little room at the stone jetty; it was filled with ships and, as I ordered the oars up I decided to go in prow first. "Erik, turn to steer board. Kurt, be ready to land and tie us up." Karl and my men had the sail down in a matter of moments and we bumped gently against the ancient stone wall. When we were tied up I turned to the crews of the knarr and shouted, "Stay in the middle of the river until we have found someone to speak with!" The four captains waved their acknowledgement.

I left my helmet and my shield on the ship. I was not going for war. "Aiden and Haaken, come with me. Cnut, command in my absence." I did not need to warn him about his belligerence. He had learned his lesson. My feet and legs were a little unsteady after so many days at sea. I looked around the huts and buildings as I steadied myself. I could see that they still had a couple of stone buildings. They were obviously from the times of the Romans. The people we had seen fleeing had run to the fort but the gates were closed and they milled around outside fearfully.

As we walked towards the fort Haaken said, "If they run from three men armed with swords alone what would they do if the whole war band landed?" I laughed. He was right.

I stopped two hundred paces from the fort. Aiden shouted, urgently, "Jarl beware, an arrow!"

I saw that someone from within the fort had loosed an arrow. I watched it as it began to arc to earth. I took one step to my left and it plunged into the ground just behind me. I leaned down to pick it up. It was a hunting arrow. I shouted, "Is this the way you greet peaceful traders? We had heard that Lundenwic welcomed all traders."

One of the men who had been milling around the gate trying to gain entry walked towards us. "When the Vikings come we have learned to run."

"We come in peace." I spread my arms. "We would trade. I am Jarl Dragon Heart of Cyninges-tūn. Who commands here?"

The man walked up to us and a few of his fellows followed. He gestured towards the hall with his thumb. "Osric of Teobernan. He is the hero who hides behind the walls of Lundenburh." He held out his hand. "I am Wiglaf of Fleta. I am a merchant and if you come to trade then I am the man you need to speak to for I can get hold of almost anything you might wish for." He put his arm around my back to guide me back to the river. I saw Haaken's look of annoyance but I gave a slight shake of the head. I was not offended. I had seen men like Wiglaf in every port we had entered. They were the ones who knew their way around. He was similar in many ways to Rorik. I just hoped he was less treacherous. Time alone would tell. "I have some ale we can try while you tell me of your needs."

The crowd behind decided that we were not a threat and they followed us back. Wiglaf saw the knarr. "They are yours?"

"We protect them and they hold the goods we would trade."

He could see that they were low in the water which suggested they were heavily laden. He rubbed his hands together. "I hope we can do some good business, Jarl." He led the three of us into a stone building. It looked Roman but I had never seen one quite like it. Two slaves appeared from a back room looking fearfully at us. "Get some ale and four horns and be quick!" He gestured towards some seats. "Now what is it that you have to trade?"

"Not so fast, Wiglaf of Fleta. First, I need to know if I have come to the right place. Do you have iron ore for trade?"

He frowned. "Iron ore? You mean swords and metal?"

"No I mean the raw iron."

"I can get you swords; the best in the land."

I took out Ragnar's Spirit. "As good as this one?"

He shook his head as he looked at it. I heard the awe in his voice, "No! Is it Frankish?"

"It was made by my smith and I ask you again, can you get us iron ore or should we go to the lands of the Cymri? I know that I can get some there but I had heard that the iron of Kent was of the highest quality. Perhaps you are not the man I need to speak with."

The ale arrived and he hurriedly went on, "Of course I am the right man. Let us drink a toast to our new friendship!" He was getting more like Rorik with every word he spoke and look he gave. "I can get iron ore but it will take a few days."

I drank some of the ale which was poor. "We have time for good iron. I hope that it is of better quality than this piss which you serve in place of ale."

"Your pardon, Jarl, it is the slaves. They have brought the wrong ale. Of course the iron will be of the best now tell me, what do you trade for it?"

I stood, "If you can find us some berths then I will show you and we will give you a horn of ale which tastes of something."

I saw Haaken and Aiden laugh as we left the building. The jetty had now filled up with the Saxons who had fled at our arrival. They parted as we headed back towards my ship. Wiglaf pointed to two men, "Move your ships so that the jarl can moor his knarr closer to the market!" They looked as though they might argue but then thought better of it. Rorik came to mind. I would watch this Wiglaf. I watched him as he stood on the jetty. He was younger than I was which was suspicious. His clothes were of the best quality and his fingers were adorned with rings. His short sword showed that he was no warrior. He was a merchant, as he had said. A voice in my head asked me, what kind?

We waited while the two captains got their crews to warp their ships upstream. There was a continuation of the jetty there but it was made of wood.

I waved my knarr over. I watched as they were sculled towards us with oars. Behind me I heard a voice, "Who gave you permission to land!"

I turned and saw a tall man with eight armed warriors behind him. I looked at Wiglaf who rolled his eyes heavenward and said, "This is Thegn Osric of Teobernan." He shook his head as though the man was not worth speaking with, "Thegn this is Jarl Dragon Heart of Cyninges-tūn. He is here to trade."

"He should have asked permission to land!"

I shook my head, "A little difficult when you were skulking inside your walls! We have landed now. Do you have any objections?"

He tried to hold my stare but this man was no warrior and he lowered his eyes. "No, of course not. We welcome peaceful traders but you are Vikings."

I gave him my wolf smile. "Sometimes we raid and sometimes we trade. Today is a fortunate one for you. We are here to trade. You would know if we were here to raid. Your women would be aboard our ships and you would lie in a pool of your own blood."

He stepped back to the protection of his guards and looked fearfully at us.

The boats had tied up. I turned to Aiden and spoke in Norse. "Fetch some of the trade items. Haaken, have two of the Ulfheonar guard each ship. Tell them not to frighten the people too much."

My men left and I turned to the two Saxons; Wiglaf and Osric. "We have woollen goods, weapons, jewellery, seal oil and spices."

I saw the eyes of the two men widen. "You have traded with someone who has been to the east?"

I shook my head, "No, we have been to Constantinopolis and traded ourselves."

Osric said, incredulously, "But the Emperor does not trade with the Norse."

I smiled, "He traded with me. If the goods are not to your taste then we also have some gold but the iron will need to be of the finest quality for us to part with either the spices or the gold."

I had Wiglaf hooked now. I could almost see him calculating how much profit he could make on the spices. He would not know that Aiden well knew the value of all of our goods. He was the master trader. After he had examined samples Wiglaf was more than pleased with the quality of all of the goods. "How much iron ore do you require?"

"As much as will fit in the holds of three knarr." I waved at the boats tied up before us.

"It will take many days to get that much ore here."

"Fear not we will wait."

"And the fourth knarr? What goods will that take back?"

"That depends upon the range of goods you have for us to trade."

"Come to my warehouse and you will not be disappointed."

He led us through the crowded huts and into two huge halls which contained all of his goods. They were stacked and arranged by type. I saw Aiden nodding. We could trade well here.

The good thoughts in our heads were disturbed a little when the night watch reported Wiglaf sending a small fast boat out to sea. If the iron was to the south, why send a ship east?

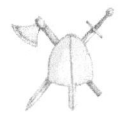

Chapter 6

We found more of the pots the women in the settlement liked and we arranged for them to be traded. I left Aiden in charge of that. Wiglaf invited my men and me to dine with him at his hall. I feigned tiredness. I did not trust him yet. When we had the iron ore in sight and settled a price then I would be happier. We slept on the deck having cooked our own food on the stone jetty. Josephus and Erik spent some time with the other captains and seafarers. They were a close community and would talk more openly without us.

The two of them came back quite late and a little unsteadily. We put Josephus to bed and Erik told us what he had learned. "You are right to worry about Wiglaf, Jarl. He is in league with Rorik. There are rumours that Rorik has designs not in Frisia but here in Lundenwic. The war between Mercia and Wessex suits him. He has made many visits here. They appear to be partners of sorts. He has the protection of Rorik." That explained his high handed attitude towards Osric.

"How far away are the Kentish mines?"

"A day's walk."

"And what of this Osric?"

"He is the younger brother of Sigered the King of Essex. I think he is not the most popular member of the king's family and most people here do not have a good word to say about him."

Haaken asked, "Perhaps we should just go to Kent for the iron ourselves."

"We could just take it!"

I shook my head. Cnut was always the one for direct action. "No, as a people, we have a bad enough reputation. If we trade then we can always get more. We choose our battles and our wars, Cnut." He nodded. You could always explain things to Cnut. "We will see what this Wiglaf brings. I will tell him tomorrow that he has but three more days to bring the iron. If it is only one day away then he should be able to fetch enough to show good faith."

When we went to him, the next day, he first said that it was impossible. I had expected that and I stood, "Then thank you for your help but we will have to seek other sources."

"No, Jarl Dragon Heart, I will send more men to bring it faster."

"That will not affect the price of course."

"You will not be disappointed, Jarl. The iron is of the finest quality."

"And we know the true value but if it is here in three days then I will pay a fair price."

When he had gone we arranged for a watch to be kept aboard the boats and then we went to explore Lundenwic. Haaken, Sigtrygg came with Josephus, Arturus, Aiden and me. Josephus was like a man newly born. He was desperate to visit as many places as he could. As we walked he spoke quietly to me.

"I wanted to thank you again, Jarl Dragon Heart for buying me and then giving me my freedom. I felt that I was to leave this earth before you came and now I cannot wait to see more of it. When I came here with Rorik I was chained to the boat to stop me fleeing. I am interested in the wonders of this ancient city."

"You do yourself a disservice; without you we would be poorer in so many ways. Erik thinks the world of you and you have brought him on so much that I hardly recognise him."

"He is like a grandson to me. It is good. What is the word you use all the time? *Wyrd*. It is truly *wyrd*. I have purpose in my life once more."

He was right for Erik was experiencing what I had had with Ragnar. It had made me a better man and it would do the same for Erik.

The town had had organisation at one time but since the Romans had left buildings had been converted, destroyed or just taken over. It was also filled with so many different people that I thought I was in Constantinopolis. We all wore our armour and I saw people shy away from us. Rorik, perhaps, had the right idea. This place was ripe for the plucking. If I had chosen I could have conquered and held the town with just my boatload of Ulfheonar. I did not want it and it held no attraction for me but I could see why Rorik might want it. Here there was no Emperor ready to send in a fleet and an army. Here there were just bands of warring Saxons. They were so busy fighting each other that an adventurer like Rorik might come in and steal the prize from under their noses.

We had a good day. The food and the ale were interesting and, once again, when we returned in the evening, poor Josephus was unsteady on his feet. The ships were as we had left them and all seemed calm. It lulled us into a sense of false security.

The following evening we were watching the sun go down in the west when Wiglaf came to my ship. "The iron will be here on the morrow." He pointed across the river to the east. There was a wooden jetty there and a handful of huts. "They will bring it to Suthriganaweorc. It will be easier to load rather than ferrying it across the river."

I was suspicious. "And what of the trade?"

"Your goods are not heavy we can ferry those easily but the iron ore is heavy. The men have struggled to bring it this quickly."

I smiled, "And I appreciate it, Wiglaf. We will have many more trades in the future."

He brightened at that.

When I told my men what he had said Haaken and Cnut were both suspicious. "I like it not. What is to stop them taking what they want and fleeing south? We would never catch them."

"You are right but we can do something about it. Firstly we will have '**Heart of the Dragon**' close by and secondly I will land with some warriors tonight and we will make our way to this Suthriganaweorc and watch. We can land beyond the bend in the river."

Arturus asked, "Will Wiglaf not be wary when we move?"

"No, for we shall tell him that we need to move the ship in order to turn the others around."

It was dark when we moved and no one saw us. I had explained to the other captains what I planned. Erik took us upriver and landed us close to a hamlet called Lambehitha. It was across the river from a church of the White Christ. I hoped it was not an omen. We made our way east along the river. I could barely see my ship as she turned around and headed back to moor in the middle of the river.

I had Snorri, Sigtrygg, Beorn Three Fingers, Erik Dog Bite and Tostig Wolf Hand with me. They were my most experienced warriors. We skirted inland a little to avoid the village and found a small wood in which we waited. Snorri found a track which led south. I assumed they would come that way.

We took it in turns to sleep but we were all wide awake before dawn broke. I wondered if the carts would come as the sun rose higher in the sky. The river was hidden from us but it was a mere thousand paces from where we waited.

Snorri clambered up a tree and it was he who spotted the approaching carts. "I can see them, Jarl Dragon Heart. They are less than a mile away. They have guards and they have horses pulling the carts."

I wondered if I had done Wiglaf a disservice. So far I could not fault his efforts.

"Do we go to greet them and escort them the last part of the journey?"

"No Snorri. We will let them pass and then follow them."

"You are suspicious, Jarl?"

"I am careful Sigtrygg Thrandson, that is all."

We stayed hidden and watched the carts struggling up the slight rise. The last part would be down hill. Once they reached the top my men would see them. I frowned as they passed for there seemed a larger number of guards than I might have expected. I saw the last cart trudging along when I spotted warriors such as us. They were hanging back. There were twenty of them. Half were mailed and all had the battle rings about their arms. There was something going on.

We allowed them to pass and then, when they reached the top of the rise, I led my men to the west. We would try to reach the river at the same time as they did. My warriors did not speak. Like me they would have known that the sight of warriors such as us was not expected. As soon as we reached the top of the rise I saw the ships. The three knarr were tied up at the jetty. The fourth was still in her original position and *'**Heart of the Dragon**'* was in the middle of the river. It looked peaceful. Perhaps the extra guards were hired mercenaries. Then sharp eyed Snorri hissed, "Jarl, there are two drekar coming up the river!"

It was a trap. I could not identify the ships but I knew who it was; it was Rorik! The crew of my ship and the knarrs would have their attention on the trade and the bank. That was where the treachery would come. Rorik and his men would be upon my ship before they even knew. "Snorri, get to the ship and warn the crews. The rest of you we will attack these guards." I saw the drekar. They were smaller than mine; they were threttanessa. They rode lower in the water than my ship and Rorik and his men would struggle to climb aboard if my warriors defended it.

This would be the first time we had tested our new armour and we would be fighting warriors trained like us. These were not farmer Saxons, these were killers and we could take no chances. The carts had reached the bank and I saw Trygg and Siggi as they stepped forward with Aiden and Arturus to examine them. Suddenly I heard a war cry and the guards from the carts and the twenty Norse charged my men.

If it had not been Aiden and Arturus there then it might have been a disaster but they both had calm minds and quick reactions. Arturus leapt forward and I saw his sword slice through the neck of the first warrior. Aiden hurried the two captains back aboard and then he yelled something. A flurry of arrows flew high in the sky. My son had bought us some time. We were less than fifty paces from our enemies. I needed to attract their attention and I yelled, "Ragnar's Spirit!" It worked for the warriors stopped in their tracks and looked behind them. Arturus lunged forward and stabbed another of the guards before Aiden pulled him aboard the knarr. The three were trying to get away. I saw Snorri as he leapt aboard one of the knarr and ran to the other side. My ship would now be warned but would the warning be in time?

I had no time for such thoughts. We had to destroy these warriors before we could rejoin our comrades who would soon be outnumbered and surrounded. I took the spear from the first warrior on my shield and brought my sword around horizontally. His shield deflected it. I kept my speed up and threw my head at his. I had my mail mask on and my helmet was strong. I heard a crack as his nose broke and I was showered in his blood. As he stumbled I stabbed down with my sword and pinned his wriggling body to the ground.

I sensed movement to my right and I spun around. The new armour was so light that it was effortless but, even so, the sword wielded by the warrior struck my shoulders. If I had worn the old mail then links would have been severed. As it was the blow hurt but the metal held. The surprised warrior lifted his sword for a second blow but I hacked across his middle before he could strike.

Ragnar's Spirit was sharp and the blow went through his poorly made mail and ripped across his stomach.

Two warriors were attacking Beorn. Like me he was saved by his armour but I made it more equal by stabbing through the back of one of his opponents. I looked up and saw Rorik's ships as they closed with my drekar. Trygg's knarr with Snorri, Aiden and Arturus was close by and the crew were preparing to sell their lives dearly. I was angry. When you are angry you do foolish things. I roared like a wolf and leapt at a knot of warriors who stood between me and Siggi's knarr. There were five of them and I should have perished but it was not meant to be. I began swinging my sword as I ran at them. They stood and waited. The blade ripped across their front. I saw the throat of one erupt in a fountain of blood as I smashed my shield into the face of another. I jabbed forward with the hilt of my sword and it crashed into the face of another. He fell backwards clutching the remains of an eye.

One lunged at me with a sword. The lamellar armour proved its worth. The blade slid along the overlapping links. A second warrior stabbed at my face. I could not get out of the way but the blade became entangled in the links. I whipped my head around and the knife came out of his hand. I was now free and I brought Ragnar's Spirit over my head. It split the helmet and skull of a warrior in two as Sigtrygg ended the life of the other.

"Jarl, the drekar!"

I looked and saw warriors swarming from the two enemy boats over the sides of mine. I could see Haaken directing the fighting. We ran to Siggi's knarr. "Get us to the enemy ship."

"Aye Jarl."

I hoped that we would be in time. The tubby little boat seemed to crawl. The disaster was unfolding before my eyes. I saw Erik Short Toe desperately fending off his enemies as he tried to hold on to the steer board. Even as we closed I saw a warrior lunge, with his spear, at Erik's unprotected back. Suddenly Josephus hurled his body between them and the old man sank to the deck. Then the side of the drekar hid us. The men on board were too concerned with trying to get aboard my drekar and did not see me and my six men leap aboard. Vengeance was in our hearts and there would be no mercy that night. I had put a dagger in my left hand as we had rowed across and, as I stabbed one attacker in the back with my sword, I plunged my dagger into the side of another. There was a wail from the crew as they realised they were being attacked from the rear.

I heard a cheer from the bow of the ship and saw Arturus and Aiden leading five of the crew of Trygg's knarr to attack the warriors at that end of the drekar. It was too much for some who flung themselves into the sea to avoid the wrath of the Ulfheonar. We scythed our way through them until we reached my ship.

"Arturus, hold this drekar!"

I heard the joy of battle in his voice as he shouted, "Aye Jarl."

I leapt aboard my ship and brought my blade down across the back of the warrior who was about to despatch Erik. The blade sliced into him and cut his spine in two. Erik was wounded but it looked as though he would live. He saw Josephus' body lying there impaled by the spear. He looked distraught. "There will be time for tears later, Erik. Secure the **'Heart'**."

"Aye Jarl!"

"Ulfheonar, let us end this now!"

My men all roared and we surged towards the men aboard our drekar. We were still outnumbered but they had expected an easy victory. This was not it. As I hacked through the thigh of one of them I looked for Rorik. He was not with them. I punched another with my shield and he tumbled, in his mail, to die in the waters below. The rest took flight and jumped aboard the remaining drekar. Whoever commanded decided to cut his losses and it began to pull away downstream. I turned to the warrior whose thigh I had cut. He was bleeding to death.

"Where is Rorik?" The man was in shock and trying to staunch the blood from his fatal wound. "Where?"

He looked up at me as though I was an apparition. Later I realised that the mail mask I wore made it look as though he was talking to a wraith. "He is waiting at Grenewic, he…" Then he died. My men were despatching the rest of the attackers and I took off my helmet and my mail mask. I had two men to pay back now, Rorik and Wiglaf. They had killed many fine warriors and ended the life of poor Josephus.

I cupped my hands and shouted to the last knarr on the other bank. "Get over here now!" I went to the other side of the ship. "Siggi, Trygg, get the iron ore loaded while we can."

"We will be overloaded!"

"Put some aboard our new drekar!"

Haaken came up to me and clasped my arm. "You came just in time, Dragon Heart."

"How many have we lost?"

"Eight Ulfheonar died but we killed more than forty of these pirates."

"And that, my friend, is a poor trade." Aiden made his way down to me. "See to the wounded. Erik has been hurt."

Arturus joined me. "This armour is worth more than gold, father."

"Aye. As are you. You fought well my son. Take charge of the drekar. You have earned the right."

I could see a crowd had gathered at the fort and that the gates were barred. We had entertained the locals. I wondered if they had had anything to do with this. Wiglaf certainly had and he would pay. Rorik's dead men were stripped of their armour, weapons and valuables and their bodies dumped into the river. The creatures there would eat well. We took our drekar and knarr to the south bank where we laid our dead on a pyre made from the carts they had used to bring the iron. The five horses we would take back with us. When the iron had been loaded we stood around the pyre and Aiden set it alight. We stood there until the flames had consumed their bodies and their spirits had ascended to the Otherworld and Valhalla. In all we had lost fifteen friends.

We had loaded the horses and were about to board our ships to pay a visit to Wiglaf when Beorn, who had been scouting to the south, came running back. "Jarl Dragon Heart the men of Wessex come. They have a banner and I think it may be their king."

I nodded, "Get everyone aboard the ships. Aiden and Haaken stand by me."

I did not replace my mask of mail nor my helmet. Both would suggest that I was ready for war. I had my shield slung around my back; I pulled it around. As I watched the column of men approach beneath the banner of Wessex I regretted not having my own banner to mark who I was.

The king marched with his men and those around him, his housecarls, were all heavily mailed and carried long axes like our Danish brethren. They halted before us and his men went into a wedge formation. I held out my hands and spoke in Saxon. "We come in peace."

The man I took to be the king laughed as he stepped forward. He was not intimidated by us and I liked that. "You are burning bodies and I can see evidence of a battle all around me. That is a strange peace, Viking," he seemed to see my shield, "wolf."

I nodded and I stepped forward to meet with this Wessex king. "The ones we fought did not come in peace. They came to ambush and attack us. I am Jarl Dragon Heart of Cyninges-tūn. We came to Lundenwic to trade for iron ore."

He stepped closer to me, "And I am King Egbert of Wessex." He looked at the hoof prints. "Did they bring the iron ore?"

"Aye they did."

"That is why I am here. The miners who dug it were slain and the ore stolen."

"Then it is you who should be paid for the iron."

He looked surprised and he laughed, "That is a strange way for a Viking to behave; to pay for something when he could fight for it."

I shrugged, "I said, King Egbert, that we came to trade and not to fight. We would buy more iron another time. We have either gold or trade goods; which would you prefer?"

He did not answer me. "I think I have heard of you, Viking. Are you not the one who changes into a wolf and bloodied the nose of Coenwulf?"

I nodded, "We are known as wolf warriors, Ulfheonar and we did fight with King Selfyn against the Mercians."

He clapped me on the back. "Good then we can talk." He waved at one of his men, "Athelstan, come and negotiate a price for the iron." A man who looked like a clerk stepped forward.

"Aiden."

"Aye Jarl." I did not need to explain to Aiden he had been listening carefully to every word.

King Egbert said, "Let us go away from prying ears and we will talk."

"My men's ears hear all that I do but if you do not trust your own warrior's discretion then let us."

He laughed, "You are blunt. I like you more and more. When I heard that Vikings were in my river I came here to fight you. I am pleased now that I did not."

We sat down on a grassy bank by the river. I took off my shield and laid my sword by my side. I pointed to the river, "There is some dispute over who does own this river, King Egbert."

"True. Let us say then, that the kings of Sussex and Kent are my subjects and soon the kingdom of Essex will join them."

"You have ambition then?"

"Do we not all?"

I shook my head, "Cyninges-tūn and the land around it are all that I desire. But I will fight to the death with any who tries to take it from me."

"Then you would not wish to fight for me? I could pay you with gold. I know the Norse love gold."

"We fight our own wars but I can promise not to raid your lands. You have been hospitable."

He laughed so loudly that his men started. "You have two long ships and you promise not to raid. You have a high opinion of your skills, Viking."

I nodded, "And it is well deserved."

He suddenly seemed to see my armour. "I have never seen armour like this before."

"The Emperor gave it to me."

"Charlemagne?"

I shook my head, "The Emperor of Byzantium, Nikephoros."

"You have been there?"

"Aye, we traded with them and did the Emperor some small service. He rewarded us with armour and friendship."

"I see that you do not boast. It makes me want you as an ally even more."

"Our land is many days to the north of here. We have mutual enemies between us." I did not wish to completely burn my bridges with this Saxon. He could be useful to us. "I will give my word to aid you in any fight against the Mercians or the Northumbrians but only at my borders. I have no ambition to rule a large land."

He gave me his hand. "Then, Jarl Dragon Heart, consider us friends." As we rose he pointed to the bodies of Rorik's men floating in an eddy at the bend of the river. "Did you kill all of these thieves?"

"Not yet. Their leader comes from Frisia although he is Norse. He and his drekar are downstream at a place called Grenewic."

"I know it. Then it seems I may yet get to fight and kill some Vikings."

"And I can bring my men to your aid."

He nodded, "Then this is *wyrd*. Let us go."

Chapter 7

Aiden and the clerk from Wessex looked to have agreed terms and goods were already being unloaded from the knarr. Both sets of warriors, mine from the boat and the Saxons on the bank, looked at us as we approached.

"Haaken, get the Ulfheonar who are not wounded from the drekar. Aiden keep the archers and the other warriors to guard the ships. We go with King Egbert to find Rorik."

That pleased my men who began banging their shields with the pommels of their swords. Although there were only forty of us we were all dressed the same way. The veteran Ulfheonar had their wolf skins and all had armour. The twenty of us who wore the new armour looked to be the bodyguards of a king and I saw Egbert looking enviously at us. We all carried our helmets and I had my mail mask with me too. We would don them when we were closer.

I diplomatically allowed the king and his men to go first. He had a hundred warriors with him although only twenty were mailed as we were. The rest had helmets, shields and spears. Egbert waved me forward. "You walk with me. I have much to ask you."

"Haaken, take charge."

"Your men have discipline."

"Warriors who do not throw their lives away recklessly have discipline and they live to fight for their jarl."

He nodded. "It is not far to Grenewic."

"Good. This man Rorik, I think he has ambitions here." I pointed to the citadel at Lundenburh. "That would be an easy place for someone to command. Thegn Osric does not seem to have much control. I would fear Rorik if he controlled such a place. He is not like me, he does harbour ambitions."

"Thank you for the warning. Unlike you I have few ships and we would need many of those to control Lundenwic."

"Then be prepared, if Rorik succeeds, for a neighbour who will raid. The land you call Kent would become a wasteland at the mercy of Rorik and his bandits."

"But he is of your blood."

"No, he comes from the same land. A weed can grow in the same field as the barley but their hearts are different. Do not judge men by their looks or their language. You need to look them in the eyes and understand their spirit. I was born of a Saxon father, a mother from Cymru and I was brought up a Norse. What does that make me?"

He laughed, "An enigma."

The king's men did not lead us in a direct line to Grenewic. We left the track and walked behind a low hill. We stopped and his men spread out in a line behind us. "Grenewic is on the other side of the hill."

"Then I will place my men on the right of yours. This Rorik has drekar and he will try to flee."

"I know. I will use my lighter men to close with him quickly then."

I was not certain that would work but it was his land and his men. I donned my mail mask and helmet and led my men to the right of the line.

"Rorik is on the other side of this hill. King Egbert is going to try to catch him."

Cnut snorted, "Then I wish him luck. Rorik will wriggle away like the slippery eel he is."

"Come Ulfheonar. Let us show these men of Wessex how we fight."

We marched up the hill. It was not a steep slope but I admired the cleverness of the Saxons. This would enable us to surprise Rorik. As we crested the rise I saw that there were three drekar and they were tied to the bank. His men were resting and having wounds dressed. I saw Rorik and his oathsworn immediately. They still had armour on. I had no doubt that he intended to sail down the river after dark and surprise us. Had King Egbert not arrived when he had then he might have succeeded. The Norns were busy their webs were complicated.

The Saxons just hurled themselves down the hill. The men without armour ran like hounds across the spongy turf. Some stumbled as they ran too quickly to keep their footing. We kept to a steadier pace. None of us wished to fall before we faced the foe. The men who had been resting on the bank leapt up and grabbed weapons. As the first of the Saxons struck them there was a clash of metal on wood. I watched as Rorik led his men to cut down the poorly armed warriors. I drew Ragnar's Spirit and pointed it at Rorik. Regardless of what King Egbert did we would go directly for Rorik. There was a blood feud and it could only end when one of us was dead.

I think that Rorik only saw the lightly armed Saxons when he charged. We struck his men from the side and his warriors were unprepared. I jabbed over the shield of a warrior with a red painted shield. The blade went through one cheek and out of the other. I twisted and pulled my sword out. His shield lowered and I ended his pain with a fatal slice to the neck.

I sought Rorik. He had just despatched a Saxon twenty paces from me and I shouted, "Rorik! Face me like a man!"

"Jarl! Watch out!"

Siggi Finehair's warning made me turn and I barely blocked the blow from the sword swung by one of Rorik's oathsworn. It was a strike delivered with all of his strength and it forced me back. However it also bent his blade. I punched with the boss of my shield three times in quick succession. It allowed me to bring my sword up and around. I delivered my blow with all of my strength and when he tried to block it his damaged sword shattered and Ragnar's Spirit continued downward to bite through his mail and into his shoulder. He fell writhing on the ground.

I looked for Rorik and saw him as he and his oathsworn jumped aboard a drekar and began to pull away from the shore. He had evaded me once more. The warriors from Wessex and my men despatched the dead. King Egbert joined me and I took off my mail mask and my helmet. He looked down at the shattered sword. "That is a marvellous weapon, Viking. Where did you get it?"

I laughed, "Where did I steal it you mean. My smith made it for me. But it was touched by the gods and that gives it added power and strength."

"Your people can make weapons such as this?"

I nodded, "And fine jewellery too. We are not savages."

"I can see that. We would trade iron for weapons such as these."

"Good." We both looked up as the drekar headed down the river towards the sea. "You have not finished with that one, King Egbert. The Emperor Charlemagne is making Frisia too uncomfortable for him." I pointed across the river. "The chaos and anarchy north of here is perfect for the likes of Rorik. "I smiled, "If I was a greedy man then I could have made the fort yonder my own. This river draws traders like bees to flowers."

I could see he was intrigued. "Where do you spend the night, Viking Wolf?"

"I have unfinished business with a merchant called Wiglaf."

"I have heard of him. His allegiance shifts with the wind. If you would take my warriors across the river we will spend the night in Lundenwic. It is time I came to an agreement with this Osric of Teobernan."

I smiled, "Of course for we are now trading partners as well as allies."

As we strode back along the river towards the setting sun he laughed, "You have opened my eyes, man of the north, to the potential of a Viking warrior."

It took three trips to ferry all of the warriors across. I went across first with my Ulfheonar. The inhabitants cowered in their homes, fearful of our retribution. I found one who had spoken truthfully to us when we first arrived. "Where is Wiglaf? Has he fled to Lundenburh?"

He shook his head, "No, my lord. He fled on the drekar." He pointed downstream.

"And did he take his goods?"

"Aye my lord. While you were burning your dead he took one of his ships and sailed down to the other raiders."

I put my face close to his. "We are not the same! If we were then you and all of your family would be dead! Remember that!"

I told the king of my news when he landed. He nodded and looked to the fort. "They have closed the gates. You say that you and your men could take such a fort?"

"Aye but it would cost me many men to do so."

He laughed, "I was not asking you to do so but I would know how would you do it?"

"Attack at night. Have archers watching both gates. If you use your shields your men can climb on the shoulders of other warriors and reach the ramparts." I smiled, "I am guessing that this Osric will not have maintained the Roman ditch."

He frowned, "Maintained?"

"A ditch only works if it is clear of rubbish, and it is deep with sharp stakes in the bottom. But if you want this fort there is an easier way."

"How?"

"Bring your men with torches and I will show you." As he hurried off I shouted, "Haaken, take the Ulfheonar to the east gate and stop anyone from leaving."

"We are attacking them?" Haaken did not mind he just needed clarification.

"No, we are frightening them." I donned my mail mask and my helmet. I led the king and his warriors to the west gate of the fort. "Have your men spread out in a line from the river to as far around the fort as we can go."

He did so, "Now what?"

"If you will come with me and allow me to be your spokesman we will see if we can frighten the Thegn of Lundenwic into handing over the fort to you."

"I will and I am intrigued."

We strode to within fifty paces of Lundenburh. I gambled that they would not try to kill the king whose standard bearer followed us. I shouted, "Osric of Teobernan."

After a few moments his face appeared. "Yes what is it you want? We have done you no harm."

"No, and you did not aid us. We have your burgh surrounded and we could take it and all of your families if we chose." I pointed across the river. "You saw how we dealt with Rorik and his pirates."

"What would you have of us?"

"I would have nothing but King Egbert here might."

I stepped aside and the king began to speak. "I want you to surrender this fort to me."

"But I hold it for my brother."

"You brother is a weak lily livered vassal of Mercia. I will let you live and leave with your arms and your families but only if you leave by dawn."

"I need to speak with my people."

"You have until dawn to give me an answer otherwise I unleash these wolves upon you!"

He disappeared and we went back to the line of warriors and torches. "What will he do?"

"One of two things; either he will surrender within the hour or send to his brother for aid."

The king waved over Athelstan, "Fetch us some ale and some food. We are hungry."

Athelstan had just returned when we heard a scream from the other side of the fort. "I think the thegn decided to send for help. I think we may see him soon."

It was almost immediately that Osric returned. "I have your word that we can leave with arms and my family?"

"I give you my word."

"Then we will leave."

"At dawn."

"At dawn."

The thegn disappeared. "And now, King Egbert I will collect my men and we will sleep. Two battles in one day are enough for any man. I would suggest you have men watch the other gate in case he tries to send for help again."

He laughed, "You are careful, Viking."

"It is why I have outlived most of my enemies. Rorik and Wiglaf will not have long on this earth."

We slept well and we missed the departure of Osric and his people. The ones who lived in Lundenwic were happy with their new king, for King Egbert encouraged them to live within the walls of the burgh and he promised to garrison it with his own men. I smiled as I saw his men clearing the ditch of rubbish. He had heeded my words.

"We will be departing for our home now, King Egbert. Would you wish me to ferry you across the river?"

He shook his head. "The men who use the port are keen to please me. They are building a ferry for us to use." He smiled, "It was *wyrd* meeting you, Jarl Dragon Heart. I now have a secure base on the northern side of the river and the trade will bring in much gold."

"Just as long as you keep a good watch for the Mercians. They will not take kindly to losing this place."

"Fear not Mercia is on the wane and Wessex is on the rise." He clasped my arm. "I look forward to trading with you."

I smiled, "Then remember that when my ships return. I expect favourable treatment."

"The wolf will always be welcome here."

"And if you hear of Rorik I would appreciate the information. I have a long memory for my enemies."

And so we sailed home. We had no need to visit with King Selfyn for our holds were full and we all adopted the wolf banner for our ships. It marked us for both friend and foe. I was confident that Rorik would emerge once more and I would be there to quash him.

Chapter 8

We had travelled back with the Ulfheonar as crew on the two drekar. We had renamed the second one '*Josephus*' in honour of the Greek who had helped us in so many ways. Poor Erik took some time to get over the death of his mentor. I spent some time with him, on the voyage back.

"He thought of you as his family, Erik. He will be in the Otherworld now feeling happy that his sacrifice saved your life."

"But he is gone!"

"Just as Ragnar died and left a space in my heart. But he is still there in spirit. If you close your eyes and open your mind you will hear him." I tapped the steering board. "He will be closest to you here. When storms rage and rocks threaten listen to your inner voice for that will be Josephus."

"Truly?"

"I am never foresworn, Erik, truly."

My words had the desired effect and I noticed that he brightened on the way home.

We had a fine welcome from both the people of Úlfarrston and Cyninges-tūn. The wealth we brought back was beyond their wildest dreams. All benefitted but it was Bjorn who was the happiest. The ore we had procured was of the highest quality and he had to take on extra workers to keep up with demand. We were also greeted by the progeny of our new animals. The cattle looked bigger and the sheep had more wool. Our voyages had been fruitful. That would have been a perfect year if we had not received ominous messages. This time they were not from the spirit world they came, instead from our brethren across the seas.

A messenger arrived from Windar. Arturus and I left directly. We left Aiden to distribute the goods we had traded and he wished to make more of the wolf pendants. Arturus was torn between helping Cnut and Haaken to train the replacement Ulfheonar and joining me. I was pleased when he accompanied me. We used the horses we had brought back from Kent. They were bigger than the ponies we normally used and allowed us to travel faster and travel with armour.

"You need to think about a wife, my son."

He looked at me as we crossed the col near our valley. "I am too young yet."

"You are never too young to father a son. I was your father at about your age. We never know what the Norns will throw at us."

"How do you know if she is the right woman for you?"

"You just know. With your mother it was clear to everyone else before us but you will know. Remember, my son, we are the guardians of the sword called Saxon Slayer. The spirits and the Norns have determined that our destiny is out of our hands. We do not decide our lives. That is done for us. We have to be prepared. I need a grandson or granddaughter so that I know our people will be cared for. Your sister has not chosen children; it is down to you."

He was silent for the rest of the journey. I had planted the seeds in his head and I knew my son well enough to know that he would ruminate and reflect on them. He was my son and he would come to the correct conclusion.

I could see from his face that Windar was worried. He was normally ebullient and without care but when he greeted us I saw the frown upon his face. "Come to my hall, Jarl Dragon Heart. I have much news to impart."

He had his slaves pour us horns of ale and then sent them hence. "There are Norse and Dane raiders in the Dunum Valley and the Tinea."

I smiled, "Slow down Windar. How do you know?"

"There were Northumbrian refugees who fled over the high divide. I had patrols out, as you suggested and they found them."

"Were they harmed?"

"Jarl Dragon Heart, I am offended. I have tried to be like you in every way." He patted his stomach. "I have failed in some but in others I do things right. They came not for war and so I welcomed them."

"I am sorry for offending you. How do they know they were Danes?"

"They do not. That is why I said Danes or Norse. They merely said that they had been driven out by raiders in long ships."

I took a swig of the ale. It was good. "Normally they come for slaves and they leave. I take it they did not leave?"

He shook his head, "They brought their families. We were told of a settlement south of the Dunum and one to the north, close to the village with the forges that you raided last year."

"It was the Norns at work again. Had my raid opened the way for invaders?"

"And on the Tinea?"

He shook his head. "They said that they had heard that the Tinea had been raided."

"Is this serious, father?"

"Aye it could be. The Dunum is a perfect artery for them to sail and conquer. It is only the waterfall which would stop them sailing here and that is less than forty miles from our borders."

"But they are of our people."

Windar and I shook our heads together. "No, my son, they are not. We are our people. The rest are looking for land that they can take. The Dunum is ripe for plucking. I think the day of the Saxon is numbered here in the north. It is no wonder that we have had little trouble from the Northumbrians of late. The raids must have been hurting them."

"Will they come here, Jarl Dragon Heart?"

"Eventually they will, Windar. It may not be this year but they will want land and the high divide is not the land for either animals or farming. They will come. We know how good this land is and they will want it. We will have to persuade them that these pastures are not for them."

I rode with Arturus towards the high divide. Windar tried to dissuade me. "Jarl, take some men with you for protection!"

"Windar, my son and I can take care of ourselves. We have our bows and we have our armour. I am confident that we can evade discovery. Do not forget that we know this land and the raiders do not. This will be the most opportune time to see how far they have come and I will be able to see who they are."

In the end he had no choice for I was Jarl Dragon Heart and we headed east. I did not travel up Ulla's Water. The land further north and east was good land but none of my people had settled it. I knew that it was empty. We went directly due east. Once we had negotiated the steep valley at the extreme east of the land we claimed we headed up the great divide. There were farmers here. They were hardy lonely folk. Some had lived here since the times of the Romans. They eked out a living alone and without defences. We sometimes found their roundhouses and their skeletons. Many had died in the wolf winter. We avoided anywhere with smoke. Smoke meant people and we wanted to be invisible until we saw signs of the Norse. I did not think that raiders would have penetrated this far so quickly.

It was when we reached the upper reaches of the Dunum that we moved with more caution. The raiders could have sailed quite a way up the Dunum. It was navigable for a small drekar almost as far as the falls. We walked rather than rode from the falls and we kept to the river. Three days after leaving Windar we had our first sight of the invaders. We saw a small ship; it was too small to be a drekar; I estimated it would have but six oars on each side but it would bring a family up the river and give them the means to both move and fish. It was, however, a Norse boat. The design was unmistakeable.

As soon as we saw the boat we took the horses away from the river, up the valley sides and tethered them. Taking our bows we made our way down to the tendril of smoke rising from their home. As soon as we saw the hut we stopped and waited. It was a Norse house. The Saxons liked their roundhouses. This one had straight sides. It had the turf roof and the familiar oblong shape. They might have come from the same fjord as Ragnar and Prince Butar. We watched until we had identified the number of settlers. It looked to be a family group. There were two women; one looked to have grey hair. There were two young children and I counted seven men. They ranged from a greybeard to two who were little older than Arturus. We only moved when night fell.

We moved a mile up the valley and we camped. We ate a cold meal of dried meat and the last of our ale. "It is just one family. They cannot worry us."

"It does not worry me if it stays at one. But I remember when we came to Mann. We sent messages to our brethren in Orkneyjar and our home fjord that we had good land without enemies. There are others though, like Harald One Eye who seeks to rule a land. They will not share the bounty of the earth. They wish to rule. When the ones like Harald One Eye come they will not just take the land, they will head west to find new lands and when they reach Windar's

Mere they will think they have found Valhalla. They will not share. They will take!"

I saw him take it in. "Then how do we stop them?"

"We meet them when they begin their migration and we stop them. We will need watchers at the steep valley to the east of Windar's Mere. This year we will not be in danger but next year we will need five men living and watching on our borders."

Surprisingly our news came as something of a relief to Windar. I think he had expected hordes of settlers pouring into his land. "No, Windar, for the present we are safe. You need to find young men who have their wits about them and can survive by hunting. I want them to keep a watch on the steep valley. Ulf can do the same at Ulla's Water. I will find others and next year they can watch for the tide which will threaten to engulf us. I want a line of watchers to the east of our land. They watch not for the Saxon but the Viking!"

Haaken and Cnut were like me; they treated the threat with respect. "If any get a toe hold then they will flood in."

"Aye. And we have too much empty land there. It will make it even more attractive to them. We need to encourage our people who want land to move to the east. The more farms we have there the safer we will all be."

"Jarl Dragon Heart, we have friends in Orkneyjar still. Siggi and Trygg came from there. Why not find if there are landless men who wish to join us."

"That is a good idea."

"I do not understand father. What is the difference between men from Orkneyjar and the ones we fear, from the east?"

"One is invited and one is not. I would welcome men like Siggi and Trygg but not men like Harald One Eye and Rorik." I could see that he was not convinced. "In this you must just trust me, my son. Haaken and I know the difference between thieves and warriors."

My oathsworn nodded as they clutched their wolf amulets.

When we reached our home again it was a hive of activity. Cheese and butter were being made with the extra milk we had from our new beasts. Bjorn and his smiths had smelted all of the iron and were now turning out armour and swords. The wool from the shorn sheep was being spun ready to be made into kyrtles.

Kara looked happy. She had grown into a confident young woman. Cyninges-tūn was the town I defended but it was Kara's to control. She was a volva and understood the harmony between man and the land. We had achieved that balance. We cut only those trees we needed and we did not clear woods just for the land. The animals grazed in the open spaces we had and not the ones we had to create for them. The Water teemed with fish but we only took enough to feed us. We had no need to salt for we could fish all year even when there was ice on the Water.

My daughter greeted me with an embrace and a smile. "We will need to trade goods again, Jarl. We have filled the huts we use for storage."

I nodded. "I had thought that too but I think we will sail to Orkneyjar instead of Lundenwic."

She looked at me curiously and then, linking me, led me down to the barrow of my dead wife and child. "You have a reason?"

"We need no more iron just yet and besides we took the best. The men of Kent will need time to mine some more and King Egbert has yet to defeat Mercia. Our stocks of seal oil are becoming low and the men of Orkneyjar will pay a high price for our weapons and our cheese."

She laughed, "And there is another reason. You need men."

"Aye, we do. We lose fine warriors and our young men are not yet ready to become Ulfheonar. Your mother came from Orkneyjar as did Siggi and Trygg."

"And so did my uncle. Look into men's hearts, father not all of our brothers are to be trusted."

"I will take the galdramenn with me. He has the ability to see beyond the words."

"You will take '**Heart**'?"

"No. I would like to try a new crew and captain for '***Josephus***'."

"That is good." She kissed me on the cheek. "I will leave you here for mother is close by." She smiled, "I will see that you are not disturbed."

After she had gone I stripped off and walked into the water. The chill soon went as the water came up to my chest. I lay on my back and sculled with my hands beneath me. It happened that the angle of the mountain was the perfect one and I saw old Olaf looking down upon me. I closed my eyes and enjoyed the feeling of isolation.

'Our son is growing and you are right, he does need a wife. Sail the seas but watch for the red sail. Peer into the hearts of men

before you trust them. Our land is rich and there are those who covet what we have. Blood will have to be spilled to hold on to what we have.'

There was silence and I asked a question in my head. *'Are you happy?'*

I thought that she had gone for there was silence, save for the lapping of the water and the distant quack of ducks.

'It is hard to see you and not to touch you but I hear your thoughts and I know your heart. I am content.'

Then the silence returned. My wife had gone. She would be back in the otherworld. I was at peace for she had spoken with me and her words comforted me.

I left the next day with Arturus and Aiden. Haaken and Cnut had wanted to come with me on my voyage but my mind was made up. "You are the crew of the '***Heart***'. This will be a new crew and captain for '***Josephus***'. I have to know how they perform in difficult circumstances. Besides you have much to do to train the new warriors. We have benches to fill and you two are the best judges of character that I know."

Haaken laughed, "You are mellowing. You have not used flattery before now to get your way."

"You know me better than that, Haaken One Eye. I speak the truth."

I had chosen the captain for the new drekar. He had been fishing with his father for some years and had shown much skill. His father would have been the perfect captain for he knew the wind and the tides better than any man. His wife had died in the Wolf Winter and he had daughters. He would not leave the Water again. Stig Haakenson was the same age as Arturus and he was delighted to be given the opportunity. Arturus and he had played together as children and Aiden knew him too. It was good that they would be able to watch him as we sailed. He could sail but he was a stranger to war.

The twenty-six young men I took with me were the best of the new warriors. They had been the ones trained by my son during the winter. As yet they had to earn their armour. I had promised them a share of the profits and given them all a Bjorn made sword. They were keen to impress and their shields all had a wolf somewhere on the leather covering. It was not the black wolf of the Ulfheonar but it showed their ambition.

I took Trygg and his knarr with me. He was somewhat wary of returning to the home he had had to flee. "This time, Trygg, you go under my banner." Kara and the women had finished my banner which had a black wolf with golden eyes on a red background. My shield was the same design and it looked striking.

"I am not worried Jarl but I would not wish you to be tainted with my punishment."

"We go to trade and not to fight."

Our stately progress up the coast suited both my captain and Arturus. He was keen to see how the warriors he had trained rowed. As we were travelling with a knarr we did not need the oars very often but the men pulled well together.

Stig was less happy about his ship. "It is slow, Jarl Dragon Heart. When we get the chance I would have her out of the water and examine her hull. I fear she has weed which is slowing her down. She should be faster."

"I have something we can paint on the hull to deter weed and we can shift the ballast around," Aiden pointed to the rowers, "and the rowers are not balanced."

"I am sorry Jarl Dragon Heart, I have much to learn."

"We all have much to learn. This ship is weregeld for Josephus. It will need a blood sacrifice. When we have made one and you and Aiden have worked together then she will fly. Bolli can also help you. This voyage is for us to see what the problems are."

The jarl with whom Trygg and Siggi had had a dispute was Sigurd the Mighty. I hoped he was less belligerent than he had been. As we headed east around the northern coast of the mainland I looked for forts and settlements. I did not know who ruled in this land. I only knew that they were not Saxon. We followed Trygg for he knew these waters well and he took us into the harbour on the island of Hrossey. I was pleased to see that the drekar there were threttanessa. Had I brought one of my other ships it might have intimidated the leader of the people who live here in the far north.

I stepped ashore with Aiden and Arturus. We left the crew on board. We were here to trade. After he had tied up his ship Trygg joined us.

"The Jarl's hall is on top of that low hill."

I could see that the island was generally low lying but the anchorage was good. I could understand why they used this as a base to raid the mainland and Norway.

There were no guards at the open gates and we walked in. An old man repairing nets just inside the gate looked up as we entered. "Trygg! You have returned! Did you hear that the old Jarl had died?"

"It is good to see you, Rognvald. Sigurd is dead?"

The old man lowered his voice, "Some say murdered." He stood. "What brings you back?"

"I serve, Jarl Dragon Heart."

The old man turned to look at me. "You are the warrior with the sword touched by the Gods?" I nodded. "Then the new Jarl will be glad to see you. Jarl Harald Blue Eye has spoken of visiting you on Mann."

"We live on Mann no longer. Where is the jarl?"

"He is in his hall."

"I will speak with you later, old friend."

"I look forward to that, Trygg. Many of us were unhappy when you and your families had to flee. Old Sigurd could be vindictive."

"What is the new Jarl like?"

The old man had a worried look and he said, "He is young." Then he went back to his work.

As we approached the hall some warriors emerged to view us. Although I wore mail I had neither helmet nor shield and there was little to identify me. I stood at the bottom of the steps leading up to the hall. "I would speak with Jarl Harald Blue Eye. We are here to trade."

The two warriors were young. They looked to be little older than Arturus. "And who are you with the strange looking armour and trimmed beard?"

Arturus started but I restrained him and smiled, "I am Jarl Dragon Heart of Cyninges-tūn. And you are a little foolish to insult a warrior whom you do not know."

I saw the one who had spoken colour and his hand went to his sword but his companion restrained him. A warrior emerged. I saw immediately that he had to be the Jarl. He had the blondest hair and the bluest eyes of anyone I have ever seen. His mail was finely made and had two golden clasps for his cloak. "Did I hear that you are Jarl Dragon Heart?"

"I am. I was just explaining that to this young man. He has a rash tongue." I glared at the young warrior. "We are here to trade."

"Come into my hall." He turned to the young warrior, "Sven, find something useful to do away from here. You have offended the jarl!"

His hall was well made and had a fire burning at one end. I nodded, "You have a comfortable home."

"This is nothing. I will improve it before too long. We will make a few more raids and I will be rich enough to build a hall of stone!"

"Good." I was not convinced by his bravado but I could be polite and diplomatic when I wanted to. "Then perhaps you need not trade with us."

"That depends what you bring and what you want."

"We want seal oil but we bring kyrtles and fine weapons."

"Weapons like the sword which was touched by the gods?"

"Made by the same smith but untouched by any gods."

"Then you are thrice welcome for we have heard of your sword and if the ones you trade are of the same quality then we will be invincible."

"Come to my drekar and I will show you. The crew have all been given the identical swords to the ones we would trade."

As we left he said, "You give your crew a sword? That is mighty generous of you."

"They fight for me, why should they not have the best?"

"And yet you wear such strange armour. Why do you not wear mail?"

"This was given to me by the Emperor of Byzantium and it suits me. Each to his own."

I could see that the young jarl was intrigued and he studied my armour as we walked to the drekar. Arturus ran ahead and his young warriors stepped ashore to show the jarl their swords.

He held his hand out and Arturus nodded to one of his warriors. Erik Stigson handed his sword over. Bjorn made excellent swords. They were light and yet immensely strong. Most importantly they were balanced. I could see that he was much taken with it. "How many do you have?"

"That depends how much seal oil you have."

"We have some here but we would need to send to other parts of the island to get sufficient for such weapons. Will you be our guests tonight? I would like to hear some of your stories."

Trygg had stayed in the background and I think that he was relieved not to be recognised. He busied himself aboard the knarr as I returned to the hall with Jarl Harald. I left Arturus and Aiden to arrange the watches on the two ships. It would not do to have our cargo stolen.

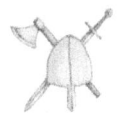

Chapter 9

The jarl offered me a chamber to change from my armour. My new armour was more comfortable than my older mail but it was still more pleasant to be in my tunic. "Come and sit by my fire. I have many questions for you."

"I will answer if I can."

"Was the story of the gods touching your word true?"

"Aye. A bolt came from the heavens and hit the sword. It threw two of us to the ground but we were unharmed."

"How was that so?"

"I have no idea. It was *wyrd*. But the sword is the strongest weapon I have ever seen. It never bends and it keeps its edge throughout a battle."

"You must be special to be touched by the gods like this."

I shrugged. "I am not special. I have good warriors and we are successful but we have losses too." He quaffed his ale and held out his horn for a refill. "And you have done well to be a jarl so young."

He gave me a quick look to see if there was any deceit in my face. I smiled. "My uncle, Sigurd the Mighty, was old and he died in his sleep. His sons were dead and the warriors chose me. I have led many successful raids to the mainland." He touched the golden clasps for his cloak. "We took much gold." He seemed to see my wolf pendant. "Is that copper or bronze?"

"Neither, it is gold!"

I could see that he realised then that the gold on his own clasp was nothing compared with the gold on the pendant. "And is that a blue stone for the eye?"

"It is."

"That is beautiful and who made this for you?"

"Aiden, one of the men I brought with me, is a galdramenn and a fine craftsman."

"I would have him make me a dragon like that."

"You can ask him but you will need to ensure you have enough gold."

"He could make it here?"

"Possibly. He is his own man you would need to ask him."

"But you are his jarl! You could command."

"I could command but I prefer to ask. It is my way."

Almost as though he had heard his name Aiden and Arturus came into the hall. "The jarl here asks if you could make him a dragon pendant like the wolves we wear."

Jarl Harald suddenly saw the pendants worn by Aiden and Arturus. "Your men have them too?"

"I give them to my oathsworn, yes."

"Then you must be rich."

"We have enough. I use what gold we have for what matters to us."

"Interesting. Well, Aiden, is it? Would you make me such a pendant?"

I gave the slightest of nods and Aiden said, "Aye Jarl if you have a smith here and sufficient gold."

He frowned, "I will get more gold for I would have one at least as big as the one which Jarl Dragon Heart wears."

I hid my smile behind my horn. The young jarl was vain and had a high opinion of himself. I noticed that Trygg was not with the other two and I hoped he would be talking to Rognvald; I would know about this young jarl of Hrossey.

As we washed before eating I said, quietly, to Arturus. "Make sure the men do not drink too much tonight. I would not have any trouble."

"I have spoken with them already."

"Aiden, keep your eyes and ears open this night. We may trade more with this jarl but I would know his intentions first."

I need not have worried about my men. They behaved impeccably. We had no Haaken to tell our tales and so it was left to Aiden. He did a good job. He had a good voice and it was pleasant on the ear. I began to relax a little and then I noticed some of the jarl's men were drinking more than was good for them. The warrior I had met earlier was particularly drunk and loud. I discovered his name was Sven Knife Tongue. It seemed appropriate. He had retained his armour and became more and more belligerent as the night went on. It appeared to me as though he had a number of young men who looked up to him.

"Jarl Harald, the young warrior Sven, he appears to be, how should I say, a little aggressive."

Jarl Harald lowered his voice. "He is. He is the grandson of Sigurd the Mighty. Some of his friends thought he should be jarl." He shrugged, "He has never led a raid and is too young." I said nothing. Jarl Harald emptied another horn and added, "Perhaps I should have had him killed when I became jarl but he is a good swordsman and a fierce warrior."

"It is more important to be a loyal warrior. Is he your oathsworn?"

The jarl looked at me and shook his head. "No."

I said nothing more for it told me that Sven Knife Tongue had ambitions. I realised then that he reminded me of Harald One Eye. His jealousy and ambition had driven Prince Butar and the rest of us west.

One of the jarl's men stood and told a tale of how the jarl and his drekar had sailed to Norway and stolen the King of Norway's treasure. He made it sound amusing and I wondered at that. The King of Norway had a long reach and Hrossey could be taken easily by a large army. I hoped that the young jarl knew what he was doing. I found myself liking the young man. He and Arturus got on well. They were laughing and joking with each other as though they had been friends their whole lives. I was so wrapped up in their interchange that I did not notice Sven Knife Tongue walking unsteadily towards me.

"Where is your fancy armour now? Are you too ashamed to wear it amongst real men?"

"Sven Knife Tongue, do not embarrass us in front of our guest. Jarl Dragon Heart is a mighty hero and a famous warrior."

I carefully watched the young man. The drunk ignored the jarl. "I have bedded young women who looked more like a warrior than this oiled and spoiled jarl." His friends all laughed and I saw Arturus colour.

"Sven! Leave us now!"

I held up my hand. "He is drunk, Jarl Harald. And I am tired. I will retire. I seem to annoy the young man and I would take away the source of the annoyance. Thank you for the feast."

I stood but Sven blocked my way. "Where are you going? I have insulted you. If you were a man and not a drekar wife you would fight me."

I put my face close to his. "I do not fight drunks and I do not fight boys. You will feel the shame of this in the morning."

"I am no boy!"

He suddenly pulled out his dagger and lunged at me. I grabbed his hand and put my elbow sharply into his stomach. The dagger fell to the floor and I felled him with one blow to the chin. I picked up the dagger and put it in my belt. I pointed to his friends. "If you are his friends then take him to his bed and keep him there until he is sober."

They staggered over and picked up his unconscious form. One of his friends held out his hand for the dagger. "When he apologises then he can have the dagger."

After they had gone the jarl said, "I will have him punished in the morning."

"Do not do so on my account. He is a young man and he is drunk. Many young men behave that way."

"You are too kind Jarl Dragon Heart but if that is your wish…"

"It is."

I went to the hall I was sharing with my men. Trygg was there. He had not stayed at the feast for too long. No-one had said anything but he wanted no trouble.

"Well?"

"It seems that the old king was in good health one day and dead the next." He shrugged, "I shall not mourn him for the vindictive old man cost me members of my family but this appears to be an even bigger nest of vipers now."

Arturus and Aiden joined us. "You are more tolerant than I am father. I would have used my sword on him."

"And that would have been a mistake. He is the grandson of the old king. He has many supporters. The last thing we need is a blood feud. I doubt that there are many warriors here who would wish to come and settle in our land or that I would want any who chose to."

"You may be wrong there Jarl. Talking to Rognvald there are many who seek a life in a place which is less harsh and where there are not so many factions."

"It is good that we came here, Jarl Dragon Heart, for we have done well with our trade. We will have enough seal oil for at least two years and it cost just ten swords." Trygg smiled more now.

"Then when the oil comes we will sail back to our own land which already seems greener, safer and more honest than here. You did well to leave here Trygg."

"I know, jarl."

Despite the words of Aiden and Trygg I did not sleep well that night. I heard warning voices all night. I awoke before dawn and I dressed in my armour. I walked down to the harbour. I had to make sure that the knarr and the drekar were safe. I was relieved when I saw Stig and my guards sitting by a lighted fire.

"As soon as the oil comes I want the swords trading and the seal oil storing. Be ready for a rapid departure."

"Is there trouble, Jarl?"

"I am not certain." I looked at the sea beyond the harbour entrance. It looked very welcoming.

The others had heard me stir and they were dressed too. We went to Jarl Harald's Hall. Most of his men were sleeping but, surprisingly the young jarl was up and about. He welcomed me with a horn of ale. "I meant to ask you last night, Jarl Dragon Heart, the drekar out there is it your only ship?" He gave me an apologetic look, "It is just that it does not seem as large as the one I have heard about."

"No this is a new one we captured in Wessex. I wanted to see the new crew and see how she sailed. I have two bigger drekar."

"How many warriors can they carry?"

"More than sixty."

He almost choked on his ale. "That is twice the size of ours. With ships that size you could threaten Norway himself."

"Aye but you would need the warriors." I spread my arm around his hall. "You can muster three perhaps four drekar?"

"Four."

"And your warriors all have mail?"

"No, Jarl Dragon Heart. It is hard to come by. I have just one drekar with mailed warriors and they are my oathsworn. Sven has ten oathsworn who have mail."

"Does he have a drekar?"

He nodded, "He does but he sails under my command."

I lowered my voice. "I would watch him. Last night's dissent was aimed as much at you as it was to me. It is a challenge to your authority."

He suddenly looked both young and distressed, "I know. I would have challenged him but…"

I thought I knew what the '*but*' meant but I would not say. "Keep your men busy and it will stop them from plotting and planning."

The hall began to wake up and we spoke of other things. He told me that the oil would arrive by sunset. We ate fresh bread and smoked herrings. Even Trygg looked at ease.

Suddenly the door to the hall was flung open and Sven Knife Tongue stood there. "Where is my dagger? You thief!"

I spread my arms for my men to remain calm. This could be a bloodbath if I spoke the wrong words. I took the dagger out. "It is here but I believe you were drunk last night and you may have said things you regretted."

He strode up to me. "You are right, I had had a drink. If I had not then you would be dead."

"You would have stabbed an unarmed man, a guest in my hall?" I heard the shock in Jarl Harald's voice.

"This is neither a man nor a warrior. I do not believe he has done any of the things he and his liars say. If he was a man he would have fought me."

My men all drew their swords. I held up my hands. "No man calls me a liar. The word of Jarl Dragon Heart is true. You will apologise now. Insults from a drunk are one thing but these words are planned and intended to insult!"

I had not yet drawn my weapon but it would be out in an instant if he said the wrong thing. I could not allow this insult to pass. I saw the look of disappointment on the face of the jarl. Sven laughed. "I will do nothing of the kind. Come outside now and I will despatch you and then your warriors! They will see what real warriors and men can do!"

"Arturus, get my shield and my helmet." I turned to the jarl. "I am sorry for this jarl. If it offends you I will go with this whelp and decide this somewhere else."

"No, Jarl Dragon Heart. He needs a lesson and you will teach him."

Sven turned and hissed, "This will be no lesson for it is to the death. Only one of us will survive and that will be me. Then we will see who the greatest warrior on Hrossey is and who is the best leader."

I glanced at the jarl. It was all clear to me now. I was being used by Sven. In killing me he would have killed a warrior with a great reputation and he would then take over as jarl. Jarl Harald had made a mistake; he should have killed him when he had the chance.

I saw the Jarl's eyes narrow. He had worked it out too. "Make a circle. Archers shoot down any man who interferes. This is in the hands of the Allfather."

The jarl's warriors made a circle in which we would fight. As Arturus fitted my shield I noticed that there were archers lined up outside the hall ready to carry out the jarls' orders. Arturus had my mail mask as well as the helmet. "I will not need the mask today."

Aiden came over to me and adjusted my helmet. He said, quietly, "I spoke with Rognvald. This Sven keeps a dagger in his left hand and he has sharpened spikes on his shield."

"Thank you, Aiden."

I saw that Sven had an open helmet with a nasal although he had a metal coif beneath it. His mail byrnie was well made, with rivets but it came down half way between his waist and his knees. That was a weakness. I saw the metal spikes on the shield. They would only be dangerous if he struck at my face. I would watch for that manoeuvre.

I walked towards him. I knew that he would want to trade insults I would not give him the opportunity. I brought my sword over my head and swung it towards his. He was not expecting the move but he had quick reactions and his shield came up. It met the blow. He might have had metal spikes but the shield was not as well made as mine and the leather covering ripped as he stepped back.

I had angered him and I wanted him angry. I wanted him to make mistakes. "You coward! I was not ready!" I did not need to look around to know that the experienced warriors would be laughing at him. He sounded like a petulant child.

He tried the same blow that I had just made. The difference was I was ready. I braced my shield with my left leg and his sword struck the shield but did no damage. I smiled at him. That was the real reason I had not worn the mail mask. I wanted him to see my face. I punched at him with my right hand. The blow caught him on the side of the face and he recoiled. He was not expecting that. I saw the side of his face begin to swell.

"How many battles have you fought in boy?" He stared at me silently. "I have been fighting warriors and winning since I was twelve summers old. You can surrender now if you wish and save your life."

I knew he would not and knew that he would do something reckless. He swung his sword overhand and tried to bring it down on my head. As he did so I saw a blade emerge from his shield as he stabbed towards me with his left hand. I lowered my own shield slightly and deflected the knife. He screamed in triumph as the sword came down at my shoulder. I brought my shield up but it would not stop the strike. I could not raise it enough. His sword hit my shoulder. I heard a crack as the bone that was across my shoulder broke but I also saw his sword bend a little. I think he expected his blade to slice through and into my flesh. His mouth dropped open as I swung my sword horizontally. It cracked into his shield and I saw wood splinters fly.

I went on the offensive. I could not use my shield arm much. I knew that if I tried to raise the shield the pain would stop me. I used my size and my superior sword to beat him back. I brought the sword at an angle towards his neck. He countered with his own sword and I saw the bend become worse. His sword had no balance now. He stepped back and I feinted at his head. When his shield came up I stabbed at his unprotected leg. He squealed like a stuck pig as my sword entered the fleshy part of his thigh. I twisted as I withdrew it.

"Surrender and live!"

"Never!"

Blood was pouring from his leg and he tried to finish it. He brought his sword over his head towards my damaged shoulder. I spun away from the blow and his sword hit air. I continued my swing and brought Ragnar's Spirit to smash into his mailed back. He was wearing good mail but the edge of my sword was sharp enough to sever the links, rip into his mail byrnie and slice into his back.

Panic set in. He turned to face me but he had a weakened leg. I could not lift my shield and so I had to use my sword and my feet only. I stepped forward and stabbed at his shield. He brought his own sword down on mine and succeeded in bending his own blade even more. He could no longer stab with it. As I was tiring I decided to end it. I shifted my body to the left and he swung his sword at what he thought was an attempt by me to punch with my shield. Instead I stabbed directly at his throat. He tried to bring his shield up but I had faster hands and I saw his eyes widen as the sword entered his throat. There was a moment when he realised he was dying before the blood flooded from him and all life left his eyes. He fell at my feet in a widening pool of blood.

I suddenly felt the air as an arrow whizzed past me. I looked up and saw one of Sven's oathsworn with an arrow between his eyes and a sword falling from his dead hands. As Arturus stepped before me Aiden took my shield. I heard the jarl's voice, suddenly commanding. "If any of you raises his weapons then he will suffer the blood eagle and die slowly. This was a fair fight and honour is satisfied. There will be no blood feud."

As if to confirm it Arturus hissed, "And if there is then you answer to me and my oathsworn and we are warriors!"

There was real venom and authority in his voice and the nine oathsworn stepped back.

"Where are you hurt, Jarl Dragon Heart?" Aiden rushed to my side.

"My shoulder. I heard something crack."

Aiden nodded. "It will be the bone the Romans call the clavicle. You will be in pain for many days and there is little that we can do to heal it but your armour saved you."

"It did that and I can see why they wear so much padding. I think we will make a few changes, Aiden."

Chapter 10

My injuries meant that we had to stay longer on the island than I would have wished but it was *wyrd* for the jarl allowed those warriors and families who wished to come with us to my land. The word had spread that I was looking for those who wished to farm in our land and he allowed me to take any who chose. I think that he was relieved to be rid of the threat of Sven. In addition, he felt guilty about the events; as a host he should have prevented the fight.

As we sailed south with a hold full of the valuable seal oil and a knarr full of farmers I forced myself to think about what had happened. It also took away the pain of the pieces of bone grinding together with the pitch of the drekar. I still did not know the truth about the death of Sigurd the Mighty. I knew that many of his people thought that the jarl had done the deed and yet, to me, he had seemed honest. He was a little vain but many young men were at that age.

I was also curious about the oathsworn of Sven Knife Tongue. If they were cast from the same mould as their leader then this was not over. I knew that I would have to suffer Haaken and Cnut telling me that I should have taken the Ulfheonar with me. They would be wrong to do so. This was the work of the sisters. I had been meant to fight and kill Sven. I could have landed at any of the islands and we had chosen Hrossey. *Wyrd*.

My left arm was strapped to my body to prevent movement. The small drekar did not help me as the motion was more pronounced than on my larger ship. That too was meant to be, for the pain was constant and a reminder of my mortality. If I had worn my old armour there was a chance that the blow, which bent Sven's sword, would have severed the mail and might have cut me. It only took one such wound to end a battle. I would have more padding made for my shoulders. I knew that even when the break healed it would be a weakness. A warrior could not fight if he could not wield a shield.

By the time we reached Úlfarrston the ache in my shoulder had eased somewhat. Aiden had apologised that the only potion he had would be drink to numb the pain. I had seen wounded warriors who had taken that course and they did not live long. I lived with the pain. I would not become a slave to drink. By the time we had trekked to Cyninges-tūn I was able to talk without grimacing.

Kara already knew of my pain. As much as she trusted Aiden and his opinion she examined me herself. Her touch on my shoulder actually made me feel less pain. She was a true volva.

"Have you spoken with the spirits in my absence, daughter?"

"Always. The danger is spreading. It is all around. The struggle you had in the north is a foretaste of what is to come. There are many Norse and Danish babies being born and they want land. You have done well for our people. This is a prosperous and rich land. This is a land which will attract those who wish to take. War will come."

"And my name and renown do not help."

She helped me put my kyrtle over my arms. She was gentler than Arturus. "That is not in your hands. The gods have touched you. That cannot be taken away. There will always be young warriors who wish to challenge you and have the fame of killing the Dragon Heart."

The thought depressed me. "I bring danger to my people."

She laughed, "You are your people. Fear not father; your armour and your skill will protect you. And you have both the spirits and the Ulfheonar watching over you too." She inclined her head. "And I believe that will be some of your wolves even now."

She had been gone but a few moments when Haaken and Cnut came in. I could see concern written all over their faces. Haaken shook his head. "I will come with you next time!"

"It would have made little difference."

"No, but I would have been able to observe, and the story would have been better. I have to make it up from the words of Arturus and Aiden!"

I laughed. It was a mistake for the bones grated and I winced. "My daughter has spoken with the spirits again and there is danger from the west as well as the east."

"Has the world gone mad?"

"No Cnut, but the sisters are spinning once more. I have learned that small events are like a stone thrown in a pond. They ripple outwards. The young jarl of Hrossey raids the King of Norway. He will retaliate. The Vikings who have settled in Hibernia and Mann, our former friends, will look to us and desire our riches. And we are the cause of much of our own mischief. Had we not damaged the Northumbrians so much then they would be as a wall against danger from the east."

Aiden came in with Arturus. They had stayed with the ship for another night and a day so that the hull could be examined.

"How is the drekar?"

"It has a bottom covered in weed. We have taken it from the water and the crew are scraping it clean." I nodded. Arturus continued, "They feel they let you down and should have protected you on Hrossey."

"You must make them know that they were wrong. It was *wyrd*." I told them of Kara's words.

Aiden look serious. "There were some traders who came to Ulfarrston while we cleaned the hull. They spoke of Mercians heading north. They have moved from Caestre. There may be danger from the south too."

"Is there any word from Egbert?"

Aiden shook his head. "Haaken I want you to escort Trygg to Lundenwic. Take some swords and seal oil to trade. We have to know what is happening. Listen and find out the way the world moves. King Egbert told me he would keep me informed of dangers. Kara and the spirits are never wrong. War is coming but we cannot defend all of our borders at the same time."

"Which crew should I take?"

"The Ulfheonar, of course."

"But that would leave you alone."

Arturus jumped up. "He has me and my men to defend him, Haaken One Eye!"

Haaken laughed but Cnut said, "I thought they were your father's men?"

"Enough! We do not squabble amongst ourselves! Thank you for your concern, Haaken. I have enough men to protect us. We will use this time to build up our strength and for me to see what we need to do."

Haaken nodded and Cnut said, "Sorry Arturus, I sometimes forget you are now a man. I still see the boy who used to follow us around."

Arturus smiled, "And I must learn to be more like my father and keep both my tongue and my temper under control."

When Haaken and Cnut had left I took Arturus to task. "I am pleased that you see your faults for you sounded, to me, a little like Sven Knife Tongue then. We are family and we do not fight each other."

"Your father is right. I can understand the concern of his oathsworn. And, it seemed to me, that you believe the crew of the '***Josephus***' are yours to command."

As soon as Arturus coloured I knew that Aiden was right.

"My son, there will come a time when you do command your own men and I look forward to that day. You need to learn how to lead." All was becoming clear. The Norns were spinning. I had been meant to meet and fight Sven so that I could see the danger for my son. I needed to plot his course so that he became a leader for my people. Arturus left us, more embarrassed than anything else.

"I will talk with him, jarl." I knew that Aiden was like Arturus' big brother. He would be able to make my son see sense.

Kara knew there was something wrong between my son and myself; how could she not? "He needs to find out for himself, father, the right and the wrong way to lead. Let him command some men."

"But I fear he will become like Sven Knife Tongue."

"Then surely it is better to find that out sooner rather than later. Haaken and Cnut just wish to serve you. That is their choice. Who will lead the people when you are in the Otherworld? Your son will make a good leader. He needs experience and guidance." She smiled as she left me. "You will find a way."

It was strange the manner in which Kara now spoke. Each day she sounded more like her mother. As I could not exercise and riding was difficult, I spent the next twenty days around Cyningestūn. I had rarely had the chance to look at it closely. I first went with Aiden to the western village for that was where we kept our animals and I was keen to see the improvements in the herds. Scanlan spent most of his time there. Since the Wolf Winter he had been almost running the village. He had come a long way since we had captured his family on Maeresea. *Wyrd*.

He was pleased to see me but I saw the concern on his face when he saw my injury. "It is nothing, Scanlan, without the armour I might be dead. How are the new animals?"

"It is still early. We have yet to slaughter any of the newly born. We will need for them to grow a little more. They will be culled after the next winter but the signs are good. They are all broader in the shoulders and the rump. The heifers give better milk and the skins look like they may make good hides. The sheep are bigger too. Perhaps we could trade for pigs?"

Aiden smiled, "You are reading my mind Scanlan. I was about to tell the jarl that they have fine pigs in Wessex. We could trade for those at the end of summer. We do not need to slaughter them here. We have food for many more animals."

He was right; the cereal crops were going to be the most bountiful yet and we had built granaries based upon the Roman style.

I put my good arm around Scanlan's shoulder and took him towards the Water. "Keep this to yourself but there may be danger from the west. We have made the north secure but enemies may come from the west and the south. How are the defences?"

"We have good weapons. Every warrior has a leather byrnie and a sword or a bow."

"That is not enough. I want each one to have a dagger and a metal helmet. We have the metal. See Bjorn." He nodded. "And the ditches should be deeper. It will stop flooding and slow down an attacker."

Aiden pointed to the Old Man. "We should use the boys who guard the flocks of sheep on the slopes. They have good eyes. They could watch for enemies coming from far away."

"See to it."

We returned to my hall and Rolf. He was a warrior and, unlike Scanlan, he was constantly improving the walls, the ditches and training the sentries. "Rolf if danger comes then I may not be here. You will command."

He nodded and then asked, "What about Arturus?"

"Do not worry about my son. I have plans for him. Make sure we have plenty of barrels; I intend to get salt from Ulfarrston and salt any surplus meat. If we are besieged I do not want the people to suffer. We have plenty of water. We save what food we have. How many men do you command? Exclude the Ulfheonar and the crew of the '*Josephus*'.

"There are twenty men who have mail. Fifteen who have no mail but weapons and who have been trained to fight in the shield wall. There are thirty boys who are either slingers or archers."

"And women?"

"Twenty of the girls can use a sling."

"I want all of them able to fight for this land. My daughter can organise them."

My final visit, before my Ulfheonar returned, was to Bjorn. I had realised the worth of the armour and, although the Emperor had given me mine Bjorn had made it for my men and I wished him rewarded. I still had half the torc I had taken from the Hibernian as well as some gold chains I had taken from Rorik's men. I gave the bundle to my smith.

"What do you wish made, Jarl Dragon Heart?"

"Nothing. This is for you. I am pleased with the work you have done. Many of my warriors would now lie dead but for the armour and the swords you made for them."

"You have no need, Jarl, I am pleased to do it for you."

"You have sons who work for you and they have wives. I know that women crave pretty things which gold can buy."

"Thank you. I am honoured."

"You will find Scanlan and Rolf asking for more helmets and weapons."

"War is coming?"

"My daughter believes so and there are rumours of other Norse Raiders looking covetously at our land."

"I do not blame them. I thought Mann was perfect until we came here and now I cannot conceive of living anywhere else."

"I feel the same. I feel at peace here especially with Old Olaf looking down."

"Aye Prince Butar and my family would have loved it here."

I tapped my heart. "I think they do."

I summoned Arturus and Aiden that evening. Arturus had been distant since I had chastised him and I needed to mend fences. One of the fishermen had caught a huge pike which had been decimating the fish stocks. It was one of the few luxuries I allowed myself and I accepted it. It seemed to please the fisherman even more than me. I think that was because they saw me as the source of all bounty. If nature was in order then our world would be well. I was seen as the one who kept that order. It helped that Kara was the volva and was a healer. As her father I seemed to have an aura of mystical power too.

My arm ached less but I could still not raise it above my head. It was another reason why I was pleased with the pike for it flaked off the bone and I was able to eat it with my right hand alone. Aiden knew what I was about. Even when I had told him what I intended he had nodded. He had the second sight. He helped me for he had been the one who had trained Arturus and taught him to read and write. He was the nearest thing to a big brother that Arturus had.

Aiden was clever and he filled the conversation with inconsequential and harmless anecdotes but all were to do with being a leader and the responsibility a leader had to his people.

"This is good fish is it not Arturus?"

"It is father. Olaf knows how to fish that is for certain."

"I also hope that he can fight."

My son looked up sharply. "You are certain that war is coming?"

"No, but your sister is. She is never wrong. The problem we have is that we do not know the direction it will come. When Haaken returns he may be able to give us news of the Mercians."

"The Mercians? Their land is many miles to the south."

I sighed, "It is not. The Northumbrians retreat. The land to the south of us is empty and easy to travel. King Coenwulf may remember me."

"Then is Ulfarrston in danger?"

"They are protected by the river and the sea. And we are but half a day from them. We would have warning. No, the danger is from the south east. The land there is empty. An enemy could approach unseen and then attack either Windar's Mere, or over the fly infested forest of Grize 's Dale to strike us here in the heart of our land and we would not know until they were upon us."

I saw Arturus taking that information in. Aiden and I had discussed this at length and both felt that a likely attack would come from that direction. "And that would be the Mercians?"

I paused before I spoke. "It could be Jarl Harald from Mann, Jarl Sihtric Silkbeard from Hibernia or Magnus Bare Legs the Dane."

"But he lives close to the land of the East Angles."

"He is greedy for land."

"How do we stop this then?" I pretended I needed to drink some more ale to allow him to come to the same conclusion that Aiden and I already had. He slapped the table, "I have it! We keep watch to the south east of here."

"That is an excellent idea. Aiden, get the old Roman maps out and let us see."

They were, of course, ready. We spread them on the table. There was a small red dot which was equidistant from Cyninges-tūn and Windar's Mere. It was the outline of an old Roman fort. Nearby was a deserted Saxon village called Cherchebi. The inhabitants had all died during the wolf winter. We all examined it closely. I waited for Arturus to jab his finger down. "Here! We rebuild the old fort. There is water nearby and it is less than twenty miles from both Cyninges-tūn and Windar's Mere. A leader could keep some ponies there and a message could be here in half a day."

I said quietly, "And who would you suggest for the commander?"

He hesitated and Aiden clapped him on the back, "You goose! Your father is thinking of you."

"I could command?"

"Could you?"

He studied my face for deceit and then nodded. "I will protect the land for you!"

"Then you need to tell your warriors tomorrow and make preparations. Some have families they will want to take with them. It will take until winter to build your new home and then you will be there, alone, for the winter. We cannot come to see if you are surviving. It will be a lonely and dangerous existence."

"I am ready. And thank you for the chance to prove myself."

I shook my head. "You need prove nothing to me, my son."

That evening saw a remarkable change in my son. His body had already become that of a man but now his mind caught up and Arturus became a leader of warriors.

Chapter 11

I saw little of my son for the next five days. He proved himself to be someone who could organise well. I suspect Aiden gave him many pointers. The two were close. I worked on my damaged shoulder to build up my strength again. As soon as I could lift my arm above my head without too much pain I started lifting stones by the water. Aiden had assured me that it was the best way to recover my strength. When Kara concurred, I gave every waking hour to the task. I had little else to do. It was high summer and all, save me, were busy. Even Kara and her women were using nature's bounty to harvest the honey and collect the abundant wild flowers and herbs she used in her potions. She had discovered that some of the spices we had brought back could also be used as effective remedies for ailments.

When the messenger brought us the news that Haaken and Cnut were on their way back I felt almost completely fit. If the enemy came now then I would be able to face them.

They looked weary as they trudged towards the hall. I clasped their arms. "Come, you look as though you need beer."

"Our friends in Wessex cannot brew decent ale to save their lives. It has neither head nor taste!"

I laughed and waved over the slave who had the horns of beer ready. As much as I wanted their news I was patient and waited. Haaken would tell me in his own time.

"The trade went well. We have more iron and some tin from Cornwall. Bjorn's swords are much sought after. Cnut here is proving to be as good a trader as Aiden."

He drank some more of the ale. "And the rumours of war?"

The Mercian rumour is just that, a rumour for he is busy fighting on two fronts. He has King Selfyn to contend with and he is trying to wrest Lundenwic from King Egbert. He is not having much luck. They are both better leaders."

"However we did hear that the Danes have begun to land in the east. The East Angles are being forced from their homes. They are flooding into Essex."

"Then we should be safe here. The land of the East Angles is many leagues hence."

"I would not count on it. When we were in Lundenwic we did as you suggested and kept our ears open. The sea captains and the traders know all that is going on. It seems that the Danes see the land to the north as a void to be filled. King Egbert has a reputation and the land of Northumbria is ripe for picking. No one will come to their aid."

"Who is the Danish leader?"

"It is a jarl called Cnut the Long. He was banished from his homeland and has been raiding Frisia and Frankia. The Emperor made life uncomfortable for him and the Kings of the East Angles just do what the Mercians wish and are weak leaders."

Haaken raised his horn to me, "You can take much credit for this, Jarl Dragon Heart. When you secured Lundenwic for Egbert it shifted the balance of power. The Mercians had retreated and the Danes have a new land."

I shrugged, "*Wyrd*. And what of Rorik and Wiglaf?"

"We heard a rumour that their long ships were seen in the Abus, the river which flows through the old Roman fort of Eboracum."

I looked up sharply and saw the frown on Aiden's face. "But that is less than eighty miles from here."

Cnut nodded, "The rumour is that he is gathering an army and he is coming to get you. He has promised all a share in the treasure which you hold."

"But we have no treasure!"

"We know that," Cnut gave a wry smile, "it is a mixture of Haaken's silver tongue and the tales he tells as well as the fact that the Ulfheonar all have golden pendants. They talk of magical swords and gold mines hidden in our lands. Every young warrior from Norway to Denmark and beyond who is not oathsworn to a Jarl is offering to sell his sword to Rorik."

The Weird Sisters had been busy. I sat in silence and watched the flames play along the logs. My three companions sat silently too. Rolf and Arturus came in and saw my pained expression.

"What ails you father? Is it your shoulder still?"

Aiden explained what we had been told. He was a clever speaker and he summarised it well. Arturus said, "Then my new command is well timed."

"Your new command?"

I explained. "Arturus and the crew of the '***Josephus***' are going to build a fort at Cherchebi to keep watch for enemies. It seems we made the right decision although we did not know the reason."

There was a sombre air. Although it was good to know that Kara was good at prophesying, her prophesy had not been comforting.

Aiden took the map from the chest in which it was kept and laid it out upon the table. "Here is the Abus. Although Northumbria is weak there are still many burghs between here and there. Eanred might be reeling from Mercian advances but he will not take kindly to raiders in his heartland. He will oppose Rorik."

Rolf shook his head, "A sound argument but Eanred is not a good leader and his men are not good warriors. Rorik will advance."

"But the jarl is right. It is many miles away and it will take him time. Our ally will be winter. The high divide will make it difficult if not impossible for him to come in winter. We have half a year to plan for this."

"We have half a year only if our other enemies leave us alone. The Hibernians and those on Mann may decide to join in. They might see us as a carcass to be picked over."

I had never seen them so depressed. Only Aiden appeared to have any hope and confidence. I stood. "Do we fear Rorik? Are these bandits and chancers any better than the men we lead?"

"Of course not. We are still the best army of any, man for man."

"And you are right, Cnut. Our problem lies in the fact that our enemies can strike from any direction. We need to be warned of an approach. Aiden will visit with Pasgen and warn him of the potential danger. He can keep a good watch there. The old Roman fort which guards the pass to the west coast can be watched. We help the shepherds in that area to rebuild a watch tower and give them each a pony. They can see all the way to the sea from the top of the pass. We tell Thorkell of the danger. He guards our northern border but he is a good warrior and his men can come to our aid. Windar will need to watch Ulla's Water and Windar's Water. We can build a wall from the mountain to the Water at Ulla's Water."

I stopped to catch breath and to take a swig of beer. Arturus smiled at me. "But you do not think he will come at us from any of those directions do you father?"

"I shook my head, "No my son. He will come through you! It is *wyrd*."

He nodded, "It is *wyrd*. Then we leave tomorrow." He looked at Haaken and Cnut. "And I would appreciate the help of the Ulfheonar. If I am to bear the brunt of an attack then I want well designed and stout defences."

Suddenly they all looked happy. All the doubts had gone. The divisions which had existed between Haaken and Arturus evaporated like morning mist on the Water. The next day we went on to a war footing. I told Kara all and she did not seem surprised. She and Rolf began to plan for the worst; an invasion by a Norse army. Messengers were sent to all the other jarls; I used my Ulfheonar for I wanted nothing to be misinterpreted. I left with the rest of my Ulfheonar and Arturus.

His men seemed even more honoured by their selection than my son had been. As we marched the twenty odd miles to the new fort I wracked my brains to think of some title I could give my son for his men needed an identity. I am not certain if it was the Weird Sisters or the spirits but as we clambered the ride through the fly infested forest which separated us from Windar's Water we suddenly stumbled upon a family of wild boars. The ferocious males and two females charged at the warriors who were at the fore. It happened to be Arturus and his men. I could not help but both wonder and admire their reaction. They went into a shield wall with their spears before them. Although one tusker broke through and gored Sven the Slow in the lower leg all four beasts were slain.

I looked up to the heavens, "Thank you Allfather for giving me the sign I sought." As Sven had his leg tended to I clapped Arturus on the shoulder. "My son you need new shields!" He looked at me in shock. "Your men are not wolves, they are the Wild Boars and yet you are still Arturus Wolf Killer!"

Even my Ulfheonar could not help but cheer the idea. We slung the dead beasts on spears and walked in a much happier frame of mind to the new fort.

The roundhouses of the former inhabitants still stood as though the villagers had just gone to the river to make a sacrifice and would be back soon. A few domestic fowl squabbled around the huts but otherwise there was a desolate air about the place. We peered in a couple of the huts and saw the bones where the villagers had perished in that icy winter which had taken so many. We carried on a little further south and found the fort on the other side of the river. The water flowed around three sides of the ruins. The Romans had chosen their site well. We crossed the river by the shallow ford. I suspected that, in winter, the ford might be difficult to cross.

The fort itself had long been abandoned and pillaged. Here there were neither stone walls nor roofed buildings. There was a stone outline of the foundation and a few broken timbers showing where the walls had been. The ditch was just a dip in the ground with nettles and thistles growing.

Haaken clapped Arturus on the back. "Well my friend, at least you can make your new home fit the picture in your head."

Arturus laughed, "Then all will be perfect."

Aiden knew how to organise. Both sets of warriors respected the galdramenn and set to willingly. The Ulfheonar marched off for the nearby wood to cut down the trees, which would make the walls, while the Wild Boars began to clear the ditch piling the spoil on the stone foundations. I went alone to view the surroundings. The woods were to the west but they were across the river and too far away to provide concealment for an enemy. The land to the east was marshy and flat. The nearest rise was more than a mile away. The fort would not be overlooked. I walked over to the rise and found another, smaller, cluster of abandoned huts. This time there were no bones and no signs of domestic animals. These villagers had fled.

As I walked back to the fort I tried to imagine what Rorik or any attacker would see. The land ahead was gentle but it rose steadily towards the ridge of trees which marked the edge of my water. The small Roman road which headed north was visible on the other side of the river. When the fort was built it would stand out and draw the enemy towards it for I could see the ford quite clearly from the rise.

By the time I reached the ditch it had been cleared. It would still need making defensible but I had an idea about that. I drew Arturus and Aiden to one side. "You can use nature to make your fort impossible to take, my son."

"How? Is there some magic which Aiden can use?"

I chuckled, "In a way. If you extend the ditch to the north and the south you can cut into the river and it will flow into the ditch. You would be surrounded by water. If you make a bridge to lower then no enemy could attack you without fording the ditch."

"And if you seed the ditch with stakes then the enemy will suffer many casualties. This is a good site my friend."

"It is."

It took four days of hard work to erect the walls. The weather was clement and we suffered no rain. Snorri and Beorn hunted for us and the river was seeded with traps to catch the fish. Another seven days saw the buildings built. They were not Roman but Norse. We took the stones we found inside to make the foundations for Arturus' hall. There were only twenty seven of them and they would all share a hall. The kitchens and the smithy they would build later. The last act we witnessed before we left for home was the breaking of the earth between the river and the ditch. Arturus and his men broke through the north eastern bank and the Ulfheonar the south western. Aiden had constructed a wooden dam so that the waters on both sides stopped at the wood. He gave the command and the two dams were raised and the water flooded and surged not just across one side of the ditch but to completely surround it. Aiden gave his last command and the bridge was lowered across the entrance. Arturus' home was finished. With a bridge over to the river; another one which could be removed he and his men would be safe. The fort was big enough to shelter all the farmers who lived close by.

There was still enough light, when we had finished, for the Ulfheonar to leave and return home. I knew that Arturus and his Wild Boars would want the time to become comfortable in their new home. My son would inspire his men and he would not want his father and the men he had admired watching him.

I turned at the top of the wooded ridge to look back. It was sad; I felt emptiness in my heart for my son had left home. He and I had been through so much together. I remembered when I had travelled to Hibernia to rescue him and his mother from the Hibernians. Since then he had been with me almost every day of his life. Now I would go for months without seeing him. I had lost my wife and Kara was now a mystery. I would be alone and it saddened me.

"It is natural, Jarl. The young bird has to fly the nest and the young wolf finds its own pack."

I shook my head, "You are becoming more skilled, Aiden. You read my mind and my heart exactly."

"It is no great trick, Jarl. I have been with Arturus since you rescued the two of us. He is like a brother to me and I too feel the ache in my heart where he used to be."

"And you have a solution to our problem? You have a potion or spell which will make the ache go away?"

He shook his head, "No Jarl, the pain will be with us for as long as we live. It is a reminder of the bond between us. Your wife feels the ache too in the Otherworld. Some pains can never be cured."

The nights began to grow longer and the days shorter. "We will have one more voyage while there is peace. I would go to visit Thorkell and then King Egbert. I fear this winter will be one where we huddle behind our walls."

Aiden nodded. Haaken asked, "Do you fear another wolf winter?"

I shrugged, "I fear the winter for we have human enemies now as well as the wolves. We will hunt the wolf this winter for it will help us to keep watch on our borders but I need to speak with our only two allies. If time allowed I would visit the land of the Bro Waroc'h but that would take too long. If the winds are right then we can sail to the court of King Egbert and back in less than fourteen days."

"We cannot reach Lundenwic and return in that time."

"No, Haaken, but we can reach Hamwic which is close to the burgh of King Egbert." I pointed to Aiden. "Our galdramenn has not been idle. If Rolf is happy with our defences then we sail on the morning tide."

Rolf nodded and wiped his beard with the back of his hand. "The new men have worked hard over the summer. The new animals have been secured. There is little for them to do until the bone burning at the start of winter."

I went to visit with Bjorn. I had not needed my armour but we were sailing perilous waters. It had not needed much repairing but he had been concerned that his armour had allowed me to become wounded.

"I have repaired your armour, Jarl Dragon Heart and I have strengthened the strips across the shoulder. It should be no heavier but it is stronger. I had my wife make you a new padded tunic to wear beneath your leather. It will cushion any blow."

"Thank you Bjorn and thank her for me." I noticed something new on his bench. "What is that?"

"I have been improving the armour. Instead of square metal plates I have made them look like fish scales. They use less metal and yet they afford the same protection. In fact I think they give more protection." He gestured towards the water. "I watch the fish sometimes and realised that the Allfather had made fish with armour too but he is cleverer than those warriors in the east. I copied nature."

As we left Úlfarrston I mentioned the new armour to Aiden and Haaken. Aiden laughed, "Bjorn is the galdramenn not I. That is something I should have seen and it makes perfect sense."

"I have asked him to make it for the Ulfheonar. We will give Arturus' boars the old armour."

Haaken looked dubious. "Will he not take that as a slight?"

"No, I know Arturus well. He will be grateful that his men will all be armoured. I gave him advice on how to improve his shields before we left and I expect that he will take whatever the jarl can give him." Aiden spoke confidently.

I caught Aiden's eye and saw inside his mind. He had spoken with Arturus. The outburst all those months ago had been on Aiden's mind. I felt happier now knowing that my son had been given sage advice. As a father I could not have done so but Aiden was in a unique position. I was grateful for the day the young Hibernian had chosen to follow my banner.

We headed north and made the short journey to Thorkell's stead. I was happy to see *'Great Serpent'* moored in the estuary. I left the crew on board and went ashore alone. I just needed to speak with Thorkell the Tall. He clasped my arm, "You look well Jarl. What brings you here?"

I told him my news and he frowned. "Your northern borders are safe. I have taken the *'Serpent'* over to raid the men of Dál Riata and Hibernia. We have taken animals and weapons."

"You did not take slaves?"

He shook his head. "They are more trouble than they are worth. We have had too many trying to swim the estuary. They drown and no one is served. We have had some settlers. They came from the east."

"They are not Northumbrians are they? Or the men of the King of Norway?"

He laughed, "You have taught me well, jarl. They were fleeing the King of Norway. The families we took had their ship destroyed in a storm. They had heard of the famous sword and Dragon Heart. They are good people and stout warriors. They managed to evade capture coming over the divide."

That was further confirmation of the impotence of Eanred. "I may need to send riders for aid. Have you someone who could lead your men under my banner?"

"Sven White hair and Harald Green Eye are still with me. They are Ulfheonar."

"I hope it will not come to that but it is good to know I have reserves here at your stead."

The relief was immense as we sailed south. I had more warriors at my disposal than I had thought. The sword and my name were now drawing likeminded folk to live in my land. There was room enough for such people. It was *wyrd*.

The sea can seem vast and empty; even when you are just a couple of miles off the coast, however, as we passed the southern tip of Mann I saw three long ships pull towards us. They had shields on their sides and they looked to be belligerent. Our experience with Mann had not been good since we left. "Erik, I think we will try to lose them. I am not in the mood for conversation."

He laughed, "Karl, Kurt, get up the stays and give us a little more sail."

Haaken took his place at his bench as Cnut said, "We are getting too fat and lazy Ulfheonar. Let us show these drekar of Mann what a real crew can do!"

They began to row and soon the drekar were dropping further behind. We slowed the rate. There was little point in tiring rowers. Who knew what the wind might do? Erik looked up at the masthead. "Jarl, the wind is veering a little. It is pushing us inshore."

The last thing that we needed was for us to be caught with no sea room. We had a lead and I wanted to use it. "Take us further west. "

We had passed Mann; to our south lay Anglesey. Once it had been a welcome anchorage but the Saxons now ruled it. I knew we could have wrested it from them but our land was perfect and I would not change perfection for anywhere else. If we headed west we might run into Hibernians or even the ships of Sihtric Silkbeard but I was confident that my ship was faster than any and my crew the best rowers.

Kirk shouted from the masthead. "The three drekar are increasing their speed, Jarl Dragon Heart. They are closing with us."

"Shall we increase the rate, Jarl?"

"No we will be turning south and east soon. The wind will take us away from them." At the time I knew not why I gave that command. Later I thought about it and remembered a voice in my head. I turned to watch the three drekar as they closed. They were rowing hard. I counted twenty oars on each side of two of them and twenty five on the one at the front. I now knew where they came from. They had the three legs on their sails; that was the sign of Jarl Erik. We had been brothers and had fought together. Since he had married and his sister, my wife, had died we had become enemies. I had many enemies but I was sad that Erik was one for many of his oathsworn had fought at my side.

Suddenly Karl shouted. "Two more drekar and they are coming from the south west. We are heading directly for them!"

"Head south east, Erik. Cnut, let us see how fast we can go!"

The ship was responsive and she heeled over. Her higher freeboard made the manoeuvre possible. I doubted that the drekar of Jarl Erik would be able to sail as close to the sea without swamping. I saw that the new drekar had Sihtric's banner at their mast. He was the closest of my enemies but I could not fight five ships and hope to win. A good leader chose his battles. Now I was glad that I had not made my men tire themselves.

"Jarl, we will run out of sea room soon." Erik Short Toe pointed to the south. There lay Anglesey. The two leaders behind me must have been anticipating when we turned to run around the west coast of Anglesey and they would have us between them.

"Head for the straits between the island and Thorkell's old fort."

Erik threw me a surprised look. "It is narrow and we are travelling quickly. It will take great skill."

"Josephus believed in you and so do I." He nodded, "Cnut we are going to risk the straits. Be ready to raise the oars on my command. You can slow the rate."

The five drekar now following us had spread out in a long line. Sihtric's drekar was the closest. They were like five beaters driving an animal towards a hunter. Whichever way we turned they would pounce upon us. I smiled to myself. They would only be able to send one drekar a time down the straits after us and they would then be spread out in a long line. It all depended on how skilful a navigator Erik Short Toe was.

The land on either side of the straits was familiar to us. The danger lay in the hidden rocks close to the island. The mainland's mountainous side looked more intimidating but a long ship could sail closer to the mainland side than the island. Normally we would have taken the sails in a little to safely negotiate the turn.

"Cnut, oars in." As soon as the oars were drawn inboard we slowed enough to allow Erik to push the steering board over. Aiden and I had to help him as we fought the drekar which threatened to smash herself on the mainland. As I pushed I looked behind me and saw that our pursuers had realised their dilemma. Sihtric dropped his sail and use his oars to turn himself into the wind. He became stationary but he saved his ship. His companion also managed to slow.

Jarl Erik's leading ship copied us. He had some good sailors aboard his ships. I know for I had sailed with them. His last drekar tried to outwit us and sailed too close to the island. As we hurtled through the straits, above the sound of the waves and the wind I heard the screech and crunch of wood on rocks and then the screams of the warriors as they were flung into the sea.

The mountain of Wyddfa loomed over me but, strangely, I felt safe for the ancestor I had recently discovered was buried there in the dream cave. I would be protected.

Our pursuers were not so fortunate. We kept our oars in and relied on the current and the wind. It meant our two remaining pursuers closed with us and they risked their oars. Inevitably some of the oarsmen bit too deep with their oars and they struck the rocks which lurked like teeth beneath the waves. I saw the ships shudder as oars were broken and the rhythm of the rowers was interrupted. Once we emerged into the open sea Erik used all the power of our huge sail and the rowers.

"Cnut, put some sea room between us."

The rest had worked in our favour and the men pulled hard. Within a few miles the two drekar were dots in the distance and Karl shouted, "They have given up!"

We sailed until we reached the island of Lundy, Puffin Island. This little rock sticking up in the middle of the sea teemed with puffins. They were an easy bird to capture and we ate well that night. We used the small beach to cook but we slept on board.

"So, Jarl Dragon Heart, it seems Sihtric and Erik are now allies."

"Birds of a feather flock together, Haaken. It is a measure of how far Erik has fallen if he consorts with such as Sihtric."

"But why now, Jarl?"

Sigtrygg had asked a question I could not answer. Had we been with the knarr and escorting goods then I would have understood but we were alone with fighting warriors on board. It was a huge risk to attack the best ship we had crewed by the finest warriors.

Aiden gave me the answer even as it came into my head. "They want you out of the way so that they can capture our land and our treasure. Five ships would be needed to take the **'Heart'** Jarl Dragon Heart."

"You are right."

"Should we return home then?"

Since he had become a father Haaken worried about his family. "I think we have time to visit with the king. One ship was damaged. Besides they will probably wait for us to return and ambush close to Anglesey again. If Aiden is right, and I think he is, then they will wait until we are eliminated before they do anything."

"But we still have to get by them."

"Aye Cnut, but Aiden and I will sleep on that. I have some ideas. Besides, the decision is at least ten days away. Let us worry about the problems we might encounter getting to Hamwic."

In the event, we had a voyage which provided Haaken with nothing in the way of stories. Four days after leaving Lundy we docked at the port which was closest to Egbert's capital, Wintanceastre. We had never been here before and I knew that we would be treated with suspicion. I spoke with the warriors who guarded the gate into the town.

"We are here to speak with King Egbert."

They were partly surprised by my tone but more with my Saxon. They lowered their weapons a little. "Wait on your ship and we will send a message to him."

I went back to the drekar. I already had much information. Hopefully this visit would complete the picture. Rorik was coming from the south east and Erik and Sihtric from the west. I wondered if there was some plan in all this. I realised that there was not. I was the honey that was drawing in the adventurers who saw a small land with a small army but one which was rich beyond belief; or so they thought.

King Egbert himself came to speak with us. "Come Jarl. Treat my hall as your home."

I shook my head. "As much as we would like to stay and enjoy your hospitality we have discovered there is danger at home."

"Well you and your wizard must come with me, at least and enjoy some of my ale."

As we went through the city of Wintan-ceastre which was the largest city I had ever seen in England the king told me of his wars and his successes.

"We now have Lundenwic ringed with burghs. Coenwulf has been forced to fall back. The kings of Kent and Essex now accept me as their liege lord. And it is all down to you."

We sat at his table and he poured me a horn of ale. I barely tasted it. "We have enemies of our own who are attacking us from the east and the west."

"Saxons from Mercia? Northumbrians?"

"No King Egbert, they are Vikings. They believe I am rich and wish to steal the treasure which I do not have."

"Then why have you come here to visit with me?" He put his huge hand on my arm, "Do not read me wrong. I am pleased to see you. You have brought my people much good fortune."

"I need to know if Mercia will attack me too. My land is wide open to such an attack."

"I do not think so but I believe I can help us both. This Coenwulf is thinking of winning back Essex to his fold. If I strike north of here then he will have to bring forces from the north to repel me. I will gain more Mercian territory and he will not have enough men to attack two of us."

I felt such relief that my face broke into a huge smile. "I would be grateful to you."

He shook his head. "It is I who should be thankful for your arrival. It was like the first stone rolling down a mountain and now we cannot be stopped. Here," he reached into a chest and took out a golden chain with a gold boar, "this is to thank you for what you did and as a mark of our friendship. This is the mark of my house."

"And I take it and swear friendship to you and Wessex. Know this King Egbert, I am never foresworn. We are your friends until the end of time."

When we sailed north I went with a much lighter heart. An attack by the men of Wessex would avert a third enemy from attacking me. All I had to contend with was two Norse armies. This would be a Viking war.

Chapter 12

As we headed west, to return home, we were caught by strong winds. They were, fortunately, in our favour. We did not need to row. Haaken asked, "What do we do about the drekar? They will be waiting for us and this time they need only put one in the straits and the rest between Anglesey and Mann. We cannot avoid them. Do we fight?"

"We could fight them. We might even defeat them but we would lose too many Ulfheonar. Aiden and I have something different in mind and this wind helps us. It has been sent by the gods."

"The wind from the east? That would just take us to the edge of the world." I said nothing and he burst out, "You are mad. I would rather take on ten drekar than risk the edge of the world."

"Think of the story you could tell."

"I would need to be alive to tell such a tale."

I laughed, "You need not fret Haaken One Eye. I will keep the coast of Hibernia in sight the whole time. We will sail around the island and take advantage of this gift of the gods. Remember we know their northern coast well and it is not a large island."

"The people who live on the west coast are supposed to be savages who eat those who are wrecked on their coast."

"And you are a wolf, you are Ulfheonar!"

I had the final say for I was jarl. Erik was quite excited. He would be doing something Josephus had only dreamt of. I think Haaken came around to deciding that it was worth the risk when we turned north and we could still see the coast to the east of us.

We used a deserted beach on the south coast for the first night in Hibernia but when we sailed further north we discovered a huge inlet. In fact it was so big that I thought it was a sea. It was almost dusk on the second night and we decided to use its sheltered anchorage for the wind was blowing stronger. Aiden checked the maps and suddenly became excited. "I know where we are. There is an island in the middle of this river and it is called King's Island. It is a holy place in my land. They say giants put stones there and my people have worshipped there since the time of the giants."

I became interested. "And are there any monasteries close by?"

"There is one at Mungret." He peered at the map. Whoever had made it had marked monasteries with a red cross. "According to the map it is half way down the river. Close to the King's Island." He pointed to the bank of the river. "It should be a mile or two down there."

Monasteries were always tempting. They were worth the risk of raiding as they contained treasure and were not normally guarded. "We will scout it out and see if it is worth the dangers we might encounter."

We kept to the southern side of the inlet as we edged our way east. We rowed inshore and I sent Snorri and Beorn to scout while the rest of us ate cold rations.

Our two scouts soon returned. "Aiden is correct. We spied it two miles along the path. It sits on a piece of high ground."

"Is it defended?"

"There is a wall but we saw no warriors."

Beorn pointed to the river. "There are guards on the island and they can see the monastery. When it is dark, however, we may be able to approach unseen."

"Then we just take twenty Ulfheonar and the rest can be with the ship. If you hear a disturbance, Haaken, then bring the *'Heart'* as quickly as you can."

I saw the disappointment on his face but he nodded. "I will be there if I hear anything."

"I know." I took Cnut, Sigtrygg, Snorri, Beorn and six of the newer Ulfheonar. It would be a test for them.

Night had fallen as we followed Snorri up the path. Like many of these monasteries there was a well worn path to the beach; no doubt the priests liked their shellfish. I smelled wood smoke and heard the gentle tolling of a bell somewhere. The White Christ liked his priests on their knees as often as possible. Even as we approached the small gate leading to the monastery I knew that we were taking a risk but the rewards could be great. The Holy Books had a high value and were worth many pieces of gold. I waved Snorri and Beorn to go around the other side of the large Church. I was a wooden structure but had a bell tower; that was unusual. It gave them some time to get into position and I glanced down to the river. I saw the fort and the small ships moored there. It was rightly called *'Island of the King'* for it had a fine fort on it and looked impregnable to me. I saw the stones placed there by giants; they ringed the buildings.

Cnut murmured, "The men are in place."

We ran forward and burst into the church. There were brown robed figures on their knees. As soon as they saw us they shouted and began to flee. There were three doors at the far end and they made for them. "After them!"

My younger warriors sped down the aisle to reach them but the monks were fast. I heard screams as two of them ran into Snorri and Beorn. "Find any treasure!"

I saw a holy book open on a carved piece of wood. The wood had been made to look like and eagle. I took both. My hands were now full. Suddenly I heard the sound of an alarm bell. Someone was calling for help. "Sigtrygg, get everyone back to the ship, now. We take what we have."

"Aye jarl."

I saw that he clutched a gold plate and a piece of fine linen. I almost tripped over the monk's body at the doorway. He had tried to defend his treasures and paid a high price. As we ran back to the ship I could hear a bell tolling on the island and I saw figures running towards the boats. Ahead of me I saw most of the others and, when I glanced behind me, I saw Snorri and Beorn. My back was covered. It was a gentle, well worn path to the ship and we soon made the *'Heart of the Dragon'*. Haaken had had her turned around and they were ready for us. I saw that Karl and Kurt were ready to lower the sail the moment that the order was given. I passed up the book to Aiden and clambered up the strakes with the wooden eagle under my arm.

"Hurry Jarl, they are coming."

As I looked astern I could see three small Hibernian boats and they were rowing as fast as they could to catch us. "Cnut, row. Sigtrygg and Aiden, get your bows and come with me."

It would take some time for the rowers to get up enough speed to lose our pursuers. Even though Kurt and Karl had raised the sail our sheltered anchorage meant that we were protected from the wind. It was down to the Ulfheonar.

"Use your arrows to discourage them." I was not looking forward to this test of my recently healed shoulder but I gritted my teeth and pulled back on the bow. My arrow fell short and landed in the boat rather than at the stern where it could have done some damage. Sigtrygg was more accurate and the warrior next to the steersman fell with an arrow in his shoulder.

The smaller river boats were faster over a shorter distance and they began to close with us. In the distance I could see more boats pulling away from the shore. These first ones would be to slow us up and to hold us until the rest could swarm around us.

"You two concentrate on the steersman."

"Aye, Jarl."

I saw that they had to pull warriors back to protect those at the stern with their shields. It raised their prow a little more and made them slower. The captain urged his rowers on. He shouted something and a huge warrior came to the prow. He carried a rope with a hook on the end. He would grapple us. They were just thirty yards from us. It would be a prodigious throw to catch us but the warrior looked confident as he whirled it above his head.

I notched another arrow and despite the pain in my shoulder, pulled back. I let fly just as his arm came back to release the hook. We were so close that the force of the arrow punched him back into the boat and he fell amongst the rowers. It almost stopped in the water as all way was lost. We began to pull away from our closest enemy. Although the others were gaining they were further back and the Ulfheonar now had the rhythm. They were chanting and singing to one of Cnut's favourite songs.

Sigtrygg and Aiden had each taken one quarter at the stern and they were relentlessly sending arrows after the next two ships. They did not cause deaths but they were so accurate that those guarding them looked like their shields had become hedgehogs.

"Open sea ahead, jarl!"

The moment the sail caught the western breeze we took flight and the Hibernian ships were left wallowing in our wake. The Allfather had been with us. "Cnut, the men did well, they can stop now."

They all gave a huge cheer as they drew the oars inboard. Sigtrygg shook his head. "I hope that the treasure was worth it Jarl."

I laughed, "We lost no men and I can feel the blood coursing through my veins again." Picking up the holy book and brandishing it aloft I said, "And this will be worth much gold. What else would we do? We are the wolves from the sea."

We hove too in the next inlet we found. We anchored in the middle of the estuary where we were sheltered from the wind. It had veered a little and was now blowing from the south east. It rarely did that and I wondered what it meant.

When I awoke I saw Aiden examining the treasures and Erik preparing the ship for sea. I plunged my head into the bucket of sea water to refresh me and dried myself on my sleeping sheepskin.

"Have we much of value?"

"The linen is good quality but the women will claim that. There are two silver candlesticks and a golden platter. We can use those to melt into coin or pendants, as you wish. There are some other candlesticks made of base metal. Bjorn can use those. The book is incomplete but it is a thing of beauty." He put them back in the chest as we began to get under way. "The trouble is, jarl, that we would have to travel to Frankia to sell them and there are dangers in that. If war is coming then we will not be trading there for a while."

"Then the book will increase in value. You must care for it back in Cyninges-tūn."

"Aye jarl."

Haaken joined me. "I wonder what the Norns have in store for us this day."

"Worrying about them will not help us. We just try to survive."

He laughed, "And we do that." He pointed to the coast to the east of us. "We had best keep well away from the land, Jarl. They will remember us well there."

I nodded, "And besides we took all of their treasures last year."

The Weird Sisters listen and it does not pay a jarl to make frivolous comments. The wind changed to come from the south west and we sped around the northern coast of Hibernia. My men and I were in high spirits. We had outwitted the men of Mann and Sihtric. We would soon be home. The winds were so favourable that we saw the mountains to the west of Cyninges-tūn just before dusk. We would be able to rest close to our land and be home by the following morning.

Sharp eyed Karl brought us back to earth and sent a shiver of fear through us all. "Jarl, there are ships drawn up on the beach and the huts are on fire!"

The Norns had been spinning their webs again. My land was being attacked.

"Erik, approach slowly. I would not have us be seen by these raiders."

"Aye, Jarl."

"Karl, are they longships?"

"I cannot tell yet for certain, Jarl, but I think not."

I felt some relief at that. If it was a party of Vikings then it meant the attack had begun earlier than we had expected. The small fishing port was called Itunocelum by the Romans who had built a fort there. Nothing remained of the fort and the handful of villagers who had settled there were a mixture of Rheged and Saxon. They kept to themselves but they lived in my land. They were my people. I hoped that the shepherds who lived on the high pass had seen them and alerted my warriors. The road from Itunocelum was like a dagger aimed at the heart of my land.

"They are Hibernian ships, jarl. I count six of them. Many of the warriors are heading inland!"

"Get the sail down, Cnut and we will slip in under oars. Land at the beach to the south of the town."

As my rowers took their places Haaken asked, "What will you do?"

I did not answer at first. I looked at the mast head. The wind was still blowing from the west and the south. "Erik, could you get the '*Heart*' back to Úlfarrston with a handful of rowers?"

He too looked at the pennant. "Aye Jarl."

I spoke to the rowers as well as Erik. "The six who came ashore with me will help Erik to row the ship home. Aiden will get to Cyninges-tūn. I want warriors to head along the road and meet us. Windar must be warned of the danger too. He will be watching the east and not the west. The rest will come with me and we will pursue these Hibernians."

It made me proud that not one warrior pointed out that we would be outnumbered. Six pirate ships would have a combined crew of over a hundred warriors. They feared no man for they were Ulfheonar and they were fighting for their own land.

Aiden helped me to adjust the straps on my armour. He held my mask of mail in his hand. "Do not send all the warriors to help us and you need to warn Pasgen about an attack from Mann. They will soon realise that we have evaded them and may decide to attack us sooner rather than later. We need to be prepared."

"And the treasure?"

The treasure suddenly seemed less important than it had. But the thought came into my head that we might not have seen the raiders had it not been for the treasure. "Put it somewhere safe for the time being."

Night had fallen as we edged into the beach which lay just a short distance from the pillaged village. We leapt ashore into the shallows. Erik did not need to be grounded with so few crewmen to row the boat away.

We ran along the beach. Snorri and Beorn led. We were drawn to the burning buildings and we heard the screams as the women were violated. They would have to suffer until we reached them. We halted when we saw Snorri with his raised arm. Beorn said, "They have left ten men with the villagers."

"Cnut, secure the ships. The rest come with me."

The Hibernians had no idea how close we were. I led my men with swords drawn out of the blackness. With our wolf cloaks and mailed faces we must have looked like daemons from the underworld to the Hibernians. One warrior had his breeks around his ankles and was standing over a young girl. He looked in horror as Ragnar's Spirit sliced towards him. His head fell from his body without a sound. I ran towards the next raider who had his back to me and was lying atop an old woman. I pulled back his head and slid my blade across his throat. I pulled his body from the old woman and held out my hand. She recoiled in terror. I did not blame her. We did not look like humans.

And then there were no raiders left. "Four of you secure the boats and guard the survivors. See what you can do for the women. Strip the dead of valuables."

I saw Haaken detail off the warriors. I waved my arm and Snorri and Beorn loped off along the Roman Road which headed east. I slung my shield. My shoulder ached still and I set off after my scouts. My Ulfheonar fell in behind me.

The raiders had almost an hour's start on us and they were without armour. Some may have left before the village was pillaged. If they ran hard they could be at Windar's Mere by dawn. We had landed enough times so that our legs were already ready for running but the steep road soon began to sap our energy. Each time I felt like we ought to stop I thought of the settlers living between Windar's Mere and Cyninges-tūn. These Hibernians would slaughter them like sheep. We had to get back before them or find them and stop them.

The shepherds at the old Roman fort had been caught by the raiders. The bodies of four of them lay in untidy heaps behind the walls. Three dead Hibernians bore testament to the courage of these boys. The moon had come out and made the fort look stark and desolate. The shepherds would watch no more sheep. I saw two dead sheep dogs. They too had paid the price. They had bought us some time and, as the road descended and it became easier Snorri saw them. He waited for us and pointed down the side of the steep, rock filled valley. "There jarl, "They are less than a mile ahead."

"You have good eyes."

He shook his head. "They passed beneath us." The road twisted and turned but the news spurred us on. We were now catching them. Once on the valley bottom they would be amongst the farms of Lang's Dale. That farmer and his family had been dead this past year, victims of the wolf winter but others had realised the benefits of farming in an east to west valley. There were many farms.

Once we reached the valley bottom we were able to keep together. Our leather boots were silent along the cobbled road and we heard the screams and shouts in the distance as the raiders found the first farm. It was frustrating not being able to run harder but if we did so then we would be in no condition to fight. We kept the same steady slog. Had my men not been as fit as they were we would have given up long ago. The Hibernians only kept ahead of us because they did not wear armour.

We found only men dead at the first farm. It was Tostig Ronaldson and his boys. They had all died well and the five dead raiders was clear evidence. The Hibernians had taken the women as slaves. Haaken said, "They have taken the cows too!"

"Then we have them! They will move too slowly!"

Sure enough we heard the shouts from ahead and this time it was closer. "Cnut, take one in three warriors to the right. Sigtrygg, take another one in three to the left!"

As they ran off Haaken joined me.

"Wedge!"

My men formed up behind me and I led the eighteen or so warriors down the road. "Let them know we are coming!"

The men banged their shields with their swords and chanted, "Ulfheonar! Ulfheonar! Ulfheonar! Ulfheonar!" as we approached. It was hypnotic. More importantly it kept us together. The Hibernians heard the noise. I wanted them to know we were coming and to draw their attention away from the farm. I could just make out the warriors milling around the Waite of Oleg Three Fingers. I heard a voice giving commands and they tried to form a wall to face us. It was futile.

I saw that they were just forty paces from us. "Charge!"

We ran hard at them. I aimed the wedge at the tall warrior who wore a winged helmet and held a double handed long sword. He whirled it above his head. Lifting my shield slightly I tucked my head beneath it and braced myself for the blow. Haaken brought his shield forward too so that the sword hit both of our shields. It was a powerful blow but we were strong. I felt a twinge of pain from my shoulder which I ignored and then I stabbed forward, blindly, at the naked torso of the leader. I felt the tip of my sword sink into flesh and then grind off his ribs; I pushed harder and then twisted it upwards. It turned off his backbone and then it was through. The weight of the warriors behind me propelled us forward and the weight of his body dragged him from my sword and we trampled over him.

His followers were enraged and they threw themselves at our wedge. A spear came towards me and I could not get out of the way. My helmet and my mail protected me and I stabbed the warrior; my sword went under his arm. The wedge was losing its shape as my men fought desperately against overwhelming odds. Bjorn's armour saved many lives that day. Poorly made Hibernian swords slid down the armour without even nicking it. Our shields deflected the powerful war axes and our swords were true. Even so the sheer weight of numbers might have gone against us had not Sigtrygg and Cnut fallen on their flanks. I heard the wail as the Ulfheonar hacked into unprotected backs. Their sheer weight of numbers was their undoing for they could not move to defend themselves. We were the anvil and Cnut and Sigtrygg hammered upon it.

By the time the first light of the new day broke it was over. The one or two who had escaped would be hunted down over the next few days but the rest lay where they had fallen and my men walked amongst them despatching the wounded. We found Tostig Ronaldson's wife and daughters. Elter Svenson and his family had all survived. They had had the foresight to build a wall and a ditch and that had slowed up the Hibernians sufficiently for us to reach the family. Oleg Three Fingers and his family had also survived. We had arrived in time for them.

The bloodied farmer limped towards me. "Thank you, Jarl,! We could not have held out for much longer."

I nodded, "I am sorry that Tostig was not as lucky."

Elter took me to one side. "I told him to build a wall and a ditch but he was convinced that he was safe." He shrugged, "*Wyrd*."

I nodded, "The shepherds who watched died too. I must give some thought to that pass."

"No Jarl, the men of Lang's Dale must watch that pass. We are your people. The Ulfheonar defend against invaders; we must protect ourselves too."

Chapter 13

It was two days later when we finally reached Cyninges-tūn. Rolf and warriors met us on the way and we sent them to collect the Hibernian boats to bring them to Úlfarrston. We gave many of the captured weapons to the men of Lang's Dale. They were all keen to protect themselves. They had thought it was just the wolves who were predators but they had learned differently. The last of the Hibernians were hunted down and killed. Homes were found for the widows and orphans.

Kara had not worried about me. She told me that she had spoken with the spirits and knew that we would be safe. For three of my Ulfheonar that was not true. They had died in the fight at Elter's stead. The Hibernian threat had gone but that did not mean we were safe. Winter was but a few weeks away and we had no idea what our enemies would do. We had fought and raided in the winter. Perhaps they would too.

Aiden brought me good news; Pasgen had added stone to the outside of his walls and he was safer. Aiden had told him of the use of water at Arturus' fort and his men were already preparing a similar defence for his stead. It would be ready by mid winter, if the weather held.

I knew that I should go and visit with my son but I felt that I had neglected Cyninges-tūn for too long. This would be the last refuge if the rest of the towns fell to attackers and raiders. The devastation along Lang's Dale and Itunocelum had been a warning of what could happen if we were not ready. I sent, instead, the Ulfheonar. Haaken could tell my son what had transpired and he and Cnut could look at the defences critically. I knew now how important the new fort was. We needed better defences and that meant more weapons.

"Bjorn, how are we for spears and arrow heads?"

"We have plenty of spear heads. We just need ash shafts to complete them but we do not have enough arrow heads." He spread his arms apologetically, "We concentrated on armour and swords."

"I am not criticising Bjorn. You did as I commanded. If we are attacked then I want enough arrows to blot out the sun."

"I will get my people working today." He hesitated, "Aiden said that Jarl Erik and his men attacked you."

"It was his ships."

"Then he has broken his oath for he swore to be your man. The gods will punish him."

"That may be Bjorn but he can still do some damage until he is punished. His wife swore no oath and she seems to hate us even more."

He shook his head, "No Jarl, I have spoken with Kara about this. The wife of Jarl Erik is jealous. You are the man she wishes her husband would be. You have the land she covets. She is a jealous and vindictive woman. I fear you are right and we will have no peace until she is dead."

As I went around the defences to look at them with an attacker's eye I realised that Bjorn was right but we did not make war on women. Perhaps that was the work of the Norns. They gave me an implacable enemy I could not kill. I reached the highest part of our wall which was to the east of the hall. The trees were too close. I remembered how the Romans had cleared all trees for almost two hundred paces from their walls. Here the trees were just forty paces from the wooden defences. They were dense enough for warriors to hide and escape our arrows. If Rorik came from the east then this would be where he would arrive.

Rolf and his men had returned. Scanlan's farmers were still out collecting the animals to bring them in for winter. I met with Aiden and the two of them in my hall.

"We need every man and boy who is neither producing weapons nor looking after animals to cut down the trees to the east. I want the forest to be a hundred paces from our walls."

Scanlan shook his head. "That is a lot of trees."

"And they can hide our enemies. We will use the smaller branches for firewood. The tree trunks can be stored for our ships and the other branches used to make shields."

That surprised Rolf. "But all of our warriors have shields already."

"Our women do not and if an enemy comes they can use them to defend themselves. They can also be used to protect the walls. It will not take long. I have Bjorn making more arrow heads. I want hundreds of arrows making this winter too."

Scanlan shook his head, "We will begin now but it will not be swift."

"It will be swifter if you start!" Rolf hid his smile as they left. I turned to Aiden. "Have some more barrels made too. I would have told Scanlan but he …"

"Maewe is with child again, Jarl and she is due to give birth soon."

"Aah, he should have said. That explains much."

"We have the staves made already but the coopers are waiting for Bjorn to make the metal bands."

"And I have ordered arrows… The Norns are spinning well."

"I will speak with Bjorn. I am sure he can produce both. The Hibernian weapons you brought back are poor quality but they will do to make arrows and metal bands." He hesitated. "We could use some of the wood to make animal pens on the western shore. We have more animals than we used to."

"You are thinking better than I am, Aiden. See to it."

After he had gone I went to the edge of the water to look across to the other settlement. Although a larger site it was prone to flooding when the rains came or the snow melted and it was harder to defend than the western citadel. It was then that the idea came to me. We would build a drekar for the Water. I did not know why I had not thought of it earlier. I went directly to the stable and rode as quickly as I could to Úlfarrston. Bolli was my shipwright and he lived close by his ships.

When I reached the estuary, I saw that he had '***Josephus***' out of the water. Stig Haakenson was up to his waist in the chilly river. He came to join me and Bolli as I approached.

"I must take you and your men away from this ship, Bolli. I have a vital task for you."

Stig smiled, "Bolli has done the hard part. My crew can finish this off."

"Good. I want a threttanessa building for the Water."

Bolli nodded and asked, "But why?"

"War is coming. If we are attacked then the Water will need to be defended. There will be no other drekar to fight and she will be able to ferry men wherever danger threatens. It will be the speediest way to get to Cyninges-tūn from here and it can connect the two settlements."

"It is a good idea. Timber?"

"It is already being felled as we speak." I hesitated. "If we were attacked then I would need you and your shipwrights to be the crew."

"It is our land too and we can fight for it."

The nights were growing longer when the new drekar took on the shape of a ship. It was a skeleton only but it was a good sign. Bolli had made a shipyard on the beach at the eastern side of the Water. It was close to my fort and to the timber. As we had been walking back Bolli had told me that he had had requests from fishermen for large fishing ships. He would build those there too. "Two shipyards; think on that. Jarl Dragon Heart, do you think my father would have been proud?"

"I know that he would."

It had been two days since the structure of the hull had been finished and still Haaken was not back with the Ulfheonar. I began to worry; not least because all of our best warriors were twenty miles away on the other side of a ridge.

Cnut and Haaken returned looking weary but unharmed. "You were there a long time."

"Your son had had trouble, Jarl. The heavy rains while we were away eroded the new ditch and made the entrance to the fort almost impassable."

"It functions now?"

"It is good and, in fact, the rains showed us how to make it even better. The ditches are wider and deeper. We have made a causeway. If Arturus is attacked then he can remove sections of the causeway and be impregnable. Your son is happy, Jarl. His men guard him jealously."

"Much as the Ulfheonar guards me."

They both laughed, "Aye, Jarl."

I mentioned the ache in my shoulder to Aiden who nodded as though he had expected to hear what I had told him. He said, "Do you remember when we were in Constantinopolis? They had hot baths where men were massaged and had oils rubbed on their muscles. The wrestlers and those who took part in the games they held told me that they helped them to recover from injury."

"When did you visit these places?"

"Whilst you were in the house of healing I explored the city. I found it interesting."

"How can we have a hot bath here?"

"We could but it would never be hot enough. We have no vessel large enough to heat the water and keep it hot but we can make a sweat room. It would serve the same function."

"A sweat room?"

"We build a small room and put a fire in it. You would sit naked and let the heat make you sweat. Then we would massage your body."

"We?"

"I am sure there is a slave we could train to perform such a task. It is what they do in the Eastern Empire." We had spare slaves but I wondered about the efficacy of such an action. My galdramenn smiled, "It would also help to clean your body. If we built it by the Water then you could step from the heat into the Water and cleanse your body too." He shrugged. "It is worth a try Jarl. If this works for you then it would also work for other warriors. If they healed quicker then it is better for us."

As with all things Aiden applied himself well to the task. He constructed the hut first. He made it large enough for six warriors to use. He spent a long time within working out how to generate enough heat to make a body sweat. When I saw him frowning I knew that he had hit a problem. Then one day, after he had emerged from the hut he had a smile as wide as the Water upon his face.

"You have solved the problem then?"

"Aye, Jarl and it was staring me in the face the whole time." He turned and pointed to the water and Bjorn's smith. "Bjorn sweats more than any man despite the fact that the air blows through the open sides of his smith. It is the stones which retain their heat. Even in winter when the coals have died down the smith is still the warmest place in Cyninges-tūn. I have used the same idea. I have built a fire pit and placed many stones around it. I will try it later on."

I left him to his experiment and joined Haaken and Cnut at the shipyard. The drekar now had strakes fitted to the frame and looked more like a longship. Bolli seemed to be enjoying the task. "I assume, Jarl, that the ship will not need to carry cargo."

"Not much why?"

"It means that we need not waste space beneath the deck. We rarely get violent storms on the Water and we never get waves. It means we can have an even shallower draft on her and we will not need as much ballast as we normally use. She will fly."

"Excellent."

"Have you a name for her yet Jarl?"

"If she will fly then she shall be the '***Eagle***'."

Haaken asked, "What put that thought into your head?"

"The wooden carving we brought back from Hibernia. It is pleasing to the eye."

Bolli nodded, "Then I will have my carver carve you an eagle at the prow."

We spent some time watching the men work. There is something satisfying in watching men turn rough trees into things of beauty. As we watched Aiden came down with a sack. He began to gather the wood chips which had fallen around the hull. When it was full he headed back to our hall. Our curiosity aroused Cnut, Haaken and myself followed him. He entered the hut.

"What is Aiden building there, Jarl Dragon Heart?"

"He calls it a sweat room and he says it will help heal my acing shoulder." They gave me a strange look and I said, "The galdramenn is rarely wrong in such matters."

He came out. "You can try it later on in the day Jarl. We just need to get it hot enough and I have an idea how to make it even more pleasant." He walked up the slope towards the gate.

Haaken said, "Let us go in and see what it looks like."

"No Haaken, you do not like to give a half finished saga. Let Aiden reveal it when he is ready. He has done all the work. We will go to my hall. We need to plan our last voyage of the year."

I took the map from the chest while Haaken poured us horns of ale. "The Holy Book is unfinished but it is well made. Deidra has looked at it and she says it is one of the best she has ever examined. Our allies, the men of Wessex are, like us, pagans and they would not appreciate such work. The Bro Waroc'h men are also pagans. That leaves us with the men of Northumbria or Frankia."

Cnut jabbed a finger at the map. "It is a long voyage to Frankia and it would be fraught with danger at this time of year. Added to which we would be leaving the Water and the people without the protection of a boat's crew."

"Then you are suggesting we go to our enemies in Northumbria?"

He emptied his horn, "I think I am. Of course we do not need to trade it at all, yet. We have gold and iron ore enough. Why not wait until the winter is over to trade?"

Haaken thumped the table. "We are meant to go to Northumbria."

"What?"

"We are worried about what is happening in the east. How far has Rorik travelled? If we went to Eboracum then we could kill two birds with one stone. We could spy out the land and trade the book. We might not get the price we would in Frankia but we would have a less dangerous journey. That way we will know who rules the city; Rorik or Eanred."

"You are suggesting we go in disguise?"

"We now have some good horses. If the three of us went with Aiden then we could reach Eboracum in a couple of days. We would not be away as long as we might if we went to Frankia on a ship. We would also have a clearer picture of how the land on the other side of the divide lies."

Cnut nodded. "Then we will see Aiden once he has finished the sweat room."

I saw smoke rising from the new hut by the Water. Aiden stood outside and waved us towards it. "Come Jarl, it is ready to try." He took us in. As soon as we entered a wall of heat hit us. He threw a horn of water on the rocks and they began to steam. "See, the air will now purify your body."

I sniffed the air. "What is that smell?"

"It is just some herbs I threw on. It is time we tried it. We need to take off our clothes and sit on these logs."

Surprisingly it did work. Not only did my aching shoulder feel better but my mind felt clearer. The four of us talked through the plan which Haaken had concocted. Aiden, who was no warrior, told us that we should not travel as warriors but merchants. "You can wear your armour but wear it beneath kyrtles and cloaks. If you have shields and helmets then we will frighten those who might have information for us. And I will take some jewellery to trade. If we try to trade the book of the White Christ first it may cause trouble."

Rolf and Sigtrygg tried to talk us out of the journey. It was Kara who had the final word. "The jarl must make this journey. We need to know what lurks behind the great divide. If he does not go now then the snows of early winter may stop him going at all."

"But why does the jarl need to go at all!"

"*Wyrd*! It is out of our hands Sigtrygg Thrandson. The Norns have plotted this course and the jarl must sail it." He had no argument to counter Kara.

We left the next day taking two ponies to carry our supplies and the holy book. It felt strange to leave my shield behind. My helmet was with the supplies but if we were attacked I would have to fight with just my sword. The kyrtles hid our armour but made us look as big as Einar Belly Shaker. Aiden smiled, "Then it is a perfect disguise, Jarl, for no one will recognise you."

He was right. We looked like well-fed merchants. Even Arturus' guards looked closely at us when we called at his fort on our way east. Like Sigtrygg he was unhappy about the risk we were taking.

"This way, my son we can travel the route which Rorik will take and we will have a clearer picture of the dangers we face."

Two days after leaving Cherchebi we looked across the vale towards the Roman City of Eboracum. The Northumbrians had expanded the settlement and it now spread along the river. There were many spirals of smoke rising from the huts. As we drew closer my heart sank. Amongst the masts of the ships on the river was the unmistakable shape of a longship. The closer we went the more we saw. We counted ten drekar. Rorik had reached Eboracum. His banner fluttered from the top of the largest.

Chapter 14

"We need to enter after dark for we will be less noticeable that way."

"Will there not be a gate and guards?"

Aiden shook his head. "No, Cnut, much of the settlement is outside the Roman walls. We find somewhere to sleep and, in the morning, we can find where they trade. That will be inside the walls."

I nodded, "There will be a market for Rorik likes to control the trade. We just need to avoid him. Luckily most of the warriors who knew us perished when we sank his drekar last year."

I knew it was a risk but this was too good an opportunity to miss. Norse warriors like to drink and when they drank they boasted. There was no such thing as a Norse secret. If we could get close enough then we would hear what we needed to know. Was Rorik coming and if so when?

We approached the city along the river and we did so slowly. It was dark when we drew close to the first knarr tied to the stump of a tree. Cnut pretended to examine the hoof of his horse. The sailors were Saxon and they addressed us first.

"Where have you four come from? They say the lands to the west are filled with fierce warriors who prey on fat merchants such as you."

I pointed to the north. "The Dunum. We would have come by ship but the one we hired sprang a leak and we could not wait. Our families need the coin our trade will bring to keep us supplied during the winter." It was a plausible story which Aiden had concocted. Ships which were not well maintained would spring leaks.

"Aye well you have come to the right place. Since the king came business is good for all." The man who spoke was obviously the captain and he leaned forward. "If I am honest he is doing a much better job than Eanred the Northumbrian did."

"King Eanred is dead? I had not heard but then we live in a remote valley. We get no news there."

He laughed, "No my friend, King Eanred lives still and hides north of the Dunum. He was chased out at the end of the last month." He laughed, "Or rather the lazy men who ran the city for him fled without even closing the gates. The new king is come from the east. He is a Viking and is the king of Frisia."

It was confirmed then that Rorik had arrived. He had even given himself titles this time. "Good then we have come to the right place. Is there a market?"

"Aye but it will not be open until they unlock the gates to the city tomorrow. They are open from sunrise to sunset." I nodded and began to leave, "You have to pay to sell your goods and to buy them too. The king likes to make a profit. They say he has golden armour."

"Is there no way to avoid paying such taxes?"

He laughed, "I can see why you have grown so fat." He nodded, "There are men who are willing to buy rare items. What do you wish to sell?"

Aiden waved his arm vaguely around the four of us, "We have a variety of goods. Some large and some small but we are keen to make a profit. And we need a place to sleep. We have travelled far."

"There is one hut which sells ale and has beds." He pointed down the river. "It is just outside the city walls. It has a stable. You will recognise it by the old saddle which hangs from the door. The owner is neither Saxon nor Norse and he can give you more information," he rubbed his thumb and fingers together, "for a price."

"What is his name?"

"Osgar." He nodded at our looks. "I know, it is a strange name but he comes from the old people of this land. They must know something to have survived all these years."

"Thank you, my friend."

We continued down the river bank which showed that this path was both well used and well worn. The ships we passed all appeared to be Saxon; we deduced that from their words. The drekar were tied up close to the walls of the old Roman fort. We heard more noise as we neared the huts and buildings which had sprung up.

We saw the saddle which hung from a hook half way up the roof. It looked to be ancient and was more wood than anything else. Most of the leather had rotted away. As I was the most renowned of the four of us and Haaken, with his one eye, also had a certain notoriety, Cnut and Aiden went in to negotiate a room and stabling. They could watch for any Norse who might know us. We watched the river but it appeared that any Norse or Danes were somewhere other than the river.

After a short while Cnut came out. "There is a stable around the back." He chuckled, "Aiden has the gift of the tongue. He wove a story there that would do the Norns credit." The stable was just an open sided byre but there was hay and water there. We took everything of value from the animals.

There was a thrall to watch over them. I took a piece of copper from my satchel and cut him a small piece from it. "If the horses are well cared for there will be another piece on the morrow."

The thrall's eyes widened. He would normally receive a beating and not a coin for his troubles. He would watch over the animals for us. When we entered the round hut I could see that it was large. There were four posts which helped to support the roof. I had seen the remains of huts like this. It was the way the old people of the land had lived. There were a few other travellers already lying on their piles of straw. Aiden was at the long table where he was drinking a horn of ale. As we approached he pointed at me and said, "This is Osric of Dunelm." I nodded. "Osgar knows of someone who may wish to buy a holy book if we can get our hands on one."

"Good. Where will he be?"

The man called Osgar who was the nearest thing to a walking skeleton I had ever seen, smiled a toothless grin. "He is careful and he will come here." He shrugged, "He does not trust many men and he would not wish to be robbed in his own home."

"I understand. If you could arrange a meeting then we would be grateful." I gestured behind me with my thumb. "I did not know that there were Vikings here."

"They only arrived recently." He lowered his voice. "They came up the river one night and slew the king's men although in truth it was not much of a fight. They left us alone and we have prospered since they arrived. Many ships now come here from Lundenwic and Frankia. So long as we can trade then we are happy." He spread his arm around, "Soon I will have two more tables in here and I can buy more slaves. I am only sorry that all of my women are taken tonight." It was only then that I realised that two of the sleeping forms were, in fact, couples who were writhing beneath their blankets. I now understood how Osgar and his family had survived. They provided what warriors needed: ale and women.

It was impossible to talk discreetly amongst others and we just slept. Aiden had paid for two nights in the hut. In the morning I went to check on the animals. They were our escape from Eboracum. I cut another sliver of copper for the thrall who nodded gratefully. While Haaken and I strolled down the river Aiden and Cnut went into the fort to visit the market. Haaken carried the holy book in a satchel whilst Cnut carried the jewellery we would trade.

Haaken and I stopped before we reached the first drekar. It was a threttanessa. I did not recognise the warriors who guarded it but some of the shields along the side looked familiar. I had seen them in Rorik's old haunt. We walked back to the gate leading to the market. There were two warriors on guard and they examined all who entered. Once again we did not recognise them but it would have been folly to risk entering before Aiden and Cnut had finished their scouting. Instead we counted the oars on the drekar in the river to ascertain numbers. I calculated that there could be as many as four hundred warriors available to Rorik. The good news was that he was here; a few days away from our home. With winter approaching I thought it unlikely that he would risk crossing land he did not know. He could sail but, as we knew, that was a long and hazardous journey. However, I also knew that he was a cunning leader and he would send scouts out. We would need to capture those scouts.

Aiden and Cnut came out of the fort but it was some time later. Haaken and I had begun to worry. We walked with them down the river bank to the boat we had seen the previous night. It meant we could talk without being overheard for it was the last one on the river.

"We saw Rorik."

"And does he have golden armour?"

"No but he has had bronze strips fitted so that it gleams like gold. His oathsworn now all wear mail too. He charges a high price for his services. I traded just four of the brooches I brought. There was little profit in them. We also saw Wiglaf. He looks prosperous. Perhaps the slippery eel brought his goods from Lundenwic to here and sold them."

"Our journey has already been worthwhile. We know the numbers of warriors and we know that Rorik and Wiglaf are here."

Cnut said, "Perhaps we are worrying over nothing. Why should Rorik bother with us? He is doing well in Eboracum."

"You may be right. We shall discover if he does have a desire to add our land to his in the winter. If he sends over his scouts then he will be coming."

Once back at Osgar's we found that we were the only ones. The others had left. His four girls were sleeping. Osgar grinned his empty smile again. "The man who is interested in the holy book will be here after dark. He is cautious."

"Good. Then bring us some food while we wait."

There was little to do but rest. When dusk approached Osgar's hut began to fill up with other visitors and we settled into a corner to wait. We knew that the deal would be done before dark if the man was to return to the safety of the fort. Two armed men came in through the door and went to Osgar. They looked to be warriors although they wore no armour. Osgar pointed to us. One walked out of the hut while the other watched us, his hand on his sword.

A small, neat looking man came back with the warrior and the three of them walked over to us. No one else appeared to take any notice of our meeting. He spoke Saxon but it was with an accent; I could not place his origins but there was something about him I did not like.

"I understand you have a holy book of the White Christ for sale?"

I had decided that Aiden would be the spokesman and he said, "We have."

"You are not monks. Three of you look like fat and prosperous merchants. Where did you acquire it?"

"We bought it from some Norse who were desperate to leave Northumbria."

He frowned, "Osgar says you came from Dunelm. Could you not have sold it there?"

It was Aiden's turn to smile enigmatically and he said, "We said many things to Osgar. Who is to say which is true? You are a careful man and so are we. Let us just say that we acquired the book. If you do not like the book or it is not of the quality you seek then we will travel further south to sell it there."

The man shrugged, "I am merely curious. Show me the book then although I do not have high expectations of it."

Haaken took it from his satchel. The man's eyes widened. "You actually have one. I thought this may have been a ploy to lure me here and rob me." We said nothing. He began to turn each page. When he reached the end he said, "This is unfinished."

"It is still a book of the White Christ."

"It affects its value."

"As you have not told us how you much you are willing to pay for it we do not know what the true value is. If you offer less than we paid for it then we shall take it elsewhere."

I could see that he wanted it. Aiden was dealing with him well. The man licked his lips and ran his fingers over the first page. "I could give you five gold pieces for this. Of course I am robbing myself but…"

Aiden closed the book and took it from him. "And you are wasting our time."

"Do not be hasty my young friend." He suddenly seemed to notice me, "Do I not know you? Have we met somewhere?"

I shook my head, "I doubt it. I rarely leave my home."

The man frowned and then said, "Ten and that is my limit."

"Fifteen."

"Twelve. Take it or leave it."

Aiden held out his hand, "You are robbing us but my friend here is anxious to get home to his wife."

The coins were counted out and the book exchanged. As he left the man looked again at me. Then they left. I nodded to the door and Cnut went to peer out. He came back in and said. "There were four more warriors outside. He was a careful man."

"I think he recognised me."

"How? I had never seen him before."

"I just have a feeling. We will need to keep watch tonight."

Haaken said, "I have done little so far. I will go to the fort and watch the gate."

When he had gone I still fretted about the potential danger. Aiden saw my frown, "We can leave this night if you wish. We have sold the book and discovered Rorik's numbers. The horses are rested. There is nothing to keep us here. We could slip out and head north along the river."

Cnut shrugged, "It makes sense to me. I found it hard to sleep last night anyway. The noises of coupling were a little off putting."

That decided me. I too had an uneasy feeling which I could not shake. "Very well. Cnut, go and fetch Haaken back."

Aiden and I went to the stables. The thrall saw us saddling the horses. "Are you leaving, master?"

"Aye, our business is concluded." I cut him another sliver of copper. "Help us with the saddling eh?"

He smiled, "I will, master, but I will miss you and your copper!"

We had just saddled them when Cnut raced in. "Quick, Haaken is behind us. He is being pursued!"

I clambered up into the saddle and we rode between the huts to the river. Haaken was running towards us and I saw some of the mailed oathsworn of Rorik behind with weapons in their hands.

I drew my sword and galloped down the path. I had not fought on a horse before but I wanted to slow down Haaken's pursuers and allow him to mount his horse. As he passed me I swung my sword at the two warriors who were closest. For some reason my horse took fright and tried to rear. I barely held on to the reins and only did so by grabbing a handful of mane and leaning forward. I almost took off one of the horse's ears with my blade. The horse's hooves did what my sword had not, it knocked one warrior into the river and made the others fall back. I whirled his head around and dug my heels in. Already frightened he took off. I felt something strike my back but I felt no pain and I carried on. When I glanced over my shoulder to see the pursuers I saw a spear hanging down from my armour. I sheathed my sword and reached around. The spear had penetrated my cloak, my armour and embedded itself in the leather byrnie. The lamellar plates had saved me once more.

Haaken was mounted. I shouted, "Ride. They are just behind me!"

Cnut and Aiden galloped ahead leading the two ponies. My mount was hurtling almost out of control it was so terrified. That saved us for the speed made the other horses hurry and soon we began to lose the warriors. Running in mail is never easy. When I saw that there was no one in sight I spoke gently to the horse to calm it and we began to slow to a canter.

We rode until we reached the ford across the river and there we rested the horses. We dismounted. I had decided that fighting on horseback was a skill I did not have.

Haaken came over to us. "When I reached the gate I saw the man who bought the book. He was talking to Rorik's men; Wiglaf was amongst them. The book dealer seemed to be known to them. Perhaps he knew you from Frisia. When I saw him pointing down the river I knew he was sending them after us but he saw me and that is when I ran."

"You were right, Jarl Dragon Heart. You were recognised. "And that means that they will pursue us." Aiden looked back down the river.

Just then we heard, in the distance, the sound of oars in the water. "They are following us."

"They cannot get further upstream." Cnut pointed to the ford we had just crossed. It would rip the hull from the drekar.

"They do not need to, Cnut; they can follow us from here. We have not got as much time as we thought."

We mounted and urged our horses up the bank. The night was pitch black but I knew that they would be able to follow us. Horses left more of a trail than a man. We would have to conserve the strength of our horses if we were to get back. We had more than a hundred miles to go. The Norns did not like being mocked. We were going to pay the price for our insolence.

The noise of our horses' hooves as we thundered up the Roman Road hid the noise of any pursuit. We rode blindly not knowing who, if anyone was following us. We had to keep going while conserving our horses. When dawn broke we had just left the road to head west over the high divide. We stopped and dismounted to let the horses recover a little and to spy out the land. We had the advantage that the lightening sky lit the road and the east. We saw, less than five miles away a knot of warriors. There looked to be about twenty of them and six of them had horses. The ones who were running had to be fit but, more importantly, they could not be wearing armour. No one wearing armour could have run after us and kept that close to us.

"We will walk the horses for a mile or so."

"That means they will close with us, Jarl Dragon Heart."

"Aye but if they do it means that they will have exhausted horses and men. The men who follow are fit but there is a limit to how far they can run. If they close with us then we stand. There are but twenty of them. If we have to then we can turn and fight. We have armour and we are Ulfheonar."

The other reason I wished to walk was to travel over more difficult ground. I wanted to make pursuit harder for Rorik's men. The ground was rocky and also had boggy parts. We went in single file. If they wished to follow us they would have to do the same. After a mile or so we mounted and looked down the valley sides. They had closed to within two miles of us. The rising land made it easy for us to see each other. The sight of us seemed to spur them on and I saw their leader urging his men after us. For the next mile there was no cover and we steadily climbed the steep slope. Our horses had enjoyed the rest and climbed energetically. As we turned a bend on the path I saw that they were even closer; perhaps a mile away but their horses were lathered and the line of warriors on foot was spread further out. From the leading rider to the rear of the column was almost half a mile.

We reached the top of the ridge and followed the ancient track west. The high divide was looming up ahead of us. It was a long slow slog up its back. It would test the endurance of all of us. The track took advantage of the terrain and it twisted back and forth. A few of the warriors who were chasing us came directly up the hill. They tugged themselves up using the tufts of long grass and bracken to do so. Four of them were closing rapidly. It was an attempt to slow us down and allow the riders to catch us up. They were almost ahead of us.

"Time to go faster, Ulfheonar." I kicked hard and my horse moved more purposefully. The four warriors saw what we were doing and they tried to hurry too and cut us off. One of them slipped and as his hand lost its grip on the bracken he tumbled down the slope. The gods were on our side for there was no way he could stop himself. He would end up below his comrades. This was our chance. I drew my sword and leapt from my mount. I did not want to risk him rearing again. If it did then I would end up at the bottom of the hill with Rorik's man.

The three climbing warriors who were the nearest were using both hands to pull themselves up. They were weaponless. I swung Ragnar's Spirit. The blade ripped up and into the throat of the first warrior. I reversed the swing and hit the second on the side of the helmet. The two tumbling warriors took out the last of the climbers. I remounted and we continued our climb. We had bought some time. The men who had survived would have to climb the hill again.

The chase went on until the rain began. The low cloud and the rain made it impossible for us to see behind us. I hoped that it hid us. It felt like we were walking through mist. We dared not stop in case they were closer than they had been. Even though we and our animals were exhausted we climbed. As darkness fell we reached the high point. It was wild and it was wet. The drizzling rain made the visibility almost nothing and we had to stop.

Cnut found a depression between four huge rocks and we camped there for the night. We could watch from between two of the rocks and, hopefully either see or hear any of Rorik's men who approached us. We all needed some sleep and I let the others sleep for an hour before waking Cnut. This way we would all get at least three hours sleep.

When we woke and looked east we saw no-one pursuing us. The low cloud had gone although the day was still overcast and threatened rain. Our dell had protected us from the cold and prying eyes. Our horses looked the worse for wear. "We will walk them for a while. The land still climbs and we are a heavy weight." I laughed, "Except, of course, for our galdramenn."

"Only because I wear no armour."

We walked and spoke of Eboracum. I had only viewed it once before and then it had been a huddle of huts around Roman walls. It now looked like it could grow into a Lundenwic. Like Lundenwic it was on a mighty river which wound its way well inland and like that southern city it was surrounded by swampy ground. Rorik had taken it easily but I could not see anyone taking it from him in a hurry. He was a careful warrior as he had shown in Frisia.

Kara was the one who spoke with the spirits but I must have inherited something from my mysterious ancestor in the cave for I felt the back of my neck prickling. I felt like someone was behind me. When I saw Aiden turning around too I knew he felt the danger.

"What is it, Aiden?"

"I am not certain, Jarl Dragon Heart but I feel that there is someone following us. My eyes are good but I cannot see anyone. Perhaps it is my mind playing tricks."

That confirmed it. "Then my mind is doing the same. Someone is following us."

Cnut asked, "How? We can see for miles down the Roman Road and there is no sign of anyone."

I pointed to the south and north of the road. "But there are dells and hollows on both sides. We stand out here for the Romans built the road to be above everything else. The road is designed to spot an ambush. They are following us still. They are not trying to catch us. We are leading them. Our pursuers want to know where our home is."

"But we are not hidden. Our homes are on the Water and the Mere."

I laughed as I mounted my horse, "Remember when we first found Cyninges-tūn? We came upon it by accident. It is not marked on maps and I doubt that Rorik has maps. All that he knows is that Cyninges-tūn lies to the west of where he is. He knows there are mountains and there is water. That is all. He cannot sail with his drekar and scout it out. He is sending his six horsemen after us so that he can find us with his warband. He is doing what we have just done. He is finding his enemy." I tightened the girths on my horse and made sure my cloak covered my body.

"Where are you going?"

"I go to scout out the enemy."

"Why you?"

I shrugged, "Because I am the best scout amongst us four. If Snorri or Beorn were here, perhaps even Arturus, then I would send one of them. As it is I am the best choice. Continue west at this pace and I will find you." They nodded, reluctantly. It was not bravado; it made perfect sense.

Perhaps the spirits were stronger in me now that I was older or it could have been my proximity to the heavens but I sensed that our followers were to the south and east of the road. I led my horse to the north of the road and headed for a depression I had spied. I mounted as soon as I was hidden and could no longer see the road. I rode east for a mile. I turned south and crossed the road. I could see the dots, in the distance, that were my companions. The road continued to rise. I hoped that Rorik's men would not count us each time they checked on our position.

I became more cautious once I reached the valley to the south of the road. I dismounted and looked to the ground. I saw nothing. I turned and headed back towards the road. I was almost at the road, just some forty paces from it, when I saw the hoof prints and the horse dung. The dung was still warm. We had not left the road there and so it had to be Rorik's men. I mounted and began to follow the tracks. The trick to tracking is to look down and ahead to get the route and then keep watch up ahead. That way you did not get surprised. Every time I glanced down I saw that the scouts who were tracking us still held the line. The only time they deviated was when the path they were following threatened to rise towards the road. I noticed that human footprints sometimes headed north to the road and then returned to the hoof prints. They were making sure where we were.

Horses are strange and almost mystical creatures. My beast's ears suddenly pricked. I stroked his mane and then held my hand over his nose. I did not want him to whinny. The horses just ahead, hidden by a strand of straggly and windblown trees did whinny. The enemy were ahead. I could have returned to my comrades then but I needed to know numbers. How many had perished when I had attacked them? I dismounted and led my horse towards the trees which hid them. When I reached them I saw, just four hundred paces away, the six horsemen I had seen when we left Eboracum. They were riding in single file and following the road. I watched them gradually disappear in the dell which followed the road. Sometimes it became almost a dry gorge and at others it was a gentle undulation leading to the ditch which ran alongside the Roman Road. I watched as one warrior, not wearing armour, dismounted and crawled to the ditch. His head popped up and then he returned to the others. There appeared to be horsemen only and there were just six of them.

I had seen enough. I turned and led my horse across the road unseen and, once on the northern side, mounted him to return to the others. The soft, springy turf had been dampened by the recent rains and the horse's hooves were almost indiscernible. I rode closer to the road this time for I knew I could not be seen. As soon as I saw the ponies I rode harder and joined them on the road. I held my finger to my lips. Now that I knew where the enemy waited I did not want to risk our words carrying on the breeze which blew from the west. It had carried the noises of the enemies' horses to me. I dismounted and held up six fingers. I pointed behind me to the left. All three nodded. I pointed west and they nodded again. We all walked our horses. If we had to hurry away then I knew we could outrun these six horses which had to be tiring for they were being ridden.

I began to concoct a plan in my head. As the afternoon wore on we saw the crest of the high divide. I knew that, beyond it, the green and fertile land to the west would unfold. This was where we would spring our trap. It was an overcast day and we could not see the sun but we saw the sky darkening behind us. We found some rocks which sheltered us from the approaching clouds and we set about making a fire. We could talk now.

"There are six of them. Five are mailed and one is not. They are to the south of the road. Once they know that we have camped I am guessing that they will keep one man to watch us while the rest sleep. We will take them."

They nodded. Cnut asked, "How?"

"We leave Aiden to maintain the illusion that we are all here. We use our cloaks to make our shapes beneath our blankets. We need no disguise now. Then we go on foot along the northern side of the road and approach from the west. There will be one watching. We need to eliminate four of them."

"Four of them?"

"Aye, Haaken, I need a prisoner."

Chapter 15

We found a spring for water and Aiden discovered some autumn berries. We used them to make a stew with the dried meat we had with us. Once Aiden put in some dried herbs the enticing smell began to drift on the breeze. I hoped it would reassure our pursuers. I wanted them to think that they had succeeded. We talked and we laughed. I needed Rorik's men complacent. They had to believe that we had no suspicions. I explained how we would slip away. Cnut and Haaken quickly understood; they were Ulfheonar. Aiden would have the hardest task for he would have to wait until he heard the sounds of combat and then reach the last guard in case we had not eliminated him.

When the fire had died to a glow I stood and went as though I would make water. I crouched down into the small hollow I had spotted. Haaken stood and pretended he was me returning to my bed. A few moments later Cnut stood and joined me. Finally, Aiden stood and went to where Cnut had been so that Haaken could rise and join me. Anyone watching would have seen each of us rise and, in the dark, assume it was the same man returning to his bed. The fire was just a glow and it would look as though we were all sleeping still.

We moved east for thirty paces and then turned south. When we reached the ditch we used it for cover and we looked south. It took some time but I identified the watcher. He was on our side of the road in the same ditch as we were. He was a hundred paces from us. He was looking in the opposite direction. He kept lifting his head to check on us and then he lowered it. I saw the glow from our fire and saw occasional sparks as the logs crumbled into the red ash and they rose into the sky.

I tapped Haaken on the shoulder and he crawled, with his dagger ready, towards their guard. Cnut and I drew our swords in case the sentry made a sound. I caught a glimpse of his white face as he turned, hearing some slight sound, but it was too late to save his life. Haaken's knife sliced across his throat. Cnut and I slipped across the road, crawling on all fours. Once in the ditch on the other side we looked and we listened. The horses told us where they were. They snorted and munched as they ate the spongy grass. Both noises alerted us to their position. They were forty paces from the road. Haaken joined us and he wiped his bloody dagger on the turf. I waved Haaken to the right and Cnut to the left. We crawled towards the sleeping forms.

They had not used a fire but they had huddled beneath blankets. I could not see them all but that did not matter; the horses were to the left. They would have to get through Cnut and me to reach them. The hard part would be sticking a sword into a sleeping body. It went against the instincts of a warrior. Inside you wanted your enemy to have a fighting chance. I steeled myself. My people would suffer unless I was totally ruthless and killed without mercy.

I saw the first warrior. He looked to have his back to me and he was ten paces from me. I moved towards him, Ragnar's Spirit held before me. I edged slowly forward. Suddenly he turned in his sleep. I saw his bare neck and I lunged at him. The tip entered his throat. His eyes opened, briefly to stare at me and I pushed harder. My sword struck a bone; I twisted and withdrew my bloody blade. No one else moved. All was silent.

I looked for my next foe. There was a warrior between Cnut and me. I turned slightly. I saw Cnut's sword raised above his victim. As he brought it down the warrior must have opened his eyes for he gave a shout of alarm before Cnut's blade took his head.

The other three were all good warriors. They were awake in an instant and, with swords in hand stood back to back to face the unseen enemy. We were in the dark and they had the fire behind them. The warrior I faced had a sword in one hand and a single bladed seax in the other. I had seen these weapons before. They were slightly curved and, because they only had a single edge they had a much thicker blade at the back. They were very strong and would neither bend nor break as easily as an ordinary sword. He had the advantage with two weapons to my one. I heard the clash of metal as Cnut and Haaken took on the last two warriors. My opponent swung his sword at me at the same time as he stabbed forward with the seax. I deflected the seax as I turned my body. His sword slid down the metal plates on my shoulder. I thanked the man who had designed such efficient armour. I stabbed forward with

Ragnar's Spirit. He tried to resist with his seax but it was his left hand and that was not as strong as his right. My sword sliced through his mail links. He was not wearing leather beneath his mail and my sword came away bloody.

I was vaguely aware of the others fighting around me but I had a dangerous opponent. Whoever made the first mistake would die. I decided to take the offensive. I swung my sword horizontally. He lifted his seax to counter it and I stepped inside his swing. The flat of his blade struck my left arm. I grabbed his belt and pulled him closer. He was not expecting it and I head butted him. His eyes watered as his nose burst. For the briefest of moments he was disorientated. I lifted my sword and struck him again with my hilt in the face. He stepped backwards. Holding Ragnar's Spirit in both hands I swung it sideways and smashed the flat of the blade into the side of his head. He fell unconscious at my feet. We had our prisoner.

I looked around and saw that the other two warriors lay dead and Cnut and Haaken were watching me. I was their jarl and they would not take away my victory. Behind them I saw Aiden approaching with his blade drawn.

"Secure the horses. Let us take this mail and their weapons."

I took the seax and stuck it in my own belt. It was a handy weapon. I began to take the mail from the unconscious warrior. Cnut looked at me curiously but did not say a word. We left the dead where they lay but we took their weapons and armour, along with their unconscious companion on their horses to our own camp. There was still some time until dawn. We built up the fire.

"Take all the warrior's clothes from him and stake him out. Aiden see to his wound. Apply honey but do not stitch him." I saw that I had aroused their curiosity but they would not question me.

By the time dawn broke we had washed the blood from our bodies and eaten. The mail and the weapons were all secured on the horses. The six horses we had captured would make a fine addition to our herd. It would make movement around my land much easier.

I heard a murmur. The warrior awoke and tried to rise. He could not move for Cnut had staked his naked body out well.

I said nothing and finished the ham I had just taken from the branch hanging over the fire. I wiped my greasy mouth with the back of my hand and swallowed some spring water. The others remained silent too.

He stared belligerently at me to show he did not fear me. "I will tell you nothing, Jarl Dragon Heart. You might as well kill me now and save yourself some time. I am oathsworn and I am a warrior. If you have killed my brothers then I will see them soon in Valhalla."

I smiled and stood over him. "We have all the time in the world. Rorik will not worry about you for many days. By then we will be safely in my home and your gnawed bones will be the last reminder to Rorik of his failure."

"You cannot frighten me. I am a warrior. I am Sven Two Swords!"

"And you will die here without a sword in your hand, Sven Two Swords. You will not go to Valhalla."

For the first time he looked worried. "Then give me a sword and kill me. I am a warrior and deserve a warrior's death."

"First you will tell me exactly how many men Rorik has and what are his plans."

He laughed, "I will not be foresworn. Leave me here to die."

"We will not leave a fellow warrior. We will watch. My healer has tended to your wound. He has applied honey. It helps the wound to heal." I saw him frown. He did not understand my motivation. "He did not stitch it and it bleeds still. It mixes with the honey and falls next to you. The flow is slow but the smell is strong. There are ants over yonder. Already they smell the honey. My healer tells me that ants are attracted by its sweetness. Soon they will come to devour the honey and the blood. That will increase the blood flow and then the rats and the foxes that are now feasting on your companions will come. By then you will be tired and weak. We will go to the rocks and watch as they enter your body and begin to eat you. The birds will come down to enjoy the feast too." I pointed to Haaken. "Haaken here wants to have honey poured on to your balls too. He wonders how long it will take the ants to eat through to the flesh. Of course Cnut just wishes to castrate you. As you can see we have lots of time and we are patient. We do not like being followed and we know the treachery of Rorik and his men."

I retired to the rock where the others waited. Aiden had found somewhere close to an ant's nest and I had not lied. The first ants were already closing with the warrior. I was not exactly certain if they would do all that I had said but it sounded reasonable. It took an hour for him to break. The ants swarmed all over his body as they sought the honey. Aiden had put a few blobs on his naked chest and his cheeks. He shook his head to try to rid himself of the crawling creatures but they were persistent. It must have been horrific to have them crawling over his body and biting him. He was a warrior and could endure much pain but this was insidious.

Eventually he said, "I will tell you! Just cut me free and give me a sword."

"When we have the information, we require." He nodded. "You are a trusted chief are you not?"

"I am one of Rorik's oathsworn."

"How many men does he have?"

"He has six hundred of his own men and his allies have the same number."

"His allies?"

The warrior laughed, "You are not a popular man Jarl Dragon Heart. Sihtric Silkbeard and Erik of Mann hate you. Ragnar Hairy-Breeches and Magnus Barelegs both owe you for past insolence. They all wish to share in the bounty of your land and to find your treasure."

"We have no treasure."

"You lie! Erik of Mann has told us of the magic sword you found as well as the blue stone and gold mines you have. How else could you afford such fine armour? How else could your men wear the golden wolf?"

Erik! He had betrayed me. "And when does he come?"

"That I do not know. I have told you all. You gave your word! Not that I believe you anymore. You have not spoken the truth. You are foresworn. You are a nithing."

I was angry. "Give him a sword and send him to Valhalla."

"You will burn my body?"

"No! The rats and the animals will feast on the flesh of Sven Two Swords."

Cnut put his sword in his hand and Haaken gave him the warrior's death. We put the armour and weapons on the horses. As we headed west I wondered about the treachery of Erik. I wondered why he had not tried to mine the gold and the blue stones for himself. It was only then I remembered that he had not gone with us to the mines themselves. He had waited in the estuary on his boat. He had received the bounty; he wore a wolf pendant around his neck and yet he had betrayed me. He had sworn an oath to follow me. He would be punished. I would need to speak with Kara. My wife would know her brother's mind and heart.

The other Norse kings who were coming were just lazy leaders. They were like the rats and foxes which would be eating the flesh of Rorik's men. They let others do the hard work and then they preyed on the ones who had toiled. I had more respect for Rorik; at least he had captured Eboracum from the Northumbrians.

"We are no wiser then, Jarl Dragon Heart?"

I shook my head but Aiden said, "We are."

"How so?"

"We knew already that Sihtric and Erik would be coming from the west. Now that we know they are allies of Rorik then we know that one attack will mean there is a second coming. This is vital information. Had we not questioned Sven Two Swords then we might have drawn all of our forces to face one foe when there was another waiting to attack. We do not know when they will come but Pasgen now has a tower. We have ships we can use to watch Mann. As soon as they sail from Mann then we will know that the attack from the east is also imminent. Where Magnus and Ragnar will come from is anyone's guess. They could join Sihtric and Erik and attack from the west but I think that Rorik will want to divide his forces." He hesitated, "The inescapable truth is that he could have a thousand warriors at his command and they will fight as your men do. They are Vikings and not Saxons!"

I could not fault Aiden's thinking. We still had time. Winter would be upon us in a matter of ten days or so. Rorik would have to wait until then to see if his scouts returned. I was even more convinced than ever that the attack would now come after the winter. We had been lucky. If we had not evaded the trap laid for us by Sihtric and Erik then Rorik would already have attacked. The ambush by his ships had been well planned and almost succeeded. There had to be communication between them. Then I remembered that Ragnar Hairy-Breeches ruled the land north of the Maeresea. With Rorik at Eboracum they now cut the land in two and Magnus Barelegs ruled Anglesey. All that they needed was to ally with the men of Strathclyde and we would be completely surrounded. Our attack on them had been judicious. We might have had to fight even more enemies else.

When we reached Cherchebi I was pleased to see that Arturus had built two tall wooden towers facing south and east. They gave a good view over the low-lying land and would warn him of an enemy's approach.

His men had hunted and we ate well. The four-day journey back had been on dried and salted food. The fresh meat and ale were welcome. We told him and his warriors of our journey. He, too, became angry when he learned of Jarl Erik's perfidy.

"Do not get angry, my son. The gods and the Norns will punish him. However, you will need more warriors here. You cannot defend this against Rorik's army."

"I have more warriors, father. There are many farmers in the dales around here and I have them come here once every five days so that they can practise with my men. They are happy to do so. I promised them that they can stay here in case of danger or bad weather. We have built storage huts and dried and salted much food. I can field fifty warriors now to defend my fort."

"It is still not enough but it is better. We will leave you the mail and the weapons we took from Rorik's men and we will leave two horses too. That way we can have news of an attack within a short time."

Arturus pointed to the ridge to the west. "My men have built a signal tower in the forest. You cannot see it but we can light a beacon which Windar will be able to see."

"Good. Then I will tell Windar when I warn him of this new danger." I pointed south. "We also face danger from the south now. Magnus and Ragnar will come that way. They will plan to assault us from every direction."

"We will be ready. I will spend the winter devising ways of slowing them down before they even get here. I have clever Wild Boars here. They will soon outshine the Ulfheonar."

Haaken laughed, "I admire your confidence, young Arturus but we shall see. I hope you have someone as talented as I am and then he can sing the songs of your great deeds!"

Arturus shook his head, "And I must get the door to my hall made bigger."

"Why?"

"So that you can get your big head in and out easier!" It was good to hear the confident banter. We were outnumbered but not downhearted.

Windar liked the idea of a signal tower and he sent his men to build one immediately. "If we have enemies from the east and the south then we will all be hard pressed."

"Do as my son is doing. Tell the farmers that if they see the beacons lit then they must come to you and Ulf for protection. Lay in supplies. You have water but you must protect it. I will send Bolli. He is building a drekar for me. He can build one for you too. Have your men cut down trees so that you have wood for your ship and you can see further. Remember these are our people we fight. They are good at what they do. These are not a Saxon warband."

The normally ebullient and cheerful Windar looked sad. "This land is perfect. I would not have it spoiled by an enemy who took all that we have worked and striven for."

"Then we fight for it. These may be our people who come but they are not of our heart."

The extra days we had spent with Arturus and Windar meant that the first winds of winter began to whip across the land bringing sleet and biting rain. I was glad to get into the relative warmth of my fort. It had been ten days since we had left but Bolli had done well and the hull of the drekar was tied up close to my hall. It was undergoing the vital soaking which would make it watertight and show if there were any leaks. He and Kara greeted me. Kara's face showed me that she had spoken with her mother's spirit. "I will speak with you later, father. I know we both have much to tell each other." She smiled at Bolli. "Your young shipwright has done well."

Bolli looked pleased at Kara's words. She was a young woman but she had an old head upon her shoulders. "The drekar looks fine. I like the eagle prow."

"It is not a dragon but it seems right somehow. We will step the mast in the next few days. Have you a crew yet?"

"We have but Rolf will need to refine his choice. When that is done you must do the same for Windar on his Mere. War is coming from the east and we need your landlocked drekar more than ever." I gave him five of the gold pieces we had received for the holy book. "Here is payment." He shook his head but I pressed the coins into his hand. "The gods like things to be paid for one way or another. I would prefer it in coin to men's lives."

Kara was waiting for me. She poured me some ale as I told her of what I had learned. "Mother's Spirit warned me of her brother. She is unhappy as is her mother and Prince Butar." She pointed across the Water to the storm clouds above the Old Man. "The weather shows their anger. It will soon descend upon Mann."

"We need to make arrangements for the farmers to have somewhere to live within our walls. When war comes I do not want families to suffer."

She pointed across the water. "There is much land over there. The men have been clearing the woods to provide grazing. The cattle and the pigs are prospering. We can use the wood to build some halls. Until the people need them they can be used to provide shelter, this winter, for the animals. The more animals we have the more people we can feed. The new bull and the ram like it here and they have many fine young. You chose well."

I took Aiden and we visited Pasgen. It was vital that he, Siggi, Trygg and Sven knew what the dangers would be. "We now have enemies all around us and you will be amongst the first to know of them. I do not want you to risk your ships. If you cannot be safe here then sail to Thorkell's Stead. The river there and his warriors will protect you. Pasgen you must lay in food and make this morsel too difficult for our enemies to digest. I believe that they will come for me. I am the target. Like our other outposts I would like you to build beacons in the forest. If we have a line from Úlfarrston to Cyninges-tūn then we can have warning of danger and we can come to your aid."

Pasgen was as loyal a man as any of my Ulfheonar. He was not of our people but he was of our heart and I could rely on him totally.

Usually our winters were spent making small but precious objects and filling in the long nights of darkness. That winter, the Wet Winter as it became known, we worked all day in the driving rain and sleet which never seemed to abate. Ditches were dug and sown with sharpened stakes. Halls were built. Drainage channels were created. All the work moved the forest away from our walls and we were safer. When night came, we were too tired for anything other than sleep.

Thorkell visited us before midwinter. The rain made travelling uncomfortable. Had it been snow and ice then it would have been impossible. He told us that he had more men now for many settlers were fleeing from the wars in the islands. The young king there was fighting for his life against the King Of Norway and the men of Dál Riata. Our attack had shifted the eyes of those warriors to the north and not the south. We had visited there at just the right time. Thorkell lived too far away for beacons to serve and so I gave him two of the better horses so that he could send us a message if danger threatened from the north.

The one luxury we enjoyed was the new sweat hut of Aiden. We could seat ten warriors in there and it became something we did each day. As we sat sweating it seemed to clear our minds as well as our bodies. I noticed that when warriors left the hut they were happier. There were more jokes and we had far less fights. Warriors are filled with aggression. The sweat hut released it. When war came my warriors would be ready to face whatever treachery our foes threw at us.

Chapter 16

I spent the winter becoming stronger. I worked on my weakened shoulder. The sweat hut helped. I also enjoyed the feeling of clean skin. Kara took to trimming my hair and beard. I liked the way it made me feel and when I looked in the Waters I liked the way I looked. Kara had learned to make oils and lotions from herbs so that I smelled as I had in Constantinopolis. I had worried what other warriors would think but now I cared not. I was Jarl Dragon Heart. I looked different and I ruled differently. I was a mixture of the old people and the Saxons and I had been raised by the Norse. There was no one like me.

Rolf and Aiden worked all winter to improve the defences of our two settlements. I visited Pasgen to see how his work went. Our new drekar, '*Eagle*' was crewed by the men who worked in the two settlements. She would only be needed in times of war. Until then she had two boys and old Einar Salt Hair as a crew. They were more than capable of sailing her up and down the Water. There was rarely a need to hurry and our well-designed ships could almost sail against the wind. The skills which Einar passed on to the boys would be invaluable. Einar had sailed with Olaf and Prince Butar when he had been a young man and he missed sailing. The two boys wanted to sail on '*Heart*' and were keen to learn from Einar. More often than not they had a crew of eight or ten for there was little else to do in winter. In the summer the experience would be invaluable.

Bolli had laid down the hull of the ship on Windar's Mere but the rains had slowed down the work. They guaranteed we would not be surprised. Every low lying piece of ground was turned into a quagmire or a new pool. The ditches which defended us became small rivers. We had to build causeways to enable people to move around. But we were safer. The gods smiled on us and the spirits protected us still.

Haaken became a father again and Cnut's wife had twins. It was taken as a good omen and the Ulfheonar celebrated for two days at the midwinter solstice. In the days following the celebration they did not drink as much as normal; we knew that after the winter war would come to our land and we had to be ready. The four of us spent time working out the numbers of warriors we had and how they would be used.

"Arturus needs more men. They do not need to be mailed warriors but he needs archers and slingers. He needs men who can stand on his walls."

Aiden had a piece of parchment. On it were the names of every man who could hold a weapon. "He has the men from the local farms but there are some warriors who have been training here with Rolf; six warriors and four archers. They came as four families last year, Jarl and they have neither land nor animals." He pointed to the southern end of our Water. "There is good land some seven miles inland from our Water. It is on the other side of Grize's Dale. Crost could farm there and become part of the garrison in times of need. Rolf says he is a good warrior."

"When we have finished then take me to him and I will give him some animals." Haaken looked at me as though surprised. "If he is willing to fight for us then I am willing to give him some of my animals."

"We do not have enough men if they all attack at the same time, Jarl. There are just not enough warriors."

"How many horses and ponies do we have Aiden?"

"We have more ponies than horses but I would say we have thirty animals. Some are needed for messengers, of course."

"Then we keep twenty five Ulfheonar as relief for wherever gets attacked."

"We cannot fight on horseback."

I laughed, "And we do not need to. Windar's Mere and Cherchebi are between two hours and a half days away on foot. By horse we can reach any of those places in an hour. If the beacons work we could arrive there at the same time as the enemy." They all nodded for it made sense to them. "The weak spot is Cherchebi, for we have a drekar on the Mere and the Water which can watch for the enemy. Arturus could be attacked from two directions."

"But he has the fort which is easiest to defend."

"And that is why I want more men for him. I will visit with Crost."

The raids to Thorkell's land had resulted in many families coming south where they thought it was safer and, I suspect, to be closer to me, Kara and the Ulfheonar. Crost was one such warrior. He was not young. He had fought alongside Prince Butar, but his sons were strong warriors. He and his family were in one of the huts Kara had had built in the western village. Crost and his sons were fletching and the women were spinning when I visited them. They stood as I entered. "No, carry on with your tasks I just need to speak with Crost."

"Have I offended you Jarl?"

"No, Crost, but you can help me out."

"Whatever I can do, I will."

"My son commands the fort twenty miles from here." He nodded. "He has just fifty men he can call upon to defend his fort. I have it in my mind to give you a parcel of land a few miles from his fort and some animals. You and your family would have the safety of the fort should danger come and my son would have the benefit of fine warriors to defend it. What say you?"

"We moved here, Jarl, because I did not want to put my family in danger."

"Where I have in mind is between here and Cherchebi. It should be safer. You will have a fort on either side of you and the land there is good farmland." I saw the doubts upon his face. "Will you ride with me tomorrow and look at the land?"

"And if I say no?"

I smiled, "You know me Crost; I am the jarl who asks. I do not command. If you stay here then I will be happy for you will defend my walls and I will ask another to farm the land."

"Then I will come with you, Jarl Dragon Heart."

Haaken came with us and we rode three of the new horses. As soon as he saw the land Crost was impressed. There was a fine stream which ran through it but it was neither boggy nor rocky. When we found the spring with the ancient altar and the standing stones he was convinced. "This is *wyrd*, Jarl Dragon Heart for my family has always made offerings to the god Icaunus and this spring is dedicated to his memory."

"Then when the weather improves we will return here and build a hall for you. This waite shall be Crost's Waite."

He shook his head. "The ground is not frozen. I shall bring my brothers and my sons. We will have a hall here within the month."

He was as good as his word and the extra warriors made me that much happier about Arturus' isolation. Haaken and I carried on to Cherchebi. I would visit with my son. He had grown even more during the short days of winter. He now had an assured confidence about him. His warriors also looked to have grown up too. They were not the callow youths we had taken to Hrossey. They reminded me of me and my Ulfheonar for Haaken, Cnut and I had begun the cult when we were even younger than Arturus was. I envied my son and the Wild Boars their time together.

"You are happy here, Arturus?"

"Yes Jarl. I feel I belong amongst these warriors." We were standing in one of his towers looking south. He had a view which, on a clear day, took in the sea and the treacherous sands that lay there. He gave me a shy smile, "Some of the decisions I have to make do not sit well."

"You cannot have favourites amongst your oathsworn. You owe all of them the same duty."

"But you favour Haaken and Cnut."

"How?"

"You choose those two for the most difficult of tasks and put them in the most dangerous places in battle."

I nodded. "They are the most experienced. They are the only two who are left from the original seven Ulfheonar. I also use Sigtrygg when I need a stalwart Ulfheonar who will hold the line. I use Snorri and Beorn to scout because no-one is better than they are." I smiled at him. "Much as I used you as a third scout when I could. That is not playing favourites, that is good leadership, using the skills of all of my men. It is why Rolf now guards my home. He cannot fight in a shield wall but he is as loyal and brave as any and I know that Kara and my people will be safe."

He nodded and stroked his beard. Like me he kept it neatly trimmed. "Now I see the error of my ways."

"You are young and you will make mistakes. I did too but your men will forgive mistakes now for they matter not. When our enemies come then you cannot make mistakes. They will cost your oathsworn their lives. I feel the loss of every oathsworn as though I had lost a brother."

"They will come here, will they not?"

"Aye. Aiden and I have looked at the maps." I pointed south. "The sands in the bay to the south are deadly. If the enemy land there then they will never reach here." I pointed to the south east. "Magnus and Ragnar will come from that direction." Shifting my finger a little more to the east I said, "Rorik, and he will be the most dangerous, will come from there. Sihtric and Erik will come from the west. They could come from the direction of Úlfarrston or Itunocelum. The beacons are vital. I am mounting my Ulfheonar; it is not to fight it is to get here quickly. Crost and the other new fighters must be summoned, with their families to this fort. You have to wait behind its wooden walls."

"I do not fight?"

"No, you defend." I saw the disappointment on his face. "You see yourself leading your warriors into battle and defeating Rorik." The sudden look of surprise told me that I had guessed correctly. "If these were Saxons, the men of Eanred, then you might be correct. Few of them have mail and they are not the warriors we command. The three kings who come here, Rorik, Magnus and Ragnar are all like us. They have smaller armies but they are all armoured and well trained. It will be like fighting your own men."

"But our men are better!"

"I know but we will be outnumbered." I pointed to the marshy ground and then the ridge rising away to the south and the east. "The gods have chosen this for you to defend. There is game yonder?"

"Aye, some."

"Enough to feed an army?"

He shook his head. "There is enough for us or we go to the forests of Grizes's Dale." He pointed to the north west.

"Then either the enemy bring their own food or they starve. If you have the farmers in here with their animals then they will starve. They may well leave you while they move further towards our homes." I laughed. "If they do then we will have won. We know the trails and the paths. We can ambush them and whittle down their numbers. That is my intent. I will wear them down until I can bring together all of our forces and defeat them."

Understanding filled his face and then he frowned. "But you will be attacked by Sihtric and Erik."

"And that is why you must hold here and keep the men watching ready to light the beacons. Rorik and the others think they have devised a cunning plan but they will find great difficulty in launching their attacks at exactly the same time. When they do attack I will summon reinforcements from Thorkell and Windar. So now you can see why you must hold. You are the dam which will hold back the flood."

"I will not let you down."

"I know and that is why I am confident that we will win."

The winter never developed into the icy monster we had suffered two years ago but the rain rarely abated. We found new stretches of water where none had existed before the winter. We had to devise both new paths and build causeways across the most treacherous of bogs and swamps. Windar and Thorkell kept me informed both about their numbers and on their defences. I was convinced that we had done all that we could. The gods were on our side. The rains helped us.

The Norns are unpredictable. We still had another two months of winter but our animals were producing young. The sheep, in particular benefitted from the lack of snow. Many of the men who guarded my walls were given permission to go on the fells and bring down their sheep. We had almost eliminated all of the wolves but we knew that the ones who remained and the foxes would prey on the young. Rolf was confident that we could summon them back in a hurry if we needed to.

I had lived alone for some time now. Kara spent most of her evenings in the house of healing. The damp weather had infected many with the coughing sickness. Kara could cure it but she needed to be on hand all of the time. Aiden also spent a great deal of time with Kara for he too was a mighty healer. They saved lives. Scanlan and his family now lived in the western settlement. He was able to run both villages successfully. Consequently I rattled around in my huge hall with just two slaves for company. Tadgh and Aed were both eager to please me. They had been taken from the Hibernians and I treated them far better than their former masters. I had thought of sending them to the thrall hall but I found it pleasant to actually speak with someone at night.

I had a routine: once I had eaten and Kara and Aiden had left, I would take down my sword and my newly acquired seax. I would clean and sharpen them with a whetstone. When they were sharpened and replaced then I took down the sword they had called Saxon Slayer. It did not need sharpening but I enjoyed running my fingers down the blade and feeling the faded writing upon it. It was ancient. If I closed my eyes I could almost hear it ringing in battle. I occasionally swung it through the air. It always seemed to sing and hum as it did so. Apart from Ragnar's Spirit it was the only blade I thought was alive. What always surprised me was how my hand fitted the hilt as though it was made for it. Ragnar's Spirit had been made specifically for me. This one had been sent to me. *Wyrd.* I looked in the fire as I held it and pictures of warriors fighting filled my head.

That night, just twenty days from Eostre, I watched the fire and held the old sword across my lap. I must have fallen asleep for I dreamed. The sword must have been ready to tell me a story. Or perhaps the spirits wished to contact me. I dreamed.

I saw half naked warriors. They looked to me like Hibernians but I was dressed as a Roman soldier and I was mounted on a horse. I charged at the head of a column of horsemen and we swept down on the warriors. The sword sang a song as it sliced into their unprotected bodies. Limbs and weapons flew through the air and they fled. I chased them and found myself alone galloping down a long tunnel of trees. Suddenly my horse stumbled and I flew through the air. Instead of striking the ground I fell into a deep and dark cavern. I managed to stop myself falling to the bottom. I pulled myself to my feet and sought a way out. There was another tunnel which twisted and climbed. Holding my sword before me I went into the dark empty place.

Ahead of me I saw a light and I headed towards it. The light grew and I saw that I was entering an enormous cavern. I heard Erika's voice as she shouted my name, over and over. I stepped out and there I saw Erika. She was tied to a stake and there were warriors around her. They held weapons to her naked body. She screamed and then shouted, "Husband! Awake!"

I opened my eyes in shock. Out of the corner of my eye I saw a sword slicing down towards me. Saxon Slayer was in my hand and I instinctively whipped it up to strike the blade away. A spear lunged towards my middle. I pushed backwards and the chair tumbled over. The spear head rammed into the thick, wooden bottom of the seat. I jumped to my feet. There were four warriors advancing towards me and all were mailed. They were Norse. I saw the bodies of Tadgh and Aed lying in a widening pool of blood. The old sword in my hand would not take combat with these warriors; Bjorn had told me that. I put my left hand behind me and found, on the table, the seax I had recently won. I put Saxon Slayer down for next to the seax was Ragnar's Spirit. I grabbed my magical sword. The four warriors advanced towards me as I held both weapons before me. I had no armour but I would sell my life dearly.

I glimpsed a wolf pendant around the neck of one warrior. I shuddered. It was one made by Aiden. In a moment of clarity, I knew who had sent these assassins; they had been sent by Jarl Erik. I had given him a pendant when we had been friends. He must have given it to the assassin as payment.

"So Jarl Erik sends others to do his treacherous work. He is afraid of me still!"

The warrior with the pendant laughed. "You are wrong Jarl Dragon Heart. We begged for the chance to kill you. I am Cnut Svenson of Hrams-a. You killed my father when his drekar attacked yours. You slew him and his body lies at the bottom of the sea. He can never rest until you are slain. Jarl Erik just gave me the pendant to make sure that you and your spawn all died!"

That put steel into my spine. They were here to kill Kara too. If it were not for the coughing sickness then she would be dead already along with Aiden. The Norns were spinning their mighty webs.

The warrior to my left suddenly lunged at me with his sword. I had no shield but the single edged seax was strong and I whipped it around. I heard the ring of metal on metal and saw the surprised look on the warrior's face as his sword bent in the middle. I sliced at him with Ragnar's Spirit. It bit through the mail and into his left shoulder. A second warrior tried to take advantage of my blow to strike at my unguarded side. I spun around holding the seax at neck height. He had to halt his charge as the recently sharpened blade headed towards his eyes. The wounded man was before me and I put my right arm around his neck and pulled him around so that his body protected me. The blood from his half severed arm was puddling before me and he would not have long to live.

The man who called himself Cnut Svenson had lunged at me while I was spinning and he plunged his sword into the body of his dying comrade. I pushed the mailed body away and it fell upon Cnut Svenson's blade. He could not strike me.

I had managed to evade my enemies up to now but I needed to strike while they were still disorganised. I turned and moved so that my back was to the fire. No one could come from behind me. The other two warriors raced at me while Cnut Svenson dragged his sword from beneath the dead warrior. For the briefest of times I only had two enemies. The only advantage I had was my speed. They were mailed; they would be tiring. I had to strike quickly before I was outnumbered three to one.

I swung Ragnar's Spirit in an arc. It was longer than their blades and I swung it at eye height. It takes a brave man to advance at a sword which is aimed at his eyes. As they recoiled I stabbed at the leg of the one on my left. I had seen that his mail shirt was not a long, knee length one. The tip of the seax's blade was like a dagger but it widened to the span of a hand. I punched as I stabbed. The blood cascaded from the wound and the warrior screamed as he fell backwards. I hoped that his scream would carry to the warrior hall for Cnut Svenson was now on his feet and advancing towards me. My trick would not work a second time; they both had long mail byrnies.

"I was told that you had not honour and were a nithing. Now I know that it is true. I will make sure that you do not go to Valhalla!"

As Cnut boasted I saw my chance. He would try to maim me and then kill me when I had no sword in my hand. It was a slim chance but a chance none the less. I had to get rid of the second warrior. I glanced at him. He was a young warrior with an open helmet and a metal byrnie. The rings had no rivets. His sword had already bent a little. His shield was well made. He approached cautiously from my right. I knew how to fell him. Someone was watching over me.

I lunged at Sven with my seax, inviting a strike from the younger warrior. I wanted him to stab at me. Cnut brought his shield down on my seax laughing. "You try to hurt me with a needle! You are growing old, Dragon Heart!"

I ignored his words and brought Ragnar's Spirit down hard on the young warrior's blade which had darted towards me. By luck or perhaps my aim was guided for Ragnar's Spirit hit the bent blade on the bend and the blade shattered. The young warrior made the mistake of staring at his broken weapon instead of punching me with his shield. I brought my sword up backhand and it tore into his face below the jaw. I hit him with the freshly sharpened blade and sliced half of his face off. I spun and stepped into the space where he had been as Cnut stabbed at where I had just stood.

The young warrior was out of the fight and it was now me against the leader of the assassins. He was warier now. He had seen me without mail and without helmet. He had anticipated his victory. He had taken it for granted. Now his three companions lay dead or dying lying in ever widening pools of blood. He must have known that he would never escape. Outside I could hear the sounds of alarm as the dead sentries on the walls were discovered. He was a brave warrior. He would avenge his father and then go to Valhalla as a hero; the warrior who had slain Dragon Heart.

He swung his sword overhand at me. That was a mistake for it caught on the beams of my hall. I stabbed forward with the deadly seax. His momentum had brought him closer to me and the sharpened edge of the seax ground against his mail and ripped into the mail rings. As I withdrew it I heard some of them fall to the floor. I stepped back as he swung his shield at me. I could move faster than normal as I was without mail. He almost overbalanced and I stabbed at his face with Ragnar's Spirit. It sliced into his cheek. He uttered not a sound but spat out blood and teeth. He stepped towards me. He would not try an overhand blow. He had to swing horizontally. I kept the wall to my left. It restricted his swing. When he did swing he could not get as much power behind it as he would have liked and the seax easily deflected it. Just then the door burst open and he half turned. I could not waste the opportunity and I brought my sword down hard across his shield. Already off balance he lurched backwards and I ripped upwards with my seax. It tore through his mail and into his stomach. The blade widened and ripped a hole as big as my fist. He slumped to the ground. Haaken, Cnut and Sigtrygg raced in with swords drawn.

I shook my head. "It is finished." I pointed Ragnar's Spirit at him. "He was sent by Jarl Erik. He is a brave warrior." I walked over to him. "Do you wish the warrior's death?"

He seemed unable to talk. Perhaps the blade through his mouth had damaged his tongue. He nodded. "Go to Valhalla." Sigtrygg stepped behind him and slit his throat.

Haaken looked at the four dead warriors. "I see you have not lost your touch."

Aiden and Kara came in. Kara looked the least surprised by the scene. I nodded to her. "Your mother saved me. She came to me in a dream."

"I too dreamed but I did not know it was of the present. When I awoke I thought it was the future and then I heard the cries."

Cnut pointed with his sword. "There are two dead outside. The sentries did all that they could but they are all slain."

"Perhaps we should not have let the others go to their sheep."

"No, Sigtrygg, this was *wyrd*. It tells me that Erik fears me. This is the second time he has tried to kill me. Rorik will want to kill me himself and this tells me that there is no unity amongst our enemies. They have merely combined to fight me. If they defeat me then they will fall out amongst themselves. They will never have this land. It is not meant for them." I pointed to the mail on the dead warriors. "Do the others have mail?"

"Aye, Jarl."

"Then he has sent six of his oathsworn. That means he has six less good warriors to fight us and we have six more sets of mail. The spirits are watching over us still."

Rolf had come in during the last part and he shook his head. "I am sorry Jarl Dragon Heart. I have failed you."

"No Rolf, the Ulfheonar have failed the jarl. We will make sure that two of us sleep at the door to the jarl's chamber to protect him."

I shook my head, "Haaken, if I am meant to die in my own hall then so be it but I think I am destined for another death and besides, my wife and Ragnar protect me still." I walked over to Saxon Slayer. "And this blade has as much magic as Ragnar's Spirit. This should be guarded when I am not here as dearly as anything. It warned me of the assassins."

Chapter 17

The attempt on my life had a number of effects. It angered all of my people and especially my sentries. They all swore vengeance on Jarl Erik. He had not followed the code of our people and they would not forgive easily and certainly never forget. He had broken his oath. I felt at peace. I had fought four warriors whilst not wearing armour and defeated them without suffering a wound. I had also seen the power of the past and the spirit world. An ancestor I had never even heard of until a few years ago had come from the past to save me; that made me feel special. I had been chosen for this task and I would make sure that I carried it out. I had known that this land was magical and I now knew my place in it. This was my home and this was where I would die.

Everyone had been energised by the attempt. When the other leaders heard of it they increased their own security as well as they finished their defences. Bolli finished the drekar for Windar's Mere and *'Hawk'* became the defender of that largest of meres.

A messenger came, a week before Eostre, from Pasgen. Siggi had sailed along the coast of Mann and seen a huge fleet gathering there. The drekar were coming. I rode to Windar while my Ulfheonar prepared for battle.

"Windar I need you to have a warband at the southern end of the Mere. I am taking the Ulfheonar to Úlfarrston. If Rorik comes to Cherchebi then I will need you here to slow down his advance."

Windar was not as experienced in war as many of my leaders and he frowned. "How?"

"Arturus and his people can hold out for at least a week. Your new drekar can ferry replacements for you as you retreat to your fort. The hills and the Mere mean that you cannot be outflanked. By retreating down the Mere you allow me the time to reach Rorik and attack his lines of communication."

"I could try to hold him here."

I patted him on the back. "This Rorik is a cunning leader and he will bring many mailed warriors. You will be outnumbered. Use your spears to hold him back and your arrows and slings to whittle him down. Draw him to your walls. It is prepared is it not?"

"Aye Jarl Dragon Heart."

"Good for we can make him hungry. Your drekar will stop him from feeding from the Mere and my warriors will destroy him. Just make sure you keep me informed of what is going on. Have your beacons manned all the time from now on!"

"It will be done as you command."

Once back at Cyninges-tūn I told Kara, Aiden and Rolf what I intended. "I will leave half of my warriors here. We have a full crew for '***Eagle***'. I will take the Ulfheonar and the other forty warriors to Ulfarrston."

Aiden nodded, "You are guessing that Sihtric and Erik will come soon."

"Erik has failed to kill me twice. In addition, he will not wish to have Sihtric and his warriors eating his supplies on Mann. If the fleet is there then they will be coming soon. I will send our ships to Thorkell. He can protect them. I would not have our ships destroyed."

"You will have to send crews with them. That will mean you will have fewer warriors."

"I know Rolf but it cannot be helped. Besides they can return by land and reinforce you here."

"And if Rorik comes?"

"We take horses and I can reach Arturus or Windar in half a day from Ulfarrston. I would defeat my enemies one by one."

"You are risking your son and his warriors."

I looked at Rolf. "He is a warrior. He leads men. Should I protect him and lose Cyninges-tūn?"

Rolf shook his head and Kara laughed. "My brother is stronger than you know, Rolf. Through his veins runs the blood of my mother and Dragon Heart."

"Aiden you have a mind like a Greek Strategos. You and Kara make the decisions necessary to keep my people safe."

He knelt. "I will, Jarl. Bjorn and all the men of the Water are sworn to defend our land. We will not fail you."

Kara pointed across the Water. "Old Olaf will watch us. He has done little yet but he will ensure that we survive."

Only half of the Ulfheonar had horses and so we walked down to Úlfarrston. The horses would only be needed in case of a disaster and Rorik attacked at the same time as Erik.

Erik Short Toe was not happy when he was ordered to sail north with the knarrs. "But Jarl Dragon Heart, my crew can fight."

"They are not warriors and I need my ships safe. I have not enough men to guard them and our town. Guard them well for me Erik." Siggi and Trygg felt the same. I told them they could return by land to fight. "The knarr will ensure our prosperity when we have defeated our enemies."

I saw the doubt on Siggi's face as he said, "There are many ships. Can we defeat them?"

I laughed, "Do not begin to doubt, my friend or we shall lose."

Once they had left with Pasgen's knarr the estuary looked empty. Pasgen put on a brave face but I could see that he, too, was worried. "We will hold them here, Jarl Dragon Heart."

"If my plan works, my friend, then you will not need to. I intended to draw our enemies through the forests. We know the land and they do not. What I want you and your people to do is destroy their ships when the warriors follow us into the forest. They will need to sleep and you know now how to make fire arrows. When their ships are destroyed then they will lose heart."

He brightened at that. The only warriors I had with me were my forty Ulfheonar. The others were already in the forest making camps. They would stay there until we drew on our enemies and then they would harass them all the way to the Water. After the second attempt on my life I saw that I was the one they wanted. I would give them what they wanted but they would pay with their lives.

Two days after our ships had sailed the enemy fleet arrived. Snorri's sharp eyes spotted the fact that there were just half the ships that Siggi had counted. It was still a sizeable number of ships and warriors. There were enough ships to carry almost two hundred warriors. The question was, where were the rest?

"We cannot worry, yet, about the others. We need to deal with these. We will meet them on the beach. I want to kill as many as I can here."

We formed up in the land between the river and Úlfarrston. I had told Pasgen not to attack the enemy. If Erik and Sihtric thought we had been abandoned by our allies it would make them overconfident. My new banner fluttered bravely above my head. Tostig Sweynson held it. His father had been as brave an Ulfheonar as any and his son would defend the banner with his life. I frowned when I saw that the ships which came were those of Sihtric and I could not see the ships of Mann. Had Erik backed out or was he up to something equally underhand?

I had no time to worry about that. My men had either bows or throwing javelins. Our shields were around our backs and our swords remained sheathed. We had spent the previous day burying sharpened spikes beneath the water line at low tide. Sihtric had come at high tide. The beach looked benign but it concealed wolf's teeth ready to rip into his drekar. His first drekar struck the obstructions and began to fill with water. His mailed warriors tried to escape but many drowned as they jumped into deep water. Four warriors perished when they hurtled themselves into the estuary and were impaled upon stakes. Half a dozen successfully scrambled ashore, wading through the shallows. Cnut led forward twelve warriors and the six were quickly despatched as they struggled up the beach.

Sihtric was a wise old warrior and he used the half submerged drekar as a bridge. They hacked down the mast and used that and the oars to make a causeway across the deepest part of the river. His men crossed with shields at the ready. The problem he had was that he could only bring twenty warriors ashore at a time.

"Ulfheonar, forward!"

The enemy braced themselves for a charge and they locked shields. We halted and made a shield wall. The arrows and the javelins came as a shock. Only a few of the missiles actually struck flesh but the ones that did not either stuck in the shields or made holes in the mail. More and more men came ashore and still they could not advance beyond the sand. To move beyond their shield wall was to invite death.

We had a limited number of javelins and, once they were used I sent my twenty archers behind us. Twelve of the attackers lay on the beach. Drawing Ragnar's Spirit I led my remaining Ulfheonar in a charge at the weakened shield wall. The weight of the javelins and the arrows made the enemy shields harder to lift and the first warriors we struck were all slain. I managed to kill the first. I raised my sword high and brought it down towards the head of the warrior whose spear had stuck in my shield. He tried, unsuccessfully, to raise his shield but it was too heavy and my sword split his skull. The warrior must have had a name for there was a collective groan as their hero died. I jabbed my sword in the sand, pulled the spear out of the shield and hurled it towards the warriors advancing across the deck of the submerged drekar. It hit a warrior in the chest.

Plucking Ragnar's Spirit from the sand I rejoined my men who were pushing back the Norse towards the ship. Once they entered the water then they found it hard to move.

Tostig Sweynson shouted, "Jarl! They have landed further up stream."

I looked to my left and saw that they had managed to reach the beach where there were no obstructions. "Ulfheonar, withdraw!"

The advantage I had was that my men would obey every command; no matter how much it went against their nature. We stepped back as one and then turned to run back towards the forest. We passed the drekar which had successfully disgorged its crew and I shouted for my men to halt and turn. I saw that two of my men had fallen. The river ran red with the blood of the many of Sihtric's men who had perished.

As I had hoped Sihtric's men ignored Úlfarrston and followed us. We locked shields and the ones to the fore drew their swords. Behind us the warriors pushed their spears between us to make a wall before us while the remaining archers drew back with their bows. Once their missiles were all used they would use their spears.

Sihtric's men were angry and they came at us without any order. I saw one, more eager than the rest, and he almost ran into the spear which penetrated the eyepiece of his helmet. He fell dead; a human barrier for the ones behind. A spear came for my masked face. I lifted my shield and then stabbed upwards with Ragnar's Spirit. The warrior had been too eager and there was a gap through which my sword jabbed. I skewered him. I punched his body away with my shield and swung my sword at the next warrior who was too busy avoiding his dead comrade. My sword sliced down across his neck.

Cnut shouted, "They are outflanking us, Jarl!"

"Back to the forest!" We had practised this manoeuvre. Every one of my men stuck out before him; spears and swords made a barrier. Then we turned and ran away. To our enemies it was totally unexpected. They stood dumbfounded. It gave us the time to reach the track through the forest. The trail which entered the forest was narrow. Eight men abreast could hold it. The men with spears formed a barrier while the rest of us went to their sides in the forest. I wanted them to outflank us. I needed them to split up and avoid the killing ground that would be the trail. With Sigtrygg holding the trail Cnut spread his men out in a line to the left while Haaken did the same to the right. We were like a long arrow with Sigtrygg as the point. Tostig and I stood behind the spearmen as a lure to draw them on.

They came on. The first warriors hurled themselves at the spears. Sigtrygg and his men slaughtered them with ruthless efficiency. I saw warriors almost fighting their own comrades to get at me. The fact that I stood there with my banner and my sword seemed to enrage them. All the time we were falling slowly back into the forest and the trap that waited them. Haaken and Cnut fell back more slowly. We were like a net catching fish. The Norse swam on oblivious to the danger from their flanks. As they tried to get around the sides they found themselves one on one with an Ulfheonar. There would be only one result from that.

After a mile or so of retreating, Sihtric halted his men. They needed the rest. All of this was normal and to be expected. Warriors could not fight in a shield wall without rest. He thought he had more reserves than I did and he moved fresh men to the front. We kept on retreating. When his men saw us falling back it must have seemed to them that we were afraid and they had defeated us. They ran at us with their cheers of victory. Their main strength lay in the centre but Sigtrygg's fourteen warriors held the trail and I still remained as a lure. At that moment the warriors I had hidden in the forest fell upon the Norse at the rear and the sides. We knew what was going on but they did not. They just heard the cries of despair from behind them and we remained a solid wall before them.

The Vikings from Hibernia began to fall back. Sigtrygg and his warriors held firm and the pressure on them began to ease.

"Now, Ulfheonar, push!"

I put my weight into Sigtrygg's back and we began to move forward. It had been many years since I had been in the second rank of a wedge but I knew what to do. As each face passed below my feet I stabbed down with Ragnar's Spirit. Soon we were not just crawling forward we were running. The warriors who had been waiting in ambush were without armour. They had not been fighting or rowing for hours and they were fresh. More than that, they were keen to show their jarl that they could fight as hard as the Ulfheonar. They fell upon the raiders like furies. Sihtric gathered the survivors who fled from the trees and they made a stand at the confluence of the two rivers. It was a dense shield wall with armoured warriors ringing it.

"Hold!" I did not want any of my men risking fighting such a formation. Sihtric had lost the battle and I would have to fight at least four other armies. I could not afford to lose a single warrior.

The men from Cyninges-tūn were desperate to get at the invaders and my Ulfheonar had to physically hold them back. Sihtric was waiting for something. I think he expected Jarl Erik to come to his aid. That worried me. Where was the treacherous ruler of Mann?

"Cnut, go to Pasgen. It is time to fire the drekar!"

Haaken and Sigtrygg joined me. "The warriors did well, Jarl Dragon Heart. They surprised Sihtric and his men."

I pointed to the warriors who were standing close to Sihtric. "Look, Haaken, he only has twenty oathsworn left. The rest are his hired men. Most of them do not even have armour. When the boats begin to burn it will be interesting to see what occurs."

The afternoon was almost over. If Sihtric and his men wanted to escape they had two choices; get to the ships or fight us. We now had parity of numbers and we had shown Sihtric that we were not easy to defeat. There were sudden shouts from the direction of Úlfarrston and then we smelled smoke. Soon we heard the crackling of fire and as we looked south we saw the flames licking the masts of two of the drekar.

It was too much for some of the warriors. The ones who were closest and had no armour jumped in the water and began to swim. Some of the archers notched bows. "Save your arrows for those who remain. They will not get far."

In a matter of moments, the hired warriors were rushing into the shallow waters to try to get to the boats. I saw a single red sail flutter down. At least one ship had escaped the fiery rainstorm and was sailing.

"Sihtric! You have lost. Surrender!"

I heard a laugh, "Surrender to a boy and a handful of warriors? If you want me come and get me. The fishes will feast on your flesh!"

I shook my head. Many fine warriors would die. "Haaken."

Haaken brought the archers all together and they began to aim at the warriors in mail who surrounded their leader. This time they were not loosing blindly. They were aiming. The slingers we had brought were even more accurate. I saw some of the boys aim at the unprotected legs. The warriors either protected their heads or their bodies. They could not protect both. Arrows found damaged mail. Stones cracked into shins and helmets. First one and then another fell to the missiles. More of those without armour risked the river as their comrades fell. The oathsworn closed around their leader and his banner. The drekar were now burning ferociously. It looked like just two had made it safely from the death trap and they were heading south.

The oathsworn began their death song and a small ring of them remained around Sihtric. "Now Sigtrygg!"

We all moved forward towards the warriors who knew they were going to Valhalla and were determined to die well. It is hard work holding a shield up and all of the shields were now ever heavier with the arrows and spears buried in them. My men were rested and we strode forward. The mailed men did not wait to be attacked; they hurled themselves at us. A Dane with a war axe brought it over his head towards me. I held up my shield and deflected the axe so that it slid down the leather cover. I stabbed forward so quickly that the Dane had no chance of bringing his shield around in time. I stepped forward with the blow and buried Ragnar's Spirit to the hilt in his mailed body.

The Dane smiled and a tendril of blood dripped from the corner of his mouth. "I will see you in Valhalla, Jarl Dragon Heart." His eyes glazed over and he fell dead at my feet. I looked up to see Sigtrygg as he dodged under Sihtric's sword and stabbed diagonally through his body. Haaken's sword took the head of the warrior holding the standard and then it was over. They had all been slaughtered.

I lefty my men to begin to strip the bodies and made my way to the burning ships. This had gone far better than I could possibly have hoped. I had just reached Pasgen and Cnut when I saw them pointing behind me. The beacons had been lit. Cyninges-tūn was being attacked! Now I knew where Jarl Erik was. He had taken the route from Itunocelum and come over Olaf. I had been outwitted.

Chapter 18

"Haaken, Cnut, mount the men." I looked around for an Ulfheonar I could rely on to organise the warriors who remained. "Tostig Wolf Hand. Bring the rest of the warriors to Cyninges-tūn as soon as you can. Issue the mail to as many warriors as possible!"

We rode north as fast as we could. For the first two miles we had to go slowly for the horses would not step on the bodies of the dead and the men Sihtric had brought littered the trail like the leaves of late summer. Once through we were able to ride quickly through the darkening forest. Reaching the end of the Water I found the drekar waiting for me. "Jarl, our scouts report an army to the west of us. They estimate more than two hundred warriors."

I doubted that there would be that number unless Jarl Erik had emptied his treasury and bought every spare mercenary that he could. However even half that number could cause us a problem, as my best warriors would be tired. Attacking over the Old Man was a clever strategy for it would give them the advantage of height. I knew that Erik possessed archers; I had trained most of them. I also knew that he knew about fire arrows. Our eastern halls could be in danger and we could not afford to lose the herds of animals there.

"Wait here for the men who are on foot. Take all the wounded directly to my daughter."

As we rode north I discussed with Haaken and Cnut what we might be able to do. "If he has any sense he will attack tonight."

"But how does he know what has happened at Úlfarrston?"

"You are both right. He should attack tonight but he may wait for word from Sihtric. He does not know our land. He would risk much by coming down the steep mountain in the dark. I agree he should attack tonight and we will prepare for such an attack but I believe he will come in the morning."

Just then the rain began. It was one of those heavy solid downpours we had at this time of the year. Sometimes they are over quickly and men are forced to march soaked. This time the rain became lighter but continued. The ground became even muddier and the Water spilled over the beach and onto the trail. When we reached the walls of our eastern halls we were soaked and the rain showed no signs of abating. Scanlan was delighted to see me and Rolf had brought over half of his garrison to bolster the defence. We had fifty men to defend the walls. I hoped that would be enough. We sent one of the boys to deliver a message to Aiden and Kara and tell them of the victory over Sihtric Silkbeard. It seemed hollow now. It took Rolf to give me the right perspective on that.

"I believe this was ordained, Jarl. It could have been that Jarl Erik arrived on time. Had he done so then he would have attacked us here and we might only have had thirty men or so to defend the walls. You could have defeated Sihtric and returned here to find your home captured."

He was right.

"I want two out of every three men to rest. They can be relieved in four hours. I do not think that they will come tonight but I wish us to be ready."

I could not sleep and I joined the sentries on the ramparts looking up at the towering head of Old Olaf. I had changed from my armour and I had my wolf cloak to shelter from the rain. The two sentries on the gate close to me stood discreetly to one side. They knew I wished to be alone with my thoughts. I closed my eyes briefly and asked, in my head, for Ragnar, Olaf and my wife to send the spirits to aid us. The men who had marched from the battle had reached us but they were exhausted and it only brought our numbers up to ninety men. This was when I needed Snorri and Beorn to be the scouts. The shepherds who had reported the numbers were used to counting sheep and not warriors. They had not differentiated between oathsworn, archers and others. The makeup of the army which faced us was important. Sihtric Silkbeard had had no archers and only a few slingers. It had made our task easier.

When dawn broke it was a dank and dismal one. The rain continued still. The light barely lit the ridge of Grize's Dale to the east. All of my available warriors waited upon the walls. The rain meant that we did not have to worry about fire however the women and the girls waited close by in case their warriors were wounded. Every boy had been used on the walls and they stood next to the warriors with their slingshots in their hands. We could not afford to ignore any potential weapon against Erik.

Snorri's sharp eyes caught the movement on the top of the Old Man. There was a ripple of conversation which ran down the walls as they were seen. They came over the top of the mountain. At first they were hard to see for there was still a little low cloud but once they descended a hundred paces we could begin to estimate their numbers. My shepherds had been accurate. There were nearly two hundred warriors. Erik had emptied his coffers to hire mercenaries. He must have been confident that we had much which was worth stealing.

The nature of the mountain meant that they disappeared from view for a while as they came down the paths. The scree slopes were treacherous. I had hoped that they would attempt to come down them and slide to their deaths in the blue water half way up the mountain. They were lucky; they used the path.

"Bring food and drink to the men on the walls."

Scanlan, standing next to me said, "They do not need it, Jarl."

"I know but it gives the women something to do and it will take the men's minds off what is to come. It will take some time for them to descend to the ridge."

The mountain flattened off towards the bottom and then ended in a ridge some eight hundred paces from the walls of the settlement. As I looked up to the Old Man I could not help but notice how much rock there was on the scree slopes. Most of it had been created during the wolf winter when it was so cold that even the rocks of the Old Man had shattered. Aiden had said at the time that it was a pity that we could not collect them. They would have made our walls much more secure. We could have had walls as high as Constantinopolis. It was not meant to be. The gods wished us to fight from behind wooden walls.

The food had been consumed, although I doubt that any had actually tasted it, and the ale drunk when the line of warriors began to assemble on the ridge above us. I saw what Jarl Erik intended. He wanted to put fear in the hearts of my people. Warriors would not fear the numbers who began to fill the ridge before us but the women and the children would. We could do little about it and his men slowly extended their line. There was one large rock which rose above the ridge and I saw Erik and his standard bearer as they climbed it. He dramatically stood atop the rock. He was going for dramatic effect.

His men began to beat their shields with their spears and stamp their feet as they chanted, "Jarl Erik! Jarl Erik! Jarl Erik! Jarl Erik!" over and over. His banner was waved. I gave a wry smile to Haaken for the effect was a little wasted in the rain which was now coming down as hard as ever.

Suddenly Snorri touched my arm and pointed to the Old Man and the scree slopes. "Jarl, look! The mountain shakes!"

At first I thought that my eyes were deceiving me. The whole of the side of the mountain appeared to ripple. The noise of the warriors began to increase. I suspect Erik had allowed them to finish off their ale and they were drunk for they began to jump up and down and scream their chants. My eyes were drawn to the slope. Rocks began to come down in a long line. They were slow at first then there was an almighty crack which made me shiver for it reminded me of the crack when the gods had touched my sword!

A wall of stones and rocks began to tumble down the side of the Old Man. The whole of the side of the mountain seemed to tumble towards the Water. At first Erik's men did not see it but my warriors touched their amulets. My Ulfheonar gripped their wolves while the ones who wore the hammer of Thor touched that for good luck.

Erik's men now began to turn. They were lulled by the fact that the wall of stones disappeared, briefly into the dead ground. The noise of the avalanche now filled the air. It was a roaring, screaming, crashing noise. I saw the girls waiting with their mothers clutch their tunics to hide their faces from the wrath of the gods.

I turned to Scanlan. "Old Olaf watches over us still. We will not be hurt."

Scanlan pointed to the warriors on the ridge who saw the wall of stone and tried to flee. Their only escape route was down the side of the steep ridge. "I am not sure, Jarl Dragon Heart."

The stones and the rocks began to scythe down the warriors who had tried to flee. Their escape attempt had been in vain. The falling rocks and stones looked like an enormous wave which rose above the ridge and then crashed down the steep slope. We could hear the screams of the dead and the dying as they were swallowed up by the stones. I saw some of the luckier, faster ones as they tried to outrun the rocks. Despite the fact that they were my enemies, I was almost willing them to make the safety of my ditch. One by one they were consumed as the rocks and the stones drew closer to my walls and my ditches. Finally there was just one warrior left and he had thrown away his shield, sword and helmet. That was a mistake. The rock wall slowed and gradually stopped. He was twenty paces from it when one last rogue rock bounced high in the air and with a wicked crunch crushed the skull of the last of the warriors.

I noticed that the rain had ceased. I had been so focussed on the avalanche I had not noticed. The sound I had taken to be rain was, in fact, the sound of small pebbles and tiny stones sliding across the slate and the rocks. I looked up as the clouds lifted and a single ray of sun came from behind us in the east to show the arms and legs protruding from the new rock field before us. Olaf had spared just two warriors. The stones had surged around the rock upon which Erik and his standard bearer stood. It was now level with the rest of the land. He would not have to climb down. He would be able to walk from it.

A silence filled the valley. All who had witnessed it were too shocked to speak. I cupped my hands around my mouth. "Your sister and Old Olaf The Toothless have spared you, Erik the Foresworn. Go now and never return!"

There was a pause and then Erik raised his hand and disappeared from view. The standard bearer lowered the standard as he followed his jarl. The attack was over and we had won without striking a blow.

I led my men to search the rocks for those who might live. There were none. Olaf had been vengeful. Warriors had been crushed into forms unrecognisable as men. Limbs had been torn from bodies. Cnut shook his head, "All those weapons and the armour are now buried. What a waste!"

"It is payment to Olaf for his work, Cnut. He deserves a share in the victory for it was his. He is one of us still."

We spent the rest of the day collecting what we could. It was a gruesome task. When rains came in the following years it sometimes shifted the rocks to reveal the skeleton of a warrior who had come to take from us. When the ice and the snows froze and shattered stones, amulets and bracelets would appear like the last flowers of winter. The last effects of the avalanche were to change the shape of our valley and provide us with the rocks and stone, shaped by the gods themselves, to make our wooden houses and halls, stone.

It was late at night when I boarded '*Eagle*' to cross the Water home and the Ulfheonar returned around the northern end with the horses. I was keen to return first and speak with Aiden and Kara. What had they had to do with the events of that morning?

They saw the approaching boat and came down to the shore to welcome me. Kara hugged me, "You have done well father."

"I could not have done it without the help of the spirits and Old Olaf."

She linked my arm as we went up the slope to the hall. "We can do nothing without the spirits." She looked at me, "Mother persuaded them to spare her brother."

I had known that in my heart and I nodded, "He has been punished and I do not think we shall see him again." I shook my head. I cannot believe we have suffered so few losses and yet we have caused so many deaths amongst our enemies."

Aiden spoke, "It is not over yet, Jarl."

I looked at Kara who nodded, "He is right father. Our enemies come from the south and the east." She spoke so confidently that I knew she had spoken with the dead again.

The hall seemed warm and inviting as I stepped inside. The two new slaves were younger than Tadgh and Aed but their presence reminded me how close I had come to death. They put ale and food on the table and left us. We sat before the fire and I drank a whole horn of beer. I was not hungry. I stared into the fire.

"We are fortunate that their plan failed. It is as you said, Jarl. It was too difficult for them to coordinate their attacks. Had Erik attacked at the same time as Sihtric they would have won. It needed another night of rain for Olaf to be able to destroy them."

"I know and tomorrow I will go to Arturus with the Ulfheonar. Even if the beacons are not lit then I know that the danger will come from that direction."

Kara was not practised in the art of war and she frowned. "You will not take all of your warriors?"

"No Kara. Magnus and Ragnar will come from the south but Rorik could come from the north east, the east or the south east. If I commit all of my warriors to the south and east then he can fall upon here and Windar's Mere. They must both be defended. My Ulfheonar are enough to watch an enemy and to aid my son.

However, I will send a rider to warn the people there. They must get within the walls of Cherchebi."

Kara laughed, "You need not worry about that. Your galdramenn took that upon himself and they were warned today."

Aiden shrugged self consciously. "I sensed that there was danger. It seemed prudent."

"Do not apologise, Aiden, you may have saved as many lives as Old Olaf! And I will to bed."

"Do you not wish to eat?" Kara was so much like her mother that it frightened me sometimes.

"I need sleep and then I will break my fast in the morning."

I needed no food. In fact I knew that I could not eat. My mind was filled with worries now. Had I used up all my luck? Olaf had helped us but he could not aid us in the east. There was simply too much I did not know and so much depended upon my son and his small fort. This would have been a test for anyone but I knew that there could be over six hundred warriors descending upon Cherchebi and this would be my son's first command. If I had not been so tired I would have mounted a horse to reach him. But I needed my Ulfheonar and they needed to be fresh. I would have to trust that his mother was watching over him.

Chapter 19

We left early the next morning. I warned Rolf that he had to keep a good watch to the north and east. I hoped that Windar had heeded my warning too and had riders ready to summon help. We had sent word to Thorkell about the battle. He would be able to judge what to do. The *'Eagle'* was a reassuring presence on the Water. She sailed faster than we rode and I watched as she headed to the south of the long stretch of Water. I glanced over to the west. The mountain now looked even more like Olaf but the shape of the land had changed forever.

We turned east to ride through Grize's Dale. The farmer, Grize, and all his family had perished in the wolf winter but the forest and the dale still bore his name. The clearing he had made remained although the house had long since fallen apart. In the summer this was filled with tiny flying insects and midges but, as yet, it was quite pleasant to ride through. Suddenly Beorn shouted, "The beacons are lit!"

The enemy had come. We urged our horses up the slope. At the top we saw the line of beacons flaring their signal. Heading south I wondered if this was Rorik or the two would be kings, Magnus and Ragnar. I was confident about fighting the latter; I had beaten them before and I had always outwitted them. They both had grandiose ambitions but lacked the skills to make them a reality. Rorik was a different proposition. He had cunning and he was devious. His men, too, were an unknown quantity.

The track we followed was not well worn but on this journey it had become a muddy morass. The heavy rains which had helped Olaf had soaked into already sodden ground. The horses sank up to their withers in the mud. We could not travel quickly. I was pleased that we had set off early.

We reached the narrow part of Windar's Mere. The horses meant we could swim across the narrow stretch of the mere. It would save at least an hour. The skill in swimming with horses is just to hang on to the saddle and let the horse swim. They are not swift but they get there. On the other side we dismounted to tighten girths and to adjust our armour. I had no idea what we would find or how soon we would be in action. For this last part of our journey we watched for signs of the enemy; whoever he was.

As we passed Crost's Waite I was happy to see neither a sign of smoke nor animals. Aiden's timely message must have ensured that they, at least were within the walls of Cherchebi. The last few miles were across undulating ground. It looked like the rain had created new pools and patches of water. In places the track was below water. The woods looked like islands in a new land of water.

"Snorri, take us to the north. We will approach from the higher ground. It will be easier on the horses and we will remain hidden."

Snorri laughed, "If I can find a way through the water. I had better use a fish than a horse."

My intrepid scout, along with Beorn Three Fingers found a route through the mud and the water. We found drier ground in the forests which lay to the north of Cherchebi. The ground rose and fell but, generally, it was drier and easier going. When we reached the hill above Cherchebi it was hard to recognise the fort we had helped my son to build. The river had burst its banks and completely surrounded the fort. Had we not used stone for the foundation layer then the inside would have been awash too. As it was I could not see the ditches we had dug. I knew they were there but even I could not have said exactly where they lay. I did see the bodies of some Norse warriors drifting in the floodwater. It seems that the defenders had been attacked. I saw that my son's banner, the Wild Boar, still fluttered from the tower and the walls were still manned. I peered to the south to see where the enemy was. I could not see them.

"Well, jarl, your son seems secure behind his walls for the moment but we cannot reach him yet either."

I nodded. "Snorri and Beorn, see if you can find the enemy but be careful!"

They scurried off the way we had come. They would have to find somewhere to cross the river and the water which separated us from whoever was besieging Cherchebi.

We dismounted to rest our weary horses. The journey had taken much longer than normal. I looked up at the sky which now had just a few clouds scudding across. Had the gods sent the rains to aid us? We now had a chance. I had not believed that we had any chance when we were fighting Sihtric. The attack by Erik and Olaf's intervention had given us all hope. However as I could see not a single living enemy I had no idea of numbers. The defence of the fort told me that there were enemies; where were they waiting?

Snorri and Beorn had had to travel far to the west to avoid the water and so we made camp. We lit fires. At first it seemed a ridiculous thing to do for it showed our enemies where we were but then I realised that it also told my son that help was at hand and it would be very difficult for our enemies to cross the swampy flood before us.

It was well after dark when a muddy and sodden pair of scouts led their weary and soaked horses into the camp.

Snorri stood next to the fire and I watched the steam rise from his leggings. "I thought, when I left the sea that I would never have to be soaked to the skin again. I was wrong."

Cnut handed him a horn of ale into which he had plunged a red hot dagger. I saw the gratitude on Snorri's face as he drank the warmed ale.

"It is Hairy-Breeches and Bare-Legs. They have a hundred and fifty warriors with them."

"It could be more," chimed in Beorn. "They were spread out over a large area. We heard them speak. No one mentioned Rorik."

"Do they have horses?"

"No, but we could not discern the type of warriors. Some were mailed. We did not wish them to know we were close."

I knew what my scouts had done. They had approached as close as they could, counted the men around one fire and then counted the fires. It was what I would have done.

"How did you know it was Magnus and Ragnar?"

Beorn laughed, "They are not hard to spot. We have met them, Jarl Dragon Heart. They are there."

"But no Rorik?"

"We did not see him and no-one used his name."

I stared into the fire. Did I stay here or return to Cyninges-tūn? My son and his people appeared to be safe and Rorik was still my most dangerous opponent. Haaken sat next to me. "You cannot fight what you cannot see, my old friend. We have to rid the land of this threat first."

I waved a hand at the Ulfheonar around the fire. "There are just over thirty of us; what can we do?"

"That is the same argument for not going back. You have left plenty of Ulfheonar with Rolf and they are guarding your home. We wait until the waters recede and we attack these before us."

He was right, of course, but I still had a bad feeling about my decision. "If they stay here…" I nodded. "We will watch. Set a line of sentries to watch their fires."

Now that it was dark we could see the pin pricks of light that were their camps. It would be a game of waiting and watching.

In the morning the sentries reported that the lights had not moved. It was a good sign. However when we looked towards Cherchebi, I saw that the waters had receded a little. There were more patches of muddy green ground to be seen. Ominously we also saw the warriors of Magnus and Ragnar as they emerged from the trees to examine the water. We could not reach my son for the river and the flood waters were still back up close to the hill upon which we stood. Snorri had told us that they had had to travel almost to Crost's Waite to find a way across.

We watched all morning and I could see that they were up to something. Just after noon, visible now that the sun was in the sky, they began to move. We saw the lines of warriors trudge from the trees and begin to head north. My strategy, to have my son hold this vital crossing, had failed. The enemy was heading north. They were heading for Windar's Mere. They would cross further upstream. We did not have enough men to stop them. We would have to get back to Windar's Mere and warn Windar of the danger.

We had one advantage, the raiders would have to cross the river. We could gain time by heading north west. Our horses would help us to get there quicker. As we spurred our horses on Snorri said, "Jarl, why not just send a messenger to Windar? We could dispute the crossing of the river and slow the enemy down."

"He is right Jarl Dragon Heart. There may not be many of us but we would be better fighting and then falling back than allowing them the freedom of our land."

They were right, of course. I sent Beorn Three Fingers to the north west and we followed the river north. Snorri knew the land well. "They will find a crossing place some five miles north of your son's fort although that is when the river is lower than this. It is a little further north than the place where the smaller river joins it."

The enemy would not know that. They would keep looking for places to cross as they headed north.

Sigtrygg said, "Do not forget, jarl, that you asked Windar to have warriors watching the trail near to the Mere. He will have warriors there to defend the approach to his stead. We may find allies to aid us soon."

"I hope he has a good leader there who will not waste his warriors."

We rode as quickly as we could and reached the ford. There we found even worse news. The ford was passable and there were the signs that a large number of men had crossed recently. Where were they?

"Jarl, we must deal with Magnus and Ragnar's warband before we can solve the mystery of the tracks."

Sigtrygg was right. We hid the horses in the tree line just above the river and we waited in the hedge which overhung the river. Snorri crossed the river and saw that we were well hidden. Magnus and Ragnar would have an unpleasant surprise when they reached the ford.

I was surprised at the speed with which the horde reached us. We had not been there long when we saw them trudging up the other side of the river. The smaller river held them up briefly; we saw that from our hiding place. I saw that both Ragnar and Magnus led their men from the front. They would be a different prospect to Jarl Erik who allowed others to do his fighting for him. His scouts saw the tracks leading to the ford and one of them ran back to Magnus to tell him. The other four all crossed. The water came up to their armpits but they crossed quickly. These were not mailed warriors. They were lightly armed youths. As they crossed they halted and looked for the signs that the other warband had made. As they ran along the muddied ground my ten archers sent their arrows to strike them to the ground. We knew that their bodies could not be seen from the other bank because of the bend in the river and my men grabbed their bodies and hid them. I hoped that the others would assume they had gone to seek a route to Windar's Mere.

We could now hear the enemy warriors as they began to sing as they marched. They were in good spirits. From my experience they would have hated waiting outside the fort for an opportunity to fight. The river crossing promised battle and they would relish that. They would be eager to cross the river.

Sure enough, thirty of them did not wait for the order, they just plunged into the water. These did not move as swiftly as the scouts. Some had mail and all had a shield and a helmet. They had to move slowly as the bottom of the ford was treacherous. I nodded to the men with bows. The arrows flew straight and true. Eight of the Vikings fell. These were not Northumbrians; these were warriors like us and they were not deterred by ambush. They tried to rush towards these hidden enemies. As they reached half way they were showered again. Four of them reached the bank safely and they ran towards us. I stepped from the hedge. I knew that I would surprise them. Few would have seen a mail mask but all would recognise my shield and know whom they faced.

I used the surprise to strike first. I brought Ragnar's Spirit down diagonally across the neck of the first warrior. He was still sodden from the crossing and was slow to raise his shield. He died quickly and his three companions fell to a flurry of arrows from my Ulfheonar.

It was Ragnar Hairy-Breeches who organised the warriors. I heard his voice roar out and no one else was tempted to cross towards us. We stayed hidden. It was the element of surprise which worked in our favour. Once they knew how few we were they would flood across the ford. Our wolf cloaks and the armour we now wore made it difficult for them to see us. They knew where we were but not our numbers. Ragnar ordered a wedge across the river. I saw that there were fifty warriors in the wedge. The best time to strike them would be when they reached the shallows on our side of the river and would feel safer.

"We attack them in the shallows. Archer, use your arrows and then go and fetch the horses. We will hit and run."

We waited behind the hedge. The wedge came on slowly and steadily. They needed to keep themselves and their shields locked together. They were just fifteen paces from the shore when the arrows flew at them. They held their shields up and kept coming forward.

"Now!"

As we ran out Tostig Wolf Hand slipped in the mud but the rest of us ran towards the wedge which now had shields held above them. Snorri struck first and his sword tore into the stomach of one warrior and he knocked a second to the river with his shield. I brought Ragnar's Spirit down to slice through the arm of a warrior. I did not wait for the next one to attack; I pushed my shield under the first warrior's shield as he tried to lower it and slid the edge of my blade into his side. As I pulled it back I punched with the shield and he fell backwards. I stabbed him in the throat as he lay in the water.

"Jarl! Back!"

I saw that my archers had returned with the horses. "Fall back!"

We left Olaf Gold Tooth in the river but the rest, some bloodied, made it back to our horses. I dragged myself into the saddle. The river was red and we had slain twelve of the warriors whilst wounding others. These were the oathsworn of Ragnar and would be grievously missed. We galloped up the hill with the warband in angry pursuit. They would waste energy following us for as soon as we made the trees we headed west towards Windar's Mere.

My Ulfheonar were in high spirits. There were just over a hundred and twenty warriors left. We could easily handle that number when we returned from Cyninges-tūn with the rest of the Ulfheonar and the reserve warriors we had left there. I could almost hear the Norns spinning. We reached the Mere and Beorn was just heading down the track which bordered the vast expanse of water. I saw the drekar, '*Hawk*' approaching too. Something inside me made me shiver in apprehension. We rode down to the shore to speak with the captain and Beorn.

"Jarl! It is Rorik. He has Windar's stead surrounded. They are in the Rye Dale and the road to Cyninges-tūn is captured."

Wyrd. "How many men does he have?"

Beorn shook his head, "I have no idea. I only know about the Rye Dale because the captain of the drekar told me."

"Haaken One Eye, go on the drekar. See if your horse will board and get to Cyninges-tūn. I want the rest of the Ulfheonar to join us from Cyninges-tūn. See if you can open the road to Windar's Stead."

"Aye, Jarl. Shall I bring more men?"

"Make that judgement yourself. We must defend our home."

He clasped my arm, "You can trust me brother!"

When he had gone I asked Beorn about Rorik. "How do you know that it was Rorik?"

"I recognised him and Wiglaf. There are at least a hundred warriors on this side of the defences. I do not think they have been there long. They were busy setting up camp."

I gathered the men around us. "There are reinforcements coming to aid Rorik but he cannot yet know about Erik and Sihtric. He will be waiting for them to join him. We have a little hope. If Thorkell saw the beacons and if Windar sent a rider then there may be warriors coming from the north. As for Ulf and his men, I do not know. My aim is to use our powers to defeat the enemy."

Some of the new Ulfheonar gave me a strange look. Snorri laughed, "We become the wolf. We use the terror of the night. We stop them sleeping. We make them look over their shoulders."

I nodded, "Snorri is right except Snorri will be doing what he does best. He and Beorn will be getting through their lines to give me an accurate count of their numbers." My two scouts nodded. It was an honour and they knew it. "We will be to the west of the fort and north of the trout beck. Meet us there at the scar above the dale."

I had two of my warriors take the horses south to safety. We would not need them for what we had to do. I glanced at the sky. It was getting on to evening. Ragnar would be hurrying to join his allies. We had to be up in the hills above Windar's Mere before that happened. We ran. Making little noise and disturbing almost nothing we ghosted up through the trees to the ridge. There was a small valley which cut to the south of Windar's fort. The beck which ran through it was full of trout. Once we had crossed the trout beck we could climb up to the slopes of the hills which led to the sacred mountain of Hel Belyn. The giants had once lived there and their spirits would protect us still. I wanted that at our back for we had an escape route to both Ulla's Water and Thorkell's Stead. Neither was easy but both routes would discourage pursuit.

We had just ascended the northern side of the trout beck when darkness fell. Rather than hindering us it actually helped us. We could both see and smell the fires of the invaders. We made our way to the steep scar which overlooked Windar's refuge. Below us we saw only darkness. The fires burning above the gates and towers of Windar's Stead marked where our friends were. There was a ring of fires to the south of the fort but north, at the Rye Dale there appeared to be many more. Below us we heard the men of Ragnar and Magnus as they made their way to join their allies. The sound of challenges and answers was reassuring. These warriors did not know each other. We could use that to aid us.

I had twenty six Ulfheonar left with me. Gathering them around me I gave them their instructions. "Tonight, when they are asleep and safe in their camps we go amongst them. Kill silently. We will use seven groups for that is a lucky number. I will go with Magnus Long Shirt. When Snorri and Beorn return they can join me. We will meet on the scar above the Rye Dale. The gorge there is so steep that if you do not know it you will fall to your death. Tonight, we spread fear here and tomorrow we disrupt their main camp."

I left the men to organise themselves. I had chosen Magnus Long Shirt because he was one of my younger Ulfheonar. Arturus had trained him and they had been good friends. He had gained his name because he captured the mail shirt of a tall warrior and it had been too long for him. In the years since he had, like Arturus, grown a whole head taller. I could see that he was honoured to be with me.

"Put your shield on your back and cover it with your cloak. You will not need your sword. Use a dagger. I shall use my seax. If I fall then do not wait for me. Find the others and tell them." He gave me a shocked look. "Arturus can lead as well as I." He nodded.

Everyone was ready. "May the Allfather be with you." I clasped arms with Cnut. "Take care, my old friend. I would watch your children grown into men as fine as their father."

Then we slipped along the path which down the slope. We walked in single file for it was a tricky journey. Once we reached the bottom we silently split up and headed towards the smell of wood smoke. As soon as I heard voices I stopped and waved Magnus to his knees. There was a fire twenty paces from us and three men lay asleep around it. Two others were talking. I saw that they had horns of ale in their hands and I could smell the ale. They would soon be asleep.

We waited. I had done this before, on Mann when we had had to relieve Hrams-a when it was attacked. It would be hard for Magnus. The waiting was worse than anything. Patience could not be taught it had to be learned. The words gradually stopped. The horns fell to the floor and the two men slumped asleep, or unconscious. It was hard to tell the difference. Soon the only sound we could hear was the sound of snoring. I held up my seax and nodded to Magnus. I began to creep forward. I went towards one of the sleeping men. The two who had just fallen into a drunken stupor would be the last to wake. The victim I had chosen was on his back and he was snoring. I put my hand over his mouth and dragged my seax across his throat in one quick movement. The warm blood gushed all over my hand.

I turned to the next warrior. He had his back to me. I lifted the seax and drove it through his ear and into his brain. This time there was no blood and only the slightest of judders showed that the man had died. Magnus had killed two other warriors; one of them was a drunk. There were two men left. I stood and made my way to the one on the far side of the fire. Behind me Magnus stuck his knife into the drunk but the man gave the slightest of cries. It might have been mistaken for someone talking in their sleep but the last warrior awoke. He turned and saw me. I leapt upon him and, with my hand over his mouth I drove the seax up into his rib cage and then his heart. I waved Magnus away and we melted into the woods. We had used up all the luck that the Norns would allow and I led him up the side of the scree slope to the gorge which led to the scar above the Rye Dale. As dawn broke we reached the safety of the dell which nestled on the northern side of the gorge. Sigtrygg and his three warriors were waiting for us.

By the time the sun had risen above the eastern mountains all my men had returned safely. I breathed a sigh of relief. My Ulfheonar were too valuable to lose. We worked out that we had killed thirty-six warriors. In itself that was no great achievement but it would terrify the others. The next night they would be looking over their shoulders and would have to set sentries to watch for us. We watched from the scar and saw Rorik's men preparing trees to make bridges and rams. They had not begun their assault yet.

Snorri arrived just as we had eaten and were preparing for sleep. "There are over two hundred men in the Rye Dale." He pointed to the west. "The land towards Cyninges-tūn is flooded. They hold the Skelwith's bridge. There are forty warriors there. Around the stead there another sixty warriors. The woods to the south have a hundred or so within them."

"Sixty-four. Have you seen anything of Beorn?"

"No, we split up to make sure we had the right numbers." He laughed. "Do not worry, Jarl, he will return. He always does."

"Then get some sleep. Sigtrygg, wake me at noon and then you can sleep."

I went to sleep listening to the sounds of Rorik and his men as they chopped down trees to make bridge across the ditches of Windar's Stead and hurled rocks into the ditches. I was happy. We had done far better than I could possibly have dreamt possible. If there were just forty men at Skelwith's bridge then Haaken and the rested Ulfheonar might just be able to open the road again.

Chapter 20

I was woken by Sigtrygg. His face looked troubled. Behind him I saw the rest of the Ulfheonar. Snorri looked as angry as I had ever seen him. "What is it?"

"We have found Beorn Three Fingers."

I followed him to the edge of the scar. There was water just to the west of the Rye Dale and two islands lay upon it. One was wooded but the smaller one was not. I saw Beorn upon it. He was naked and he had suffered the blood eagle. Rorik had left me a message. Another of the Ulfheonar had paid the price for serving me. I put my arm around Snorri. "We will have our vengeance." Looking at them all I said, "Get some rest. I will watch now. When it is dark we will go amongst them again. Then we will have our revenge."

I sat on the rock looking down on the island. Snorri joined me. Before I could speak he said, "I cannot sleep. I blame myself for Beorn's death. We should have stayed together and then he would be alive."

"Or you could both be dead and we would not know that hope remains. It is *wyrd*, Snorri and Beorn is in Valhalla now. The blood eagle is a noble death."

I was not certain that I had convinced him but he sat in silence and I remembered all the times we had fought together. I remembered him losing his fingers when Arturus achieved his name of Wolf Killer. I found myself smiling for Beorn had ever been brave and he would not wish us to mourn such a noble death.

After we had eaten I gave them their instructions. "We go into the Rye Dale. I want terror here in the heart of Rorik's camp. I have watched and they have almost finished their bridges across the ditches. They will attack tomorrow. We weaken them tonight. We meet in the cave of the wolf to the west. It was there that Beorn lost his fingers and his spirit will be there. We will join with Haaken and open the road to Cyninges-tūn. Rorik thinks he has frightened us. He thinks he outnumbers us. He thinks he will win. He does not know the Ulfheonar!"

They did not cheer but their eyes did. Everyone clasped arms as we descended through the trees towards their camp. They had chosen to camp where Dargh had had his tower and his stead. His spirit and those of his men would be there and they would aid us. The gods showed their approval by hiding the moon behind a thick cloud which threatened more rain. *Wyrd*!

This time it would not be as easy. There were fewer trees in which to hide and more warriors. Rorik had positioned guards at the north and the south of the camp. The scar protected the east and the river the west. I pulled my wolf cloak above my head. I slipped my dagger into my left hand and held my seax in my right. Snorri took my right and Magnus my left as we began to crawl through the darkness. The fires had died a little which helped. We had the most dangerous route for we were closest to the sentries at the northern edge of the camp.

I smelled warriors. I held my hand up to halt the other two. Lifting my head above the ferns through which we were moving I saw the four men sleeping. Their feet were towards the fire. They looked like a human cross. I did not need to signal where my two Ulfheonar were to move. The position of the men had determined that. I saw that the warrior I was to kill was lying on his back and his mouth was open as he snored. I lifted the seax high and brought it down into his open mouth. His body convulsed involuntarily as he died. Snorri had slit the throat of one warrior and the last died with Snorri's dagger through his eye.

We stood and began to move through the camp. We passed little knots of men asleep. Had they woken they would have seen three walking wolves or shadows seemingly floating through their camp. There were too many in each group to risk another killing. As we neared the river we heard the sound of the bubbling beck racing over the stones. It would cover any noise that we made. I saw five men asleep close to the hedge which ran by the river. It arched over a little and gave them shelter. These five were veterans.

We dropped to all fours and moved slowly towards them. The man I chose to kill was on his side. His blanket came up to his shoulder but his neck was bare. I saw that the other two were in position and I sliced across the side of his neck. His body shuddered a little as he died. That was when our luck ran out. One man must have heard something or perhaps he needed to make water. He rose and saw me. I hurled my dagger at him as he stood and began to shout. The blade entered his throat and he tried to pull it out. I leapt at him with my seax. Magnus killed his warrior. The fifth man awoke and gave a shout before Snorri silenced him.

I waved to Magnus and we jumped over the low hedge and landed on the rocks next to the water. I did not hesitate. I knew that we could ford it and we slipped into the water and made our way across. There was only the noise of the stream and I thought that we had escaped notice until I heard a cry from the far side of the camp. Someone had discovered the first bodies. As we scrambled to the bank I waved the other two to lie flat. We just made it. Torches appeared as Rorik's men began to search the other side of the stream for signs of us. We had landed on rocks and left no tracks. They searched up and down for a while but then gave up. I wondered how they had missed the other Ulfheonar. I watched as they put sentries all around and each was holding a torch. We crawled away using very small movements. As soon as we reached the trees we stood. I led them up the trail to the cave we had used before. It was the one where poor Beorn had lost his fingers to the wolves. I hoped there were none within and that Beorn's spirit watched over us.

I drew my sword as I stepped into the cave. I heard a movement. I could not smell wolf. That did not mean there were none within. Then I heard Cnut's voice, "It is us, jarl."

We did not risk lights but lay down to rest. I discovered that our eyes became accustomed to the dark and we watched as, in twos and threes the rest arrived. Harald Magnusson did not return. We found his body some days later. He had been wounded in the attack but silently held the pain until it overcame him on the path to the cave of the wolf.

We rested until dawn. We should have left whilst it was still dark but we had waited for Harald. We owed him that. The ground around Windar's Stead was drying out but it was still difficult terrain to travel over and we kept to the high ground. I decided to take us by Elter's Water. That way we could approach the bridge from the same side as Haaken. I was also unsure of the condition of the road leading to Windar's Mere.

Elter's stead was deserted but it looked to have been left in some sort of order and I was hopeful that he and his people had escaped to Cyninges-tūn. The road from Cyninges-tūn was higher than the other roads and firmer. We made good time. I hoped that Haaken had been successful but I took no chances and I spread out my remaining warriors to filter through the trees while Cnut, Sigtrygg and I came down the road.

Warriors stepped out from the trees. They were mailed. "I wondered when you would reach us Jarl Dragon Heart but I assumed you would come from the east."

I clasped Haaken's hand. "I was not certain of the road. The ground around Windar's Stead is still muddy. How many men do we have?"

He gave a low whistle and more warriors emerged. "We have the twelve Ulfheonar and forty more warriors beside. Kara and Aiden concurred with Rolf that they could hold Cyninges-tūn now that the threat was from this direction."

He was looking at the Ulfheonar who remained. "Is Beorn scouting?"

Snorri answered him. Snorri had grown older in the last few days and his normal smile was gone. It had been replaced by a scowl. "He is in Valhalla." He paused. "Rorik gave him the blood eagle."

Haaken nodded, "When this is over you must tell me the story and we will honour him in the warrior hall."

I began to formulate a plan in my head. Although we were still out numbered more than fifty warriors had died in the last two nights. Rorik and his allies would be searching for us. If they followed us to the wolf cave they would soon lose our trail for we had walked on stones for eight hundred paces. Even Snorri could not track over such ground.

"Have you sent word to Thorkell?"

"Your sister did. The messenger should have reached there by the night before last. He should have sent men by now. What do you intend?"

"I am hoping that Rorik assumes this bridge is still held and that his allies have, at least, pinned us in Cyninges-tūn. The few numbers we have used in the last few nights should have confirmed this. It will be safe for us to approach Windar's Stead."

"You intend to join them inside and fight from there?"

"No, Cnut, that would be a waste. I want Snorri to go within the walls and tell Windar that we are close at hand. We will return by Elter's Stead and the wolf cave. If we head for the Grassy Mere then we should find Thorkell. I intend to attack the warriors in the Rye Dale. They will be the most nervous. If Thorkell is there then we can attack this night. They will think we are the small raiding party of the last few nights and we will surprise them." I looked at Snorri. "Can you do this?"

He nodded and looked at Haaken. "Did you send '*Hawk*' back to the stead?"

"I did. It patrols the western side of Windar's Mere."

"Good, then I will use that to gain entry."

I knew that Snorri would be able to do what I asked. "Snorri, we will avenge Beorn. It is Rorik who must pay!"

"I know and do not worry, Jarl Dragon Heart, I am no berserker; I am Ulfheonar and the wolf is not reckless. It is cunning."

He turned and melted into the woods. "Did you bring food and arrows?"

Haaken waved forward four boys who brought ponies. Two distributed food while those with bows replenished their quivers. Although we only had eight archers left amongst the Ulfheonar they could be used with deadly effect. As we ate we told Haaken of our experiences over the last two nights.

He nodded, "We reached here in the afternoon of yesterday. I sent the Ulfheonar across the river and we attacked from two sides. We killed them all. None escaped."

"Did you lose any?"

"Five warriors we had brought with us and one boy who got too close the enemy." He pointed to the ridge above the bridge. "We buried them there with their weapons."

I chewed and reflected on our losses. They may have been small but the ones we had lost were irreplaceable. This war was expensive. It had been begun by the greed of others who wished to take what we had worked for.

"And what of Arturus and his men?"

"What about them?"

"They would swell our numbers."

"I know Cnut but there are too many warriors between us and him. Besides I am not certain that the waters around his fort will have subsided. When this is over we will have to build causeways. I fear Cherchebi will always be prone to such inundation."

Once we had eaten we set off. I was more confident on the way back for I knew where the enemy were. We did not go to the cave but headed up the ridge which bordered the Water of Rye Dale. We dropped down at the neck of land which separated it from the Grassy Mere and headed for the old Roman Road which led through the dale. Haaken used his scouts and they found the road unguarded. The land to the left rose steeply to the scar from which we had watched Rorik. I thought it unlikely that he would have moved north. If anything, he would have strengthened his watch on the east and the west. I knew that he would now be beginning his assault on Windar's Mere. I hoped that Snorri had reached him to give him hope but we could do little until Thorkell and his men arrived.

Siggi Thorson was watching from the tree line above the road. He slithered down to us. "There are warriors coming down from the slopes above."

"Thorkell and his men?"

"I did not recognise their leader."

I quickly organised the men and we hid in the trees. There were thirty odd warriors. Five had mail and all wore helmets. The faces of the men were obscured by their helmets and, with their shields on their left arms I could not identify them that way. I could see what Siggi meant. Their leader was not a tall man. Thorkell the Tall stood out. It was not my former Ulfheonar.

Suddenly the voice of one of the men from Cyninges-tūn broke the silence, "Sven Ullason!" The warriors turned as one and began to descend.

Haaken strode over to the man who had shouted, "Why did you break silence?"

"They are men from Ulla's Water. I know them!"

It was then that I recognised Sven. I had fought with him against the Northumbrians the year before last. I walked over to him and took off my helmet and mask. "It is good to see you."

"We tried to come to Windar's aid but the raiders have blocked the road. We were heading around to Skelwith's bridge. We hoped to find you."

Just then I heard a noise from behind me. All of us whipped around and drew our weapons. Thorkell stepped out leading his warriors. He laughed, "We saw the strange warriors coming from the fells and thought they were the enemy."

Sven looked offended, "We are warriors who fight for Dragon Heart just as you do!"

I put my arms around them both. "I am just grateful that you are here. Thorkell, how many men did you bring?"

"Thirty-six warriors and six slingers. I brought the eight men too who rowed the '***Heart***' north. I left the archers to watch my stead."

"Erik reached you then?"

"Aye. He was unhappy about being left in the river but I am more settled for we have a fleet there now and any of the men of Dál Riata will think twice before attacking."

"We now have enough men to attack them."

Thorkell asked, "Who are they? Erik told us of the attack by Sihtric."

"Jarl Erik tried to attack over the Old Man but Olaf the Toothless destroyed him. The men we face are Rorik from Frisia, Magnus Barelegs and Ragnar Hairy-Breeches."

"It is time that treacherous Ragnar Hairy-Breeches was destroyed! I have never trusted him."

"And we will destroy him. Beorn is dead. He suffered the Blood Eagle."

"He was the best of scouts. I remember him well hiding close to Hrams-a so that no-one could find him. I will see him in Valhalla."

I nodded and pointed to the south. "We have spent the last two nights as wolves slipping into his camp and killing their men. We have whittled down their numbers. Rorik has the largest number. They are attacking the walls of Windar's stead. I had intended to attack tonight but the timely arrival of your men means we can go to the aid of Windar now." I pointed to the south. "His main camp is in the Rye Dale. His men should be attacking Windar and, I hope that they will be tiring. It will be dark in less than two hours. If we attack now we may dishearten them." I looked at the faces of Sven and Thorkell. "Are your men fit enough to fight?"

Thorkell smiled. "We may not all be Ulfheonar but we have the hearts and the courage to fight alongside them. The journey south has just made us eager to get to grips with this enemy who dares to threaten our land. We are ready."

"Then let us go to war!"

Chapter 21

I led the Ulfheonar and the others followed. It was a narrow pass into the Rye Dale but we were familiar with it. As we dropped over the top I saw the wounded warriors lying in the field. I pointed to the wounded warriors with my sword and shouted, "Sven, have your men despatch the wounded, take their armour and follow us." I sheathed my sword and picked up a spear which was stacked with others. "Grab a spear!"

Their camp was mainly on the higher ground to the east of the river. We avoided the area to the west. It was swampy and wet. It meant that we had to travel on the narrow strip of land which bordered the steep slope which rose to the scar. It suited my formation for we had thirty odd Ulfheonar leading. Dressed in mail and with my banner above us they told the enemy that Dragon Heart was coming for them.

As we neared the mere we heard the clash of arms and we smelled the smoke. Rorik and his men were trying to burn the walls of Windar's Stead. We had arrived just in time. We waded across the narrow Stock Ghyll and clambered up the slope on the other side. There, before us, we saw the warriors who were battering the walls of Windar's Stead. Rorik and his men had built stout causeways and they were protecting his battering rams with shields. It was pointless to estimate numbers and an even bigger waste of time to pause. The enemy had been fighting all day having had little or no sleep. I raised my spear yelling, "Ulfheonar!" and led my screaming band down the gentle slope towards the enemy.

They heard our war cries and they turned. It was then that I could begin to estimate numbers. The three warbands were attacking the three sides of the ramparts. Rorik was to the south and the east. Ragnar was before us and Magnus to the west of us. I saw their banners. There looked to be over eighty in each warband. The two rivers and the Mere had narrowed the attack but I could see that they were close to breaching one of the walls.

My men had formed a wedge behind me. We had a wall of spears before us and we had the slope in our favour. I took in that the ground ahead was churned up and boggy. Cnut had begun a chant to keep the rhythm. "Dragon Heart! Dragon Heart! Dragon Heart!"

The enemy did what I expected them to. They fought as all Vikings did; wildly and on their own. We had learned from the Northumbrians and the Saxons. The wedge worked if you had discipline. I jabbed forward at the first warrior who came directly for me. I was the flower they all wanted to pick! He impaled himself upon my spear and I twisted as I pulled it from his dead body. A spear clattered into my shield before Haaken speared the warrior. I felt something crack beneath my feet as I stepped heavily on the first body. I slowed down. It was getting muddier and we needed to keep our formation. I saw Snorri wave from the gate. He had got through.

The walls of the stead were less than a hundred paces from us but every part was covered by a warrior. The water was replaced by a sea of warriors. They now turned to face us. A wave of warriors rushed at us with an assortment of weapons. We still had momentum and there was an enormous crack as the two bands met. My spear shattered as I thrust it through the mailed body of the leading warrior. It must have penetrated through to his back and lodged in the shield of the man behind. The press of warriors meant I could not draw Ragnar's Spirit and I drew the seax instead. I had not had time to clean the blood from the previous night and its stained tip ripped up into the guts of the warrior who was close enough for me to smell his breath. He cursed at me as I disembowelled him.

We were all so close that it was not combat; it was a fight to the death. What saved us was our mail. I saw a seax come directly at my face. I tried to turn away and raise my shield at the same time but the warrior was strong. I managed to put my helmet and my mail mask in the way. The tip tangled in the mail mask. I lifted my seax and ripped across the bare arm which was before me. I severed it and the dagger fell as the man tried to staunch the bleeding with his other hand. Haaken despatched him and, as he fell back a small space was cleared. I put the seax in my left hand and drew Ragnar's Spirit. I used the space to whirl the long blade in front of me. One foolish warrior stepped forwards at the wrong time and the edge smashed into the side of his head. It was like being struck by an iron bar and he fell stunned at my feet. As I stepped over him I stamped hard on his neck and heard it break.

One of Ragnar's warriors stepped forward. He had a shield which was more kite shaped than round and he had a long handled axe. Although it had a small head it looked to be well made.
"Now face a real warrior, Dragon Heart and prepare to die! I am Olaf the Skull Splitter and your head will belong to me!"

The problem with some warrior's names is that they tell you how they fight. I already had my shield rising as he swung his axe. He would go for my head. Instead of stabbing at him or going for his shield I brought my sword backhand from under my shield. I could not have done it had he not swung at my head and allowed me to raise my shield. The sharpened edge ripped upwards towards his armpit. His axe clattered and crashed upon my shield making me step back a little and then his motion took his right arm off at the shoulder. Olaf the Skull Splitter had a surprised look upon his face as he began to bleed to death. I used my shield to push his dying body away.

He must have been expected to win for the men behind him stood, briefly and stared at his corpse and my bloody sword. Although I was tiring this was not the time to stop. "Ulfheonar!" I lunged at the next man with my sword but the action took me in the middle of the waiting warriors. I felt a rain of blows on my shield and helmet. If I had not had such good mail and padding I might have perished there and then. I still held my seax and, as I swung shield out to push away one warrior the seax ripped through the stomach of the warrior who stepped forward to finish me off. I twisted Ragnar's Spirit to block the sword which came down to strike my unguarded side. I smiled as the poorly made blade shattered on Ragnar's Spirit. Cnut lunged and gutted the warrior.

The Ulfheonar formed a protective wall around me. Haaken laughed, "Slow down, Dragon Heart. There are more than enough for all of us."

We needed the break to gather our breath. I looked up and saw that Ragnar Hairy-Breeches was edging his standard towards that of Rorik. He had borne the brunt of our attack. Suddenly the gates opened and I saw Snorri lead the garrison to attack the rear of

Ragnar's war band. It proved to be too much and they ran towards Rorik, following their banner.

I turned to my men. "Let us finish Magnus now and eliminate one of our enemies."

I saw, as I looked at them, that there were warriors missing. Thorkell and his men protected our left and Sven and his men had joined the warriors from Cyninges-tūn. We had over eighty warriors and ahead of us Magnus had barely sixty. The wedge was reformed with the extra men at the rear and we hurled ourselves at Magnus' banner.

Magnus Bare-Legs was not a tall man but he was a big man and he and his oathsworn were a solid wall of mail around his banner. Their backs were to the rivers and the ditches. They had nowhere to go. The archers behind the walls of Windar's Stead rained arrows upon them and they decided to meet us head on. We clashed with the lightly armed mercenaries between us. It cushioned the blow but all of them died as the Ulfheonar's blades cut into unprotected bodies.

I aimed myself at Magnus. He had a double handed war axe which he swung over his head. It was meant to intimidate. To reach him there were four warriors we would have to kill first. They had spears which had yet to taste blood. I angled my body to take as much protection as I could get from my shield. Cnut's shield overlapped my own and I felt the edge of Haaken's on the other side. The spear head jabbed through my guard but the edge of the seax held it. The metal jammed between the seax and my shield. I slid my sword along the spear haft. The men behind me pushed and the ones between the oathsworn held firm. Ragnar's Spirit tore through the mail links of his byrnie and into the padded tunic. I saw him brace himself for the blow he knew was coming. He bravely tried to work his spear into me but it was jammed tightly and I thanked Ragnar once more for teaching how to make a metal rim for my shield. I felt the sword sink into flesh and I saw him grimace. When the blood began to drip from his mouth and the spear fell to the ground I withdrew my sword and punched with my shield. Like his jarl he was not a big man but a wide one and he collapsed back, creating a hole large enough for Haaken, Cnut and me to step into. The warrior behind was not quick enough with his shield and Ragnar's Spirit tore into his throat.

"Magnus Bare Legs, you should have stayed where you were safe. The Mercians and the Cymri are easier to defeat. You have been led astray by Hairy-Breeches again!"

He swung the axe easily over his head in a circular motion. "When Sihtric Silkbeard and Erik of Mann have finished with your people you will have nothing to go back to!"

"Then it is fortunate that they were both defeated."

His face showed that they did not know of the disaster which had befallen them. "You lie!"

I shook my head, "The world knows that Jarl Dragon Heart is never foresworn. There is no-one coming to aid you and," I inclined my head to the left, "your allies are deserting you."

As he glanced to his right I jabbed forward with Ragnar's Spirit. For such a big man he had quick reactions and his axe head swung down to strike Ragnar's Spirit. Instead of tearing through his stomach it sliced along his famously bare legs. The blood flowed.

"Are you Loki now to play tricks?"

"No, I am the warrior who will kill Magnus Barelegs."

His axe swung around. I did the unexpected; I stepped into the blow and dropped to one knee. I raised my shield as I stabbed upwards. It went upwards through his groin and out of his back. I must have struck his heart on the way through for all life went from his eyes and his axe fell to the ground. His oathsworn roared in rage and I was knocked backwards by an axe blow. Had I not had such a good helmet then it would have felled me. I sat back, stunned.

They dragged his body back next to his banner and stood in a determined circle. They would die protecting it. My men moved forward. "No! Bring archers!"

Siggi shouted, "Where is the honour?"

"You can have the honour when Rorik and Ragnar Hairy-Breeches are dead. Archers and javelins!"

Haaken helped me to my feet as Cnut took charge. It was not pleasant but it had to be done. The arrows and the javelins were loosed from such close range that each one was deadly. Magnus Bare-Legs oathsworn died singing his praises. The last to die was the standard bearer. His body was riddled with arrows but he hung on to the last until his body and the standard fell on the body of Magnus Bare-Legs.

I looked to the east and saw Rorik and Ragnar Hairy-Breeches withdrawing down the road which bordered the Mere. They still had a hundred and fifty warriors. "Haaken, recall the warriors. Night is falling and I want no more losses. We have saved Windar's Stead. Tomorrow we can pursue Rorik."

The end of a battle is never a pleasant place. The enemy wounded were despatched as were those of our own folk who were too badly wounded to live. Bodies were stripped of valuables. Normally the enemy were despoiled but Magnus and his men had died well and we made a pyre from the wood they had cut to build their causeways and rams. In the dead of night the Mere was lit with the flames from the funeral pyre of eighty warriors.

There were too many of our men to rest inside the Stead and so we camped on the higher ground, now cleared of bodies. I was the only one of my warriors to go inside Windar's Stead and that was to see the damage that our enemies had done to us.

Windar had fought bravely as had his people. He had lost his right hand in the fighting. Snorri had been on hand with a burning brand and had staunched the bleeding. Over fifty warriors, women and children had perished in the fighting. As Windar told me that was much less than would have died had they not been able to bring them all within the walls.

We had lost fewer warriors than I might have expected but we would still be outnumbered when we pursed them on the morrow. I left Windar to repair his damage and went, with Snorri, to sleep amongst my warriors. My last task, before I slept was to send Snorri to the drekar. He would be able to follow the Norse invader safely and find where they went.

I was aching as I lay down to sleep. Bjorn would have much work to do on my helmet and armour when I returned to Cyningestūn. However, no matter how much damage my armour had suffered, I knew that those we followed would be in an even worse state. I had taken the opportunity, whilst in Windar's Stead, of having my sword and my seax sharpened. I knew that I would need them soon.

I was woken, deep into my slumber, by Snorri. "Jarl, they are camped at the far end of the Mere."

I sat up, suddenly awake. "They did not take the road close to Cherchebi?"

He smiled, "No jarl. I am not certain if they missed it by accident or by intention but they carried on south."

Haaken and Cnut were listening. "Then they have made a mistake. They could still head east but the land there will be as flooded as the land around Cherchebi. We can get ahead of them!"

I went back to my bed to get another couple of hours sleep. I ran through the events as I drifted back to sleep. Magnus and Ragnar would have travelled further inland when they had headed north. Ragnar would have told Rorik of the flooding around Cherchebi and they would have assumed they could miss out the swampy area and the garrison and cross further south. We knew our own land. We had cursed the rain we had had for some many days but it had been for a purpose. The gods were working for us and the Norns were being as complicated as ever.

Chapter 22

I filled the '*Hawk*' with archers and sent it down to the end of the Mere. They could watch the enemy and harass them, if possible. We marched towards my son. I wondered what he would be thinking. He had been isolated for many days. The enemy had come and gone. He had not seen us. I knew that he would be worried and I hoped that his mother had seen fit to visit his dreams.

The sleep had been our first one which had been uninterrupted. It showed for my men marched with purpose. Crost's Waite was still empty which meant that the farmer and his family were still in Arturus' fort. The ground was now merely damp rather than being a quagmire. The river, however, was still high. We would need to build a bridge once we reached the fort.

We waved to the men on the walls as we approached. I sent some of the men from Ulla's Water to cut down trees to make a bridge across the river to the fort. While they did so we went to speak with Arturus across the river.

He looked relieved to see us, "What happened?"

"The short answer is that we have defeated the men who besieged you." I pointed to the south east. "They went down the Mere and I fear they will be heading east. We go to cut them off. We are building a bridge to reach you."

I could see that he was happier and I heard it in his voice. "We worried when they left and went north along the river. Some of the guards thought that they had seen you leave and follow them but we heard nothing and I feared the worst. Is it over?"

"Almost but I would not send your farmers back. Let them garrison the fort and we will take your Wild Boar with us."

It did not take my men long to throw together a bridge. We used rope to tie it together and we quickly crossed the swampy ground. I embraced my son. "You have done well Arturus."

He shook his head. "I did nothing save stay in my fort and hide."

"No, you denied them the crossing. And it has made them avoid you and travel south. Now we must leave and catch them. I do not want to have to fight these again. I want their trail home to be marked by their bones."

It did not take the Wild Boars long to ready themselves. "Crost, you are a good warrior. Watch over the fort. We will be seven days at the most and then you can return home."

He nodded and said, quietly, "Your son is a good leader. He may be young but he has your head on his shoulders. He will make a good jarl."

I sent Snorri off with two others who had skill in scouting. They headed south east. As we walked I spoke to my son and my leaders of my thoughts. "They will have to cross the great divide further south. They cannot use the Dunum for it is too far north. They will think we are following and will try to out run us. Rorik has his home, now, in Eboracum. That will be his direction."

"And Ragnar Hairy-Breeches?"

"I am not worried about him. Besides we can visit him in his home. He was not the instigator of this attack. That was Rorik."

When Arturus heard about his uncle and his treachery, he was all for going after him too. I shook my head. "Your mother, as well as Olaf and the spirits protected us. They spared him. He did no harm, none whatsoever. We did not have to blunt one weapon to destroy him. The mountains did that. Jarl Erik will spend long lonely nights in Mann fearing that the spirits will revisit him there. The best vengeance we can have is to do nothing and he will punish himself."

Haaken laughed, "And that harpy he is married to will make his life seem like Hel! I agree with your father. He will have a worse punishment than mere death."

Snorri found us in the middle of the afternoon. There was a deep almost dry valley which ran for many miles south. On the far side the high divide rose like a huge scar running north to south. There was a trail which twisted north and then headed east. He had found them. Rorik was heading that way. It acted like a spur for my men. They almost began to run. Snorri led the way and his speed was almost too fast for us. He had Beorn's death on his mind. He wanted to be the one to capture Rorik.

We had found few of Rorik's men on the battlefield. The ones we had killed had been in his camps. It seemed that Magnus Bare-Legs men had borne the brunt of the deaths. We had found a few followers of Hairy-Breeches but he still had many men.

We found them in the late afternoon. They had had a longer journey and shorter rations than we had and they were camping on the north side of the valley, close to a stream which tumbled from the steep valley sides. This was no time for strategy. We could not risk them fleeing. We formed up in two wedges. The Ulfheonar were to the left and the Wild Boars to the right. The warriors we had brought from Cyninges-tūn and Ulla's Water filled the space behind.

When Rorik saw us he formed his men into a shield wall. I suspected that they were too exhausted to run. As we marched, rather than ran, across the valley and the shallow stream I realised that Ragnar Hairy-Breeches was not with him. It was a smaller band that we faced but there still remained one enemy who would have to be dealt with; another enemy who had to be taught to leave the wolf alone.

The formation we were using was appropriate. It was a Saxon one called the wild boar. The two points would strike deep into the enemy line and overlap the centre. Rorik would watch his men being killed and he would be safe in the middle until we turned our teeth upon him. We slowed once we crossed the stream to make sure that all the shields were still locked and we had lost no one. Rorik had chosen his defensive site well. There were small rocks which threatened to trip us and he was up hill. His men hurled their spare spears as we began to trudge the last ten paces. They clattered into our shields but we were all well armoured. They did no damage and we moved relentlessly uphill.

"Now!" My Ulfheonar ran the last eight paces so that we had some momentum when we struck their line. The Wild Boars had spears but Rorik's men and mine had shattered theirs. It was sword on sword. The difference was that we were rested and we had sharpened weapons.

A sword arced down towards me. The men of Frisia were in a double row and had the room to swing. I blocked it with my sword held horizontally. I smiled as the warrior's sword bent. I pulled Ragnar's Spirit back and then slid it forward. It sank deep into his body. I twisted it as I pulled it out. The men on either side were felled by Cnut and Haaken and I punched at the warrior behind. The boss of my shield cracked into the knuckles on his hand. His hand went back and I brought my blade down diagonally towards his neck. I was moving forward already even as his body slipped before me. The centre of Rorik's line was now surrounded by the two wedges and he stood with ten of his oathsworn.

Arturus ran at him, flanked by two of his Wild Boars. I put my seax in my left hand and I ran to aid him. The warrior, who had been felled by Haaken, reached a hand out to grab my foot as I ran by him. Haaken quickly finished him off but I was already falling forward. Three of Rorik's men raced towards me with weapons ready to hack at me. Cnut stepped quickly to aid me and took the blow of one sword on his shield. I just managed to get my sword in the way of the axe which swooped down from above. I slashed out wildly along the ground with Ragnar's Spirit and felt it bite into the ankle of the third warrior. I rolled over as the axe descended again and I was on my feet before the warrior could strike a third time. Stepping back, I raised my shield and feinted to the warrior's left. As he brought his axe to block it I spun around and brought my blade to gouge into the side of his body.

As he fell dead I looked up and saw that the two warriors who had been with Arturus lay dead and my son was being attacked by both Rorik and his standard bearer. I ran and launched myself like a human spear. I held Ragnar's Spirit before me. Rorik saw me at the last moment. He turned and my sword slid along his shield. I crashed to the ground and was briefly winded. Rorik gave a cry of triumph and brought his sword down. I tried to move but it was in slow motion. My shield would not come round in time and the sword was slicing towards my stomach. The armour had been designed to stop blows from above. This one was coming from the side. I knew that it would tear through the wires holding the plates in place, then through the padded tunic and I would die the slow death of a stomach wound.

I forgot that I still clutched the seax and Rorik's sword clanged against the thick metal. I twisted my left hand and stabbed blindly with my sword. The spirits guided my hand and my sword sank into his knee. I twisted and heard him scream in pain. I jumped to my feet and punched at him with my shield and seax at the same time. This time it was his turn to be winded. I swung my sword around in a horizontal arc and it bit through the mail and into his shoulder. Fear was in his eyes. I remembered Bcorn as I hit him again. This time it was a diagonal blow. It went through his mail and jarred on the bone in his shoulder. I knew that pain! He staggered and I repeated the blow. This time it went into the flesh and he screamed, falling to the ground.

He lay on the ground, gripping his sword and his body shuddering as he slowly died. I had given him four or five wounds and he was bleeding to death. He tried to curse me but the curse was in his eyes only. The light went from them and Rorik perished. He should have stayed in Frisia.

I looked around and saw my son leaning on his sword. The standard bearer lay dead but Arturus had been wounded by a sword. A flap of skin hung down from his cheek. Haaken ran to him. "Fear not Jarl. I have learned from Aiden. Your son will not die." He took some of the spirit that the men of Dál Riata distilled and poured some on the wound. Arturus gritted his teeth at the pain. He began to stitch the flap of flesh in place. I turned and saw our victorious men despatching the enemy.

Snorri pointed to the valley side. Thirty odd warriors were fleeing. "It looks like Wiglaf has escaped."

I shook my head. "We have killed the snake and taken its head. The body will die. It is time to go home. The Viking War is over and we can enjoy our celebration of victory.

Epilogue

We had lost more men in the last battle than in the ones which preceded it. Six more Ulfheonar went to Valhalla and the Wild Boars had lost half of their number. It was a harsh lesson for my son to learn. His face was healed but he would bear the scar to his grave. Haaken blushed when both Kara and Aiden praised him as a healer. He had prevented a worse wound. Arturus was equally adamant that he would return to his fort. The loss of his men had made him more determined than ever to become a better leader and he returned within the month with ten volunteers who were eager to become Wild Boars.

Our ships returned and we wasted no time in sending them out to trade and to spread the word about our victory. We wanted all to know whom we had defeated. I sent a personal message to Ragnar Hairy-Breeches. I told him to find some corner of the world where I would not find him for when I did then I would finally rid the world of his treachery. As far as I was concerned he could sail across the sea to the edge of the world and I would find him.

As I stood on the shore, watching the sunset in the west, I thanked Olaf the Toothless and all the spirits who had saved our people. Cyninges-tūn was still our home and it was stronger than ever. We would have to defend it again and I knew that it would be people like us who would come to wrest from us this most perfect of homes. I swore an oath that night that I would give my life before we would lose one part of my land. I was Jarl Dragon Heart and my people were the people of the wolf. We would make the stone of the land become the bedrock of our homes. We would become stronger and we would survive.

The End

Glossary

Names and words in *italics* are fictional

Áed Oirdnide –King of Tara 797
Afon Hafron- River Severn in Welsh
Aiden- a former Hibernian slave and a galdramenn
Arturus- Dragon Heart's son
Bardanes Tourkos- Rebel Byzantine General
Bebbanburgh- Bamburgh Castle, Northumbria
Blót – a blood sacrifice made by a jarl
Bro Waroc'h- one of the Brythionic tribes who settled in Brittany
Byrnie- a mail shirt reaching down to the knees
Caerlleon- Welsh for Chester
Casnewydd –Newport, Wales
Cephas- Greek for Simon Peter (St. Peter)
Chape- the tip of a scabbard
Charlemagne- Holy Roman Emperor at the end of the 8th and beginning of the 9th centuries
Cherchebi- Kendal (Cumbria)
Cherestanc- Garstang (Lancashire)
Cnut- The warrior who was with Dragon Heart when his sword was struck by lighting
Cymri- Welsh
Cymru- Wales
Cyninges-tūn – Coniston. It means the estate of the king (Cumbria)
Drekar- a Dragon ship (a Viking warship)
Duboglassio –Douglas, Isle of Man
Dyflin- Old Norse for Dublin
Ein-mánuðr- middle of March to the middle of April
Fey- having second sight
Fleot- a tidal estuary (River Fleet in London)
Frankia- France and part of Germany
Garth- Dragon heart
Gaill- Irish for foreigners
Galdramenn- wizard
Glaesum –amber
Gói- the end of February to the middle of March

Grenewic – Greenwich
Gwened- Brittany
Haaken One Eye- Dragon Heart's oldest friend
Hamwic- Southampton
Haughs- small hills in Norse (As in Tarn Hows)
Heels- when a ship leans to one side under the pressure of the wind
Hel - Queen of Niflheim, the Norse underworld.
Hel Belyn- Helvellyn
Hetaereiarch – Byzantine general
Hibernia- Ireland
Hoggs or Hogging- when the pressure of the wind causes the stern or the bow to droop
Hrams-a – Ramsey, Isle of Man
Itouna- River Eden Cumbria
Jarl- Norse earl or lord
Joro-goddess of the earth
Kara- Dragon Heart's daughter
Knarr- a merchant ship or a coastal vessel
Kyrtle-woven top
Lambehitha- Lambeth
Legacaestir- Anglo Saxon for Chester
Lochlannach – Irish for Northerners (Vikings)
Lundenwic –London
Lundenburh- the fort in London
Mammceaster- Manchester
Manau – The Isle of Man (Saxon)
Marcia Hispanic- Spanish Marches (the land around Barcelona)
Mast fish- two large racks on a ship for the mast
Melita- Malta
Midden- a place where they dumped human waste
Nikephoros- Emperor of Byzantium 802-811
Njoror- God of the sea
Nithing- A man without honour (Saxon)
Odin - The "All Father" God of war, also associated with wisdom, poetry, and magic (The Ruler of the gods).
On Corn Walum –Cornwall
Olissipo- Lisbon

Orkneyjar-Orkney
Pillars of Hercules- Straits of Gibraltar
Ran- Goddess of the sea
Roof rock- slate
Rinaz –The Rhine
Sabrina- Latin and Celtic for the River Severn. Also the name of a female Celtic deity
St.Cybi- Holyhead
Scanlan- A former slave and Dragon Heart's Steward
Scar- a cliff
Scillonia Insula- Scilly Isles
Seax – short sword
Skeggox – an axe with a shorter beard on one side of the blade
Sheerstrake- the uppermost strake in the hull
Sheet- a rope fastened to the lower corner of a sail
Shroud- a rope from the masthead to the hull amidships
Suthriganaweorc – Southwark
Stad- Norse settlement
Stays- ropes running from the mast-head to the bow
Strake- the wood on the side of a drekar
Syllingar- Scilly Isles
Tamese –River Thames
Tarn- small lake (Norse)
Teobernan –Tyburn (London)
The Norns- The three sisters who weave webs of intrigue for men
Thing-Norse for a parliament or a debate (Tynwald)
Thor's day- Thursday
Threttanessa- a drekar with 13 oars on each side.
Thrall- slave
Trenail- a round wooden peg used to secure strakes
Tynwald- the Parliament on the Isle of Man
Úlfarrberg- Helvellyn
Úlfarrland- Cumbria
Úlfarr- Wolf Warrior
Úlfarrston- Ulverston
Ullr-Norse God of Hunting
Ulfheonar-an elite Norse warrior who wore a wolf skin over his armour

Veturnætur- In October when winter began
Volva- a witch or healing woman in Norse culture
Waite- farm
Windar's Mere- Windermere
Windar's Stead- Ambleside
Wintan-ceastre -Winchester
Woden's day- Wednesday
Wulfhere-Old English for Wolf Army
Wyrd- Fate
Yard- a timber from which the sail is suspended

Maps
Courtesy of Wikipedia

Anglo-Saxon London

Historical note

The Viking raids began, according to records left by the monks, in the 790s when Lindisfarne was pillaged. However, there were many small settlements along the east coast and most were undefended. I have chosen a fictitious village on the Tees as the home of Garth who is enslaved and then, when he gains his freedom, becomes Dragon Heart. As buildings were all made of wood then any evidence of their existence would have rotted long ago, save for a few post holes. The Norse began to raid well before 790. There was a rise in the populations of Norway and Denmark and Britain was not well prepared for defence against such random attacks.

My raiders represent the Norse warriors who wanted the plunder of the soft Saxon kingdom. There is a myth that the Vikings raided in large numbers but this is not so. It was only in the tenth and eleventh centuries that the numbers grew. They also did not have allegiances to kings. The Norse settlements were often isolated family groups. The term Viking was not used in what we now term the Viking age beyond the lands of Norway and Denmark. Warriors went a-Viking which meant that they sailed for adventure or pirating. Their lives were hard. Slavery was commonplace. The Norse for slave is thrall and I have used both terms. The Norse only had Winter and Summer; Autumn and Spring did not exist for them.

The ship, *'Heart of the Dragon'* is based on the Gokstad ship which was found in 1880 in Norway. It is 23.24 metres long and 5.25 metres wide at its widest point. It was made entirely of oak except for the pine decking. There are 16 strakes on each side and from the base to the gunwale is 2.02 metres giving it a high freeboard. The keel is cut from a piece of oak 17.6 metres long. There are 19 ribs. The pine mast was 13 metres high. The ship could carry 70 men although there were just sixteen oars on each side. This meant that half the crew could rest while the other half rowed. Sea battles could be brutal.

The Vikings raided far and wide. They raided and subsequently conquered much of Western France and made serious inroads into Spain. They even travelled up the Rhone River as well as raiding North Africa. The sailors and warriors we call Vikings were very adaptable and could, indeed, carry their long ships over hills to travel from one river to the next. The Viking ships are quite remarkable. Replicas of the smaller ones have managed speeds of 10-15 knots. The experts estimate that even against the wind a good crew could keep up a speed of 5-5.5 knots. The sea going ferries, which ply the Bay of Biscay, travel at 14-16 knots. The journey the *'Heart of the Dragon'* makes from Santander to the Isles of Scilly in a day and a half would have been possible with the oars and a favourable wind and, of course, the cooperation of the Goddess of the sea, Ran! The journey from the Rhine to Istanbul is 1188 nautical miles. If the *'Heart of the Dragon'* had had favourable winds and travelled nonstop she might have made the journey in 6 days! Sailing during the day only and with some adverse winds means that 18 or 20 days would be more realistic.

The Vikings only had two seasons, summer and winter. Winter began round about October. Veturnætur was the time of sacrifices, offerings and weddings.

Nikephoros was Emperor from 802-811. Bardanes Tourkos did revolt although he did not attempt a coup in the palace as I used in my book. He was later defeated, blinded and sent to a monastery. Nikephoros did well until he went to war with Krum, the Khan of Bulgaria. He died in battle and Krum made a drinking vessel from his skull!

I have recently used the British Museum book and research about the Vikings. Apparently, rather like punks and Goths, the men did wear eye makeup. It would make them appear more frightening. There is also evidence that they filed their teeth. The leaders of warriors built up a large retinue by paying them and giving them gifts such as the wolf arm ring. This was seen as a sort of bond between leader and warrior. There was no national identity. They operated in small bands of free booters loyal to their leader. The idea of sword killing was to render a weapon unusable by anyone else. On a simplistic level this could just be a bend but I have seen examples which are tightly curled like a spring.

The length of the swords in this period was not the same as in the later medieval period. By the year 850 they were only 76cm long and in the eighth century they were shorter still. The first sword Dragon Heart used, Ragnar's, was probably only 60-65cm long. This would only have been slightly longer than a Roman gladius. At this time the sword, not the axe was the main weapon. The best swords came from Frankia, and were probably German in origin. A sword was considered a special weapon and a good one would be handed from father to son. A warrior with a famous blade would be sought out on the battlefield. There was little mail around at the time and warriors learned to be agile to avoid being struck. A skeggox was an axe with a shorter edge on one side. The use of an aventail (a chain mail extension of a helmet) began at about this time. The highly decorated scabbard also began at this time.

The blood eagle was performed by cutting the skin of the victim by the spine, breaking the ribs so they resembled blood-stained wings, and pulling the lungs out through the wounds in the victim's back.

It was more dangerous to drink the water in those times and so most people, including children drank beer or ale. The process killed the bacteria which could hurt them. It might sound as though they were on a permanent pub crawl but in reality they were drinking the healthiest drink that was available to them. Honey was used as an antiseptic in both ancient and modern times. Yarrow was a widely used herb. It had a variety of uses in ancient times. It was frequently mixed with other herbs as well as being used with honey to treat wounds. Its Latin name is **Achillea millefolium**. Achilles was reported to have carried the herb with him in battle to treat wounds. Its traditional names include arrowroot, bad man's plaything, bloodwort, carpenter's weed, death flower, devil's nettle, eerie, field hops, gearwe, hundred leaved grass, knight's milefoil, knyghten, milefolium, milfoil, millefoil, noble yarrow, nosebleed, old man's mustard, old man's pepper, sanguinary, seven year's love, snake's grass, soldier, soldier's woundwort, stanchweed, thousand seal, woundwort, yarroway, yerw. I suspect Tolkien used it in the Lord of the Rings books as Kingsfoil, another ubiquitous and often overlooked herb in Middle Earth.

The Vikings were not sentimental about their children. A son would expect nothing from his father once he became a man. He had more chance of reward from his jarl than his father. Leaders gave gifts to their followers. It was expected. Therefore the more successful you were as a leader the more loyal followers you might have.

The word lake is a French/Norman word. The Norse called lakes either waters or meres. They sometimes used the old English term, tarn. The Irish and the Scots call them Lough/lochs. There is only one actual lake in the Lake District. All the rest are waters, meres or tarns.

The seax which Dragon Heart captures is based on one found in Sittingbourne, Kent. I have made a poor drawing of it merely to show its unique shape. The fact that it only had one edge meant it could be thicker along the back and therefore stronger. It has much in common with the Roman Gladius.

The Bangor I refer to (there were many) was called Bangor is-y-coed by the Welsh but I assumed that the Vikings would just use the first part of the place name. From the seventeenth century the place was known as Bangor of the Monks (Bangor Monachorum). Dolgellau was mined for gold by people as far back as the Romans and deposits have been discovered as late as the twenty first century. Having found gold in a stream at Mungrisedale in the Lake District I know how exciting it is to see the golden flecks in the black sand. The siege of the fort is not in itself remarkable. When Harlech was besieged in the middle ages two knights and fifteen men at arms held off a large army.

Anglesey was considered the bread basket of Wales even as far back as the Roman Invasion; the combination of the Gulf Stream and the soil meant that it could provide grain for many people. In the eighth to tenth centuries, grain was more valuable than gold.

When writing about the raids I have tried to recreate those early days of the Viking raider. The Saxons had driven the native inhabitants to the extremes of Wales, Cornwall and Scotland. The Irish were always too busy fighting amongst themselves. It must have come as a real shock to be attacked in their own settlements. By the time of King Alfred almost sixty years later they were better prepared. This was also about the time that Saxon England converted completely to Christianity. The last place to do so was the Isle of Wight. There is no reason to believe that the Vikings would have had any sympathy for their religion and would, in fact, have taken advantage of their ceremonies and rituals not to mention their riches.

There was a warrior called Ragnar Hairy-Breeches. Although he lived a little later than my book is set I could not resist using the name of such an interesting sounding character. Most of the names such as Silkbeard, Hairy-Breeches etc are genuine Viking names. I have merely transported them all into one book. I also amended some of my names- I used Eric in the earlier books and it should have been Erik. I have now changed the later editions of the first two books in the series.

Eardwulf was king of Northumbria twice: first from 796-806 and from 808-810. The king who deposed him was Elfwald II. This period was a turbulent one for the kings of Northumbria and marked a decline in their fortunes until it was taken over by the Danes in 867. This was the time of power for Mercia and East Anglia. Coenwulf ruled East Anglia and his son Cynhelm, Mercia. Wessex had yet to rise.

Slavery was far more common in the ancient world. When the Normans finally made England their own they showed that they understood the power of words and propaganda by making the slaves into serfs. This was a brilliant strategy as it forced their former slaves to provide their own food whilst still working for their lords and masters for nothing. Manumission was possible as Garth showed in the first book in this series. Scanlan's training is also a sign that not all of the slaves suffered. It was a hard and cruel time- it was ruled by the strong.

The Vikings did use trickery when besieging their enemies and would use any means possible. They did not have siege weapons and had to rely on guile and courage to prevail. The siege of Paris in 845 A.D. was one such example.

The Isle of Man is reputed to have the earliest surviving Parliament, the Tynwald although there is evidence that there were others amongst the Viking colonies on Orkney and in Iceland. I have used this idea for Prince Butar's meetings of Jarls.

The blue stone they seek is aquamarine or beryl. It is found in granite. The rocks around the Mawddach are largely granite and although I have no evidence of beryl being found there, I have used the idea of a small deposit being found to tic the story together.

There was a famous witch who lived on one of the islands of Scilly. Famously Olaf Tryggvasson, who became King Olaf 1 of Norway, visited her. She told him that if he converted to Christianity then he would become king of Norway.

The early ninth century saw Britain converted to Christianity and there were many monasteries which flourished. These were often mixed. These were not the huge stone edifices such as Whitby and

Fountain's Abbey; these were wooden structures. As such their remains have disappeared, along with the bones of those early Christian priests. Hexham was a major monastery in the early Saxon period. I do not know if they had warriors to protect the priests but having given them a treasure to watch over I thought that some warriors might be useful too.

I use Roman forts in all of my books. Although we now see ruins when they were abandoned the only things which would have been damaged at the time the books are set would have been the gates. The Saxons rarely used stone for building. Anything of value would have been buried in case they wished to return. By '*of value*' I do not mean coins but things such as nails and weapons. Such objects have been discovered. Many of the forts were abandoned in a hurry. Hardknott fort, for example, was built in the 120s but abandoned twenty or so years later. When the Antonine Wall was abandoned in the 180s Hardknott was reoccupied until Roman soldiers finally withdrew from northern Britain. I think that, until the late Saxon period and early Norman period, there would have been many forts which would have looked habitable. The Vikings like Saxons did not build generally in stone. It was only when the castle builders, the Normans, arrived that stone would be robbed from Roman forts and those defences destroyed by an invader who was in the minority and yet conquered a much more numerous population. It was their stone castles which achieved that. The Vikings also liked to move their homes every few years; this was, perhaps, only a few miles, but it explains how difficult it is to find the remains of early Viking settlements.

London began to become more important at this time. It was fought over between Mercia and Wessex. Over the next fifty years Wessex increased its power culminating in the reign of Alfred the Great at the end of the century. The kingdoms of Essex and Kent gradually disappeared. They had been part of the Anglo-Saxon heptarchy but they had never been one of the major players. The balance of power had shifted from Northumbria to Mercia and would culminate in Wessex which became England. The shift allowed the Danes in the east and the Norse in the north to gain both land and power until by the middle of the ninth century the country was effectively divided in two; Danelaw was in the north and the east of Britain and England (Wessex) in the south and the west.

The place names are accurate and the mountain above Coniston is called the Old Man. The river is not navigable up to Windermere but I have allowed my warriors to carry their drekar as the Vikings did in the land of the Rus when travelling to Miklagård. The ninth century saw the beginning of the reign of the Viking. They raided Spain, the Rhone, Africa and even Constantinople. They believed they could beat anyone!

I used the following books for research

- Vikings- Life and Legends- British Museum
- Saxon, Norman and Viking by Terence Wise (Osprey)
- The Vikings. (Osprey) Ian Heath
- Byzantine Armies 668-1118 (Osprey) Ian Heath
- Romano-Byzantine Armies 4th-9th Century (Osprey) David Nicholle
- The Walls of Constantinople AD 324-1453 (Osprey) Stephen Turnbull
- Viking Longship (Osprey) Keith Durham
- Anglo Saxon Thegn AD 449-1066 (Osprey) Mark Harrison

Griff Hosker **January2015**

Other books by Griff Hosker

If you enjoyed reading this book, then why not read another one by the author?

Ancient History

The Sword of Cartimandua Series
(Germania and Britannia 50– 128 A.D.)
Ulpius Felix- Roman Warrior (prequel)
Book 1 The Sword of Cartimandua
Book 2 The Horse Warriors
Book 3 Invasion Caledonia
Book 4 Roman Retreat
Book 5 Revolt of the Red Witch
Book 6 Druid's Gold
Book 7 Trajan's Hunters
Book 8 The Last Frontier
Book 9 Hero of Rome
Book 10 Roman Hawk
Book 11 Roman Treachery
Book 12 Roman Wall
Book 13 Roman Courage

The Aelfraed Series
(Britain and Byzantium 1050 A.D. - 1085 A.D.)
Book 1 Housecarl
Book 2 Outlaw
Book 3 Varangian

The Wolf Warrior series
(Britain in the late 6th Century)
Book 1 Saxon Dawn
Book 2 Saxon Revenge
Book 3 Saxon England
Book 4 Saxon Blood
Book 5 Saxon Slayer
Book 6 Saxon Slaughter
Book 7 Saxon Bane

Book 8 Saxon Fall: Rise of the Warlord
Book 9 Saxon Throne
Book 10 Saxon Sword

The Dragon Heart Series
Book 1 Viking Slave
Book 2 Viking Warrior
Book 3 Viking Jarl
Book 4 Viking Kingdom
Book 5 Viking Wolf
Book 6 Viking War
Book 7 Viking Sword
Book 8 Viking Wrath
Book 9 Viking Raid
Book 10 Viking Legend
Book 11 Viking Vengeance
Book 12 Viking Dragon
Book 13 Viking Treasure
Book 14 Viking Enemy
Book 15 Viking Witch
Book 16 Viking Blood
Book 17 Viking Weregeld
Book 18 Viking Storm
Book 19 Viking Warband
Book 20 Viking Shadow
Book 21 Viking Legacy
Book 22 Viking Clan

The Norman Genesis Series
Hrolf the Viking
Horseman
The Battle for a Home
Revenge of the Franks
The Land of the Northmen
Ragnvald Hrolfsson
Brothers in Blood
Lord of Rouen
Drekar in the Seine
Duke of Normandy

New World Series
(Iceland and America- 10th-11th Century)
Blood on the Blade

The Anarchy Series
(England 1120-1180)
English Knight
Knight of the Empress
Northern Knight
Baron of the North
Earl
King Henry's Champion
The King is Dead
Warlord of the North
Enemy at the Gate
The Fallen Crown
Warlord's War
Kingmaker
Henry II
Crusader
The Welsh Marches
Irish War
Poisonous Plots
Prince's Revolt
Earl Marshal

Border Knight
1182-1300
Sword for Hire
Return of the Knight
Baron's War
Magna Carta
Welsh War
Henry III

Struggle for a Crown
1360- 1485
Blood on the Crown

To Murder a King

Modern History

The Napoleonic Horseman Series
Book 1 Chasseur a Cheval
Book 2 Napoleon's Guard
Book 3 British Light Dragoon
Book 4 Soldier Spy
Book 5 1808: The Road to Corunna
Waterloo

The Lucky Jack American Civil War series
Rebel Raiders
Confederate Rangers
The Road to Gettysburg

The British Ace Series
1914
1915 Fokker Scourge
1916 Angels over the Somme
1917 Eagles Fall
1918 We will remember them
From Arctic Snow to Desert Sand
Wings over Persia

Combined Operations series
1940-1945
Commando
Raider
Behind Enemy Lines
Dieppe
Toehold in Europe
Sword Beach
Breakout
The Battle for Antwerp
King Tiger
Beyond the Rhine
Korea

Other Books
Carnage at Cannes (a thriller)
Great Granny's Ghost (Aimed at 9-14-year-old young people)
Adventure at 63-Backpacking to Istanbul

For more information on all of the books then please visit the author's web site at http://www.griffhosker.com where there is a link to contact him.

Printed in Great Britain
by Amazon